'Tell me to stop.'

But she didn't. She had broken so many rules today.

His gaze was heated, his eyes burning with a warning she couldn't heed. Something about this man drew her in, tantalising her with the promise of physical pleasure.

'Don't stop. I need this...' Hannah didn't even understand what she was asking for.

'So innocent.' His mouth moved over her skin, caressing her with his warm breath. As before, her body came alive, needing him to touch. To taste.

Michael pulled her against him, though he didn't hold her tight. 'This is your last chance to run away. I'm not above taking what's offered.'

'Show me what it's supposed to be like,' she murmured.

The words were all the encouragement he needed, and he covered her breathless mouth with his own. Instinct took over and Hannah kissed him back, ignoring every warning that flew into her mind. She didn't care. Soon enough, she'd never see him again.

And, by Heaven, if she was going to be ruined after today she might as well have a memory to show for it.

Michelle Willingham grew up living in places all over the world, including Germany, England and Thailand. When her parents hauled her to antiques shows in manor houses and castles Michelle entertained herself by making up stories and pondering whether she could afford a broadsword with her allowance. She graduated *summa cum laude* from the University of Notre Dame, with a degree in English, and received her master's degree in Education from George Mason University. Currently she teaches American History and English. She lives in south-eastern Virginia with her husband and children. She still doesn't have her broadsword.

Visit her website at: www.michellewillingham.com, or e-mail her at michelle@michellewillingham.com

Previous novels by this author:

HER IRISH WARRIOR*
THE WARRIOR'S TOUCH*
HER WARRIOR KING*
HER WARRIOR SLAVE†
THE ACCIDENTAL COUNTESS**

**Also available in eBook format in
Mills & Boon® Historical *Undone*:**

THE VIKING'S FORBIDDEN LOVE-SLAVE
THE WARRIOR'S FORBIDDEN VIRGIN
AN ACCIDENTAL SEDUCTION**

The MacEgan Brothers
†prequel to *The MacEgan Brothers* trilogy
**linked by character

THE ACCIDENTAL PRINCESS

Michelle Willingham

First published in Great Britain 2010
Large Print edition 2011
Harlequin Mills & Boon Limited,
Eton House, 18-24 Paradise Road, Richmond, Surrey TW9 1SR

© Michelle Willingham 2010

ISBN: 978 0 263 22304 0

Harlequin Mills & Boon policy is to use papers that are natural,
renewable and recyclable products and made from wood grown in
sustainable forests. The logging and manufacturing process conform
to the legal environmental regulations of the country of origin.

Printed and bound in Great Britain
by CPI Antony Rowe, Chippenham, Wiltshire

3226755X

AUTHOR NOTE

I've always loved princess stories, ever since I was a little girl. I devoured Grimm's fairytales and other classics such as *A Little Princess* by Frances Hodgson Burnett and *The Prince and the Pauper* by Mark Twain. I wanted to explore the idea of a soldier hero, Michael Thorpe, who looks nearly identical to a crown prince. Throughout the book Michael must question his past and discover whether he was an illegitimate son or the true prince.

Lady Hannah Chesterfield, the daughter of a marquess, is drawn to Lieutenant Thorpe, though she knows she can never wed a soldier. As Michael's secrets unfold, Hannah is forced into a fascinating world of intrigue and royalty. Ultimately she must decide whether or not to face her greatest fear: surrendering to her hidden desires.

I hope you enjoy THE ACCIDENTAL PRINCESS, and I invite you to try its companion book, THE ACCIDENTAL COUNTESS, about Hannah's older brother Stephen Chesterfield, the Earl of Whitmore. You can also find behind-the-scenes information about my books on my website: www.michellewillingham.com.

I love to hear from readers, and you may e-mail me at michelle@michellewillingham.com, or write to me at: PO Box 2242 Poquoson, VA 23662, United States.

Warmest wishes.

ACKNOWLEDGEMENTS

I'd like to thank the library staff of the Mariner's Museum in Newport News, Virginia, for their invaluable help in researching the interior of a steamship. In particular, thanks to Library Researcher Bill Edwards-Bodmer, who guided me in choosing the best steamship to use as a model for my own ship. I had a great time poring over old photographs and I was very inspired by the luxurious interiors of these historic vessels.

DEDICATION

To Elizabeth, my own special princess.

Chapter One

London, 1855

She could feel his eyes watching her from across the room. Like an invisible protector, warning away anyone who would bother her. Lady Hannah Chesterfield smiled at one of the ballroom guests, but she hadn't heard a word the woman had said. Instead, she was all too aware of Lieutenant Thorpe's gaze and the forbidden nature of his thoughts.

Though she'd only met him a few weeks ago, she hadn't forgotten his intensity. Nor the way he'd stared at her like a delectable sweet he wanted but couldn't have.

He'd brushed his lips upon the back of her hand when her brother had introduced them. The unexpected kiss had made her skin flush, awakening the strange desire to move closer to him. He looked as though he wanted to kiss every inch of her, and the thought made her body tremble. His interest had been undeniable.

It was nearing midnight, the hour of secret liaisons. More than a few ladies had disappeared into the garden with a companion, only to return with twigs in their hair and swollen lips.

Hannah wondered what it would be like to indulge in such wickedness, feeling a man's mouth against her lips, his hands touching her the way a lover would. There was something about the Lieutenant that was dangerous. Unpredictable. He didn't belong here among London's elite, and yet he fascinated her.

She risked a glance and saw him leaning against the back wall, a glass of lemonade in one hand. His black tailcoat was too snug across his broad shoulders, as though he couldn't afford one that fit. His matching waistcoat accentuated his lean form, while the white cravat he wore had a careless tilt to it. His dark hair was too long, and he was clean-shaven, unlike the current fashion.

His mouth gave a slight lift, as though daring her to come and speak to him. She couldn't possibly do such a thing.

Why was he here tonight? It wasn't as if Lieutenant Thorpe could seek a wife from among the ladies. He might be an officer, but he did not possess a title. Furthermore, if it weren't for his unlikely friendship with her brother Stephen, the

Lieutenant wouldn't have been allowed inside Rothburne House.

'Hannah!' A hand waved in front of her face, and she forced herself to pay heed to her mother, who had crossed the room to speak with her.

'You're woolgathering again, my dear. Stand up straight and smile. The Baron of Belgrave is coming to claim his dance with you.' With a slight titter, Christine Chesterfield added, 'Oh, I do hope the two of you get on. He would make such a dashing husband for you. He's so handsome and well-mannered.'

An unsettled feeling rose up in her stomach. 'Mother, I don't want to wed the baron.'

'Why? Whatever is wrong with Lord Belgrave?' Christine demanded.

'I don't know. Something. It feels wrong.'

'Oh, for heaven's sake.' Her mother rolled her eyes. 'Hannah, you're imagining things. There is absolutely nothing wrong with the baron, and I have little doubt that he would make an excellent husband.'

A sour feeling caught up in her stomach, but Hannah didn't protest. She'd learned, long ago, that her mother and father had carved-in-stone ideas about the man she would marry. The gentleman had to be well-bred, wealthy and titled. A saint who had never transgressed against anyone, who treated women with the utmost respect.

And likely rescued kittens in his spare time, she thought sourly. Men of that nature didn't exist. She knew it for a fact, being cursed with two older brothers.

Though she wanted to get married more than anything, Hannah was beginning to wonder if she'd ever find the right man. Having her own home and a husband was her dream, for she could finally have the freedom she wanted.

She craved the moment when she could make her own choices without having to ask permission or worry about whether or not she was behaving like a proper lady. Although she was twenty years old, she might as well have been a girl of five, for all that she'd been sheltered from the world.

'Now, Hannah,' her mother chided. 'The baron has been nothing but the soul of kindness this entire week. He's brought you flowers every day.'

It was true that Lord Belgrave had made his courtship intentions clear. But despite his outward courtesy, Hannah couldn't shake the feeling that something was wrong. He was almost *too* perfect.

'I'm not feeling up to a dance just now,' she said, though she knew the excuse would never hold.

'You are perfectly well,' her mother insisted. 'And you cannot turn down an invitation to dance. It would be rude.'

Hannah clamped her lips together, suppressing the urge to argue. Her mother would never bend when it came to appropriate behaviour. With any luck, the dance would be over in three minutes.

'Smile, for the love of heaven,' her mother repeated. 'You look as though you're about to faint.'

Without waiting for her reply, Lady Rothburne flounced away, just as the Baron of Belgrave arrived to claim his dance.

Hannah forced a smile upon her face and prayed that the remaining hours would pass quickly. And as the baron swept her into the next dance, she caught a glimpse of the Lieutenant watching them, an unreadable darkness upon his face.

Michael Thorpe had a sixth sense for trouble. He often perceived it before it struck, which had served him well on the battlefield.

It was happening again. Intuition pricked at his conscience, when he saw Lady Hannah about to dance with the Baron of Belgrave. Whether she knew it or not, the suitors were circling her like sharks. There wasn't a man among them who didn't want to claim her.

Including himself.

She was an untouched angel. Innocent of the world, and yet he recognised the weariness in her green eyes. Her caramel-brown hair had been artfully arranged with sprigs of jasmine, while her gown was purest white. It irritated him that her parents treated her as a marital offering to be served out to debauched males.

Like the dog that he was, he wanted to snarl at her suitors, warning them to stay the hell away. But what good would come of it, except to embarrass her among her family and friends?

No. Better to remain in the shadows and keep watch over her. He'd seen so much death and war in the past few months, he felt the need to protect something fragile and good. Soon enough, he'd have to go back to the Crimean Peninsula. He'd have to face the demons and ghosts he'd left behind, and, more than likely, a bullet would end his life.

For now, he would savour this last taste of freedom before the Army ordered him back to the battleground. He glared at Belgrave, watching the pair of them on the dance floor. For a brief moment he imagined himself holding a woman like Hannah in his arms.

His good friend, the Earl of Whitmore, approached with an intent glare upon his face. A moment later, Whitmore's younger brother, Lord Quentin Chesterfield, joined them.

'I hope, for your sake, Thorpe, that you weren't eyeing my sister.' The Earl spoke the words in a calm, deliberate fashion. 'Otherwise, I'll have to kill you.'

Lord Quentin leaned in, a mischievous smile on his face. 'I'll help.'

Michael ignored their threats, though he didn't doubt that they meant them. 'Your sister shouldn't be dancing with Belgrave. I don't trust him.'

'He might be a baron, but he looks a bit too polished, doesn't he?' Lord Quentin agreed. 'Like he's trying too hard to impress the women.'

'You could try a bit harder with your own attire.' Whitmore grimaced at his younger brother's dark purple jacket and yellow waistcoat.

'I like colourful clothing.' Lord Quentin shrugged and turned his attention back to the dancing couple. 'I suppose we shouldn't worry. Our father isn't going to allow Hannah to wed a man like Belgrave, even if he does propose.'

Glancing at the ceiling as if calculating a vast number, Lord Quentin thought to himself. 'Now how many proposals does that make for her this Season…seventeen? Or was it twenty-seven?'

'Five,' Whitmore replied. 'Thankfully, from no one appropriate. But I'll agree with you that Belgrave wouldn't be my first choice.' Crossing his arms, the Earl added, 'I'll be glad when she finds a husband. One less matter to worry about.'

From the tension in Whitmore's face, Michael suspected that impending fatherhood was his greater fear. 'How is the Countess?' he asked.

'One more month of confinement, and then, pray God, we'll have this child. Emily begged me to take her to Falkirk for the birth. We're leaving at dawn. Still, I'm not certain I want her to travel in her condition. Our last baby arrived weeks earlier than we'd expected.'

'Emily *is* approaching the size of a small carriage,' Lord Quentin interjected.

Whitmore sent his brother a blistering look, and Michael offered, 'I'll hold him down while you break his nose.'

A smile cracked over the Earl's face. 'Excellent idea, Thorpe.'

Changing the subject, Michael studied Lady Hannah once more. 'Do you think the Marquess will choose a husband for her this Season?'

'It's doubtful,' Whitmore replied. 'Hannah might as well have a note upon her forehead, telling the unmarried gentleman: "Don't Even Bother Asking."'

'Or, "The Marquess Will Kill You If You Ogle His Daughter",' Quentin added.

The brothers continued to joke about their sister, but Michael ignored their banter. Beneath it all, he understood their fierce desire to protect her. In that, they held common ground.

But regardless of what he might desire, he knew the truth. A Marquess's daughter could never be with a soldier.

No matter how badly he might want her.

'Lady Hannah, you are truly the loveliest woman in this room.' Robert Mortmain, the Baron of

Belgrave, led her in the steps of the polka, his smile broad.

'Thank you,' she murmured without looking at him.

She couldn't deny that Lord Belgrave was indeed charming and handsome, with dark brown hair and blue eyes. Born into wealth, nearly every unmarried woman had cast her snare for him—all except herself. There was something about him, a haughtiness that made Hannah uncomfortable.

Don't worry about it, she told herself. *Papa isn't going to force you to marry him, so there's no need to be rude.* The problem of Lord Belgrave would solve itself.

Hannah's skin crawled when the baron touched the small of her back, even with gloved hands. As they moved across the floor, she tensed. The smug air upon his face was of a man boasting to his friends. He didn't want to be with her; he wanted to show her off. A subtle ache began to swell through her temples.

Just a few minutes more, and the dance will be over, Hannah consoled herself. Then she could escape to the comfort of her room. It was nearly midnight, and though she was expected to remain until after two o'clock, she might be able to convince her father that she didn't feel well.

Lord Belgrave scowled when they danced past

the refreshment table. 'I didn't realise *he* would be here tonight.'

He was speaking of Lieutenant Thorpe, who was now openly staring at them. Displeasure lined the Lieutenant's face and he gripped the lemonade glass as though he intended to hurl it towards the Baron.

'Why did your father invite him, I wonder?' Lord Belgrave asked.

'Lieutenant Thorpe saved my brother Stephen's life a few years ago,' she admitted. 'They are friends.'

Though how Stephen had even encountered such a man, she'd never understand. Despite his military rank, Thorpe was a commoner—not the second son of a viscount or earl, as was customary for officers in the Army. And were it not for her brother's insistence, she knew the Lieutenant would never have been invited.

There was nothing humble or uncertain about the way he was watching them. Anger ridged his features, and though the Lieutenant kept himself in control, he looked like he wanted to drag her away from Belgrave.

'He's trying to better himself, isn't he?' Belgrave remarked. 'A man of his poor breeding only poisons his surroundings.'

From his intensity and defensive stance, the Lieutenant appeared as though he were still standing on a battlefield. Likely he'd be more comfortable holding a gun instead of a glass of lemonade.

'I don't want you near a man like him.' The baron scowled.

Lord Belgrave's possessive tone didn't sit well with her, but Hannah said nothing. It wasn't as if she intended to go anywhere near the Lieutenant. Even so, what right did Belgrave have to dictate her actions?

None whatsoever. The dance was nearly finished, and she was grateful for that. Her headache was growing worse, and she longed for an escape to her room. When the music ended, she thanked Lord Belgrave, but he held her hands a moment longer.

'Lady Hannah, I would be honoured if you'd consent to becoming my wife.'

She couldn't believe he'd asked it of her. Here? In the middle of a ballroom? Hannah's smile grew strained, but she simply answered, 'You'll have to speak with my father.'

No. No. A thousand times, no.

The baron's fingers tightened when she tried to pull away. 'But what of your wishes? If you did not require the Marquess's permission, what would you say?'

I would say absolutely not.

Hannah kept her face completely neutral. She didn't like the look in his eyes. There was a desperate glint in them, and she wondered if Belgrave's fortunes were as secure as he'd claimed. Forcing a laugh she didn't feel, Hannah managed, 'You flatter me, my lord. Any woman would be glad to call you her husband.'

Just not me. But then, a word to her father would take care of that. Although the Marquess presented an autocratic façade to his peers, he was softer towards her, probably because she'd never embarrassed him in public, or even hinted at rebellion. Obedient and demure, she'd made him proud.

Or at least, that's what she hoped.

Hannah managed to pry her hand free. Even so, she could feel the baron's eyes boring into the back of her gown. She walked towards her father and brothers, who were standing near the entrance to the terrace. From the serious expressions on their faces, she didn't want to interrupt the conversation. She took a glass of lemonade and waited outside the ballroom, in the darkened shadows near the terrace. It wasn't good to be standing alone, but she hoped she was near enough to her brothers that no one would bother her.

Everyone else was still inside, dancing and mingling with one another. Her head was aching even more, a dreadful pressure that seemed to spread.

Oh, please, not tonight, Hannah prayed. She'd suffered headaches such as these before, and they were wretched, attacking her until she was bedridden for a full day or longer.

'You don't look well,' came a male voice from behind her.

Without turning around, she knew it was Lieutenant Thorpe. His voice lacked the cultured tones of the upper class, making his identity obvious. Hannah contemplated ignoring him and approaching her father, but then that would be rude. And whether or not she wanted to speak to him, good manners were ingrained within her.

'I am fine, Lieutenant Thorpe. Thank you for asking.'

Despite her unspoken dismissal, he didn't move away. She could feel him watching her, and, beneath his attention, her body began to respond. It felt too hot, even outside on the terrace. The silk of her dress felt confining. She fanned herself, not knowing why his very presence seemed to unnerve her so.

She didn't turn around, for it wasn't proper for her to be speaking with him alone. Even if he was completely hidden behind her, she didn't want to take a chance of someone seeing them. 'Was there something you wanted?'

He gave a low laugh, a husky sound that was far too intimate. 'Nothing you can give, sweet.'

Her face flushed scarlet, not knowing what he'd meant by that. She took a hesitant step closer to her father, sensing the Lieutenant's presence like a warm breeze upon her nape. Her gown rested off her shoulders, baring her skin before him. The strand of diamonds she wore grew heavy, and she forgot about her aching head. Instead, she was intensely conscious of the man standing behind her.

'You look tired.'

It was so true. She was tired of attending balls and dinner parties. Tired of being paraded around like a porcelain doll, waiting for the right marriage offer.

'I'm all right,' she insisted. 'You needn't worry about me.' She wanted him to leave her alone. He shouldn't be standing behind her, not where anyone could come upon them. She was about to step away when a gloved hand touched her back. The heat of his palm warmed her skin, and she jerked away out of instinct.

'Don't touch me,' she pleaded.

'Is that what you want?'

Her shoulders rose and fell, her breathing unsteady. Of course that's what she wanted. A man like Michael Thorpe was nothing but trouble.

But before she could say another word, his hand moved to her shoulders. Caressing the skin, gently easing the tension in her nape.

Step away from him. Scream, her brain insisted. But it was as though her mouth were stuffed with cotton. Her limbs were frozen in place, unable to move.

Her breasts prickled beneath the ivory silk,

becoming aroused. He'd removed a single glove, and the vibrant intimacy of his bare palm on her flesh made her tremble.

'Don't do this,' she pleaded. Her voice was a slight whisper, barely audible. 'You—you shouldn't.'

Well-mannered ladies did *not* stand still while they were accosted by a soldier. She could only imagine what her mother would say. But she had never been touched by a man like this, and the sensation was a secret thrill.

The Lieutenant's fingers slipped beneath the chain of her necklace, teasing her neck before winding into the strands of her coiffeur. 'You're right.'

His fingers were melting her resistance, making her feel alive. She was beginning to understand how a woman might cast off propriety, surrendering to a stranger's seduction.

'My apologies. You were too much temptation to resist.'

Her fingers clenched at her sides. 'Sir, keep your hands to yourself. Or you'll answer to my brother.'

'I'll try.'

Then she felt the lightest brush of his mouth upon her nape, a kiss he shouldn't have stolen. Wicked heat poured through her, and she gasped at the sensation.

Hannah whirled around, prepared to chastise him. But he'd already gone. She stared out at the gardens, but there was not a trace that he'd been there.

Only the gooseflesh on her arms and the storm of churning fire inside her skin.

'Why are you out here alone, Hannah?' The Marquess of Rothburne approached, having finished his conversation with her brothers. Her father frowned at her, as though she'd transgressed by avoiding a chaperone.

She prayed he didn't see her flushed cheeks or suspect the improper thoughts racing through her head. 'I would like permission to retire,' she said calmly. 'It's been a long evening. My head hurts, and I need to lie down.'

'Do you want me to send your maid with laudanum?' he asked, becoming concerned.

Hannah shook her head. 'No, I don't think it's going to be one of those headaches. But if you please, Papa, I'm very tired.'

Her father offered his arm. 'Walk with me for a few minutes, if you will.'

Hannah was hesitant, but she suspected her father had something else to discuss with her. He led her outside the terrace and down the gravel walkway toward her mother's rose garden. The canes held hints of new growth, though it would be early summer before the first blooms came. She raised her eyes to look out at the glittering stars, wishing she had brought a shawl.

Her skin was still sensitive from the Lieutenant's touch, her mind in turmoil. He'd awakened a restless side to her, and she didn't like it. Even while she walked, the shifting of her legs sent an uneasy ache within her body.

What had he done to her? And did that make her a wanton, for enjoying his fleeting touch?

Her father led her through the gardens toward the stables, their feet crunching upon the gravel as they walked. Hannah found herself comparing the two men. James Chesterfield was every inch a Marquess, displaying a haughty exterior that intimidated almost everyone except herself. Never did he stray from the rules of propriety. In contrast, Lieutenant Thorpe had a devil-may-care attitude, a man who did exactly as he pleased.

She shivered at the memory.

When her father's silence stretched on, Hannah guessed at the reason. 'You turned another proposal down, didn't you?'

James paused. 'Not yet. But the Baron of Belgrave asked for permission to call upon me tomorrow.'

It wasn't a surprise, but she felt it best to make her feelings known. 'I don't want to marry him, Papa.'

'He possesses a large estate, and comes from an excellent family,' her father argued. 'He seems to have a genuine interest in you.' He escorted her back to the house.

'Something about him bothers me.' Hannah paused, trying to find the right words. 'I can't quite explain it.'

'That isn't a good enough reason to reject his suit,' the Marquess protested.

She knew that, but was counting on her father to take her side. To change the subject, she asked, 'What sort of man are you hoping I'll wed? I do want to get married.'

The Marquess cleared his throat. 'I'll know him when I see him. Someone who will take care of you and make you happy.' He took her hand and gave it a gentle squeeze, though he didn't smile. Streaks of grey marred his bearded face, his hair silvery in the moonlight.

He led her back to the house, where they passed the ballroom filled with people. Music crescendoed amidst the laughter of guests, but it only made her headache worsen. Finally, her father escorted her to her room, bidding her good night.

At the door he added gruffly, 'Lady Whitmore brought over some ginger biscuits earlier this afternoon, when she visited. I had a servant place some in your room. Don't tell your mother.' Shaking his head in exasperation, he added, 'You would think that a woman in her condition would know better than to work like a scullery maid. It's ridiculous that she wants to bake treats, like a common servant.'

While most women rested in their final month of pregnancy, her sister-in-law Emily had gone into a flurry of baking during the past several weeks.

Stephen humoured his wife, allowing her to do as she wished during her confinement.

Acting upon her father's unspoken hint, Hannah slipped inside her room for a moment and returned with two of the ginger biscuits. She handed them to her father, who devoured them.

'If I see Emily, I'll tell her how much you liked them,' she said.

He grimaced. 'She shouldn't be in the kitchens. Her ankles are swelling, so she said. If you see her, order her to put her feet up.'

'I will,' Hannah promised. Though he would never admit it, the Marquess thoroughly enjoyed his arguments with Stephen's wife.

After her father left, Hannah rang for her maid. She sat down at her dressing table, wondering if she would need the laudanum after all. Her headache hadn't abated and seemed to be worsening.

She massaged her temples in an attempt to block out the pain. It frustrated her, being unable to control this aspect of her life.

Then again, so much of her life was out of her hands. She should be accustomed to it by now. Her mother made every decision concerning her wardrobe and which balls and dinner parties she attended. Christine controlled what she ate, which calls she made…even when she was allowed to retire for the night.

Hannah ran her hands over a silver hairbrush,

praying for the day when she could make those decisions for herself. Though she supposed it was her mother's way of showing she cared about her welfare, as time went on, her home felt more and more like a prison.

Her gaze fell upon the list of reminders her mother had left behind. She'd received one every day since the age of nine, since, quite often, she didn't see her mother until the evening.

1. Wear the white silk gown and the Rothburne diamonds.
2. Wait for your father and brothers to introduce suitors to you.
3. Do not refuse any invitation to dance.
4. Never argue with any gentleman. A true lady is agreeable.

Hannah could almost imagine instruction number five: Never allow strange gentlemen to touch you. Her eyes closed, her head pounding with pain.

Folding the list away, she rested her forehead upon her palm. A slow ache built up in her stomach when she saw a morning dress the colour of butter laid out for tomorrow. She had never cared for the gown, and would have been quite happy to see it burned. It made her feel as though she were six years old.

But she would never dream of arguing with Christine Chesterfield. Her mother alternated the colours of her dresses, selecting gowns of white, rose and yellow. When Hannah had tried to suggest another colour once, Christine had put her foot down. It wouldn't surprise her if her mother measured each and every one of her necklines, to be sure that she wasn't revealing too much skin.

Just once, Hannah wished to have a scarlet dress. Or amethyst. A wild burst of colour to liven up her wardrobe. But she supposed real ladies weren't supposed to wear colours like that.

Hannah raised the hem of her gown, and at the glimpse of her petticoats, she thought of the man who would one day become her husband. Would he treat her with tenderness, bringing friendship and possibly love into their marriage?

Or was there…something more? Her mother had not breathed a word about the intimacy between a man and a woman. Only that she would learn of it, the night before her wedding. Any mention of the marriage bed made her mother blush and stammer.

The unexpected memory of Lieutenant's Thorpe's kiss made Hannah shiver. He never should have caressed her, especially with an ungloved hand, but then that was the sort of man he was. A man who made his own rules and broke them when he liked. The Lieutenant hadn't offered tired compliments or begged her father for permission to call upon her. Instead, he'd touched her in the shadows, and she'd come alive.

Nothing you can give, sweet.

What had he meant by those words? Her hands moved to her shoulders, over the sensitised skin. Her mother would have a fit of the vapours if she knew the Lieutenant had stolen a kiss. His mouth had touched her here, on the nape. Almost like a lover's kiss. A cold realisation dawned upon her when her fingers touched bare skin.

Her diamond necklace was gone. *No. Oh, no.* Panic shot through her, for the diamonds were worth nearly a thousand pounds.

Hannah threw open the door to her room and fled down the stairs. Keeping towards the wall, she tried to avoid notice.

She hid behind the doorway, searching the floor of the ballroom, but saw nothing. Nothing by the refreshment table, either.

Thoughts of the Lieutenant's hands around her throat made her wonder. Had he unfastened the clasp? She didn't want to believe that he'd taken the diamonds, but the last time she remembered wearing the necklace was in his presence.

With fear in her throat, she sought him out. The Lieutenant wasn't among the ballroom guests, but instead stood alone on the edge of the terrace. Before him, the boxwood hedges rose tall, like silent sentries.

His arms were crossed in the ill-fitting formal wear, causing the seams of the coat to stretch against his shoulders.

'I beg your pardon,' she murmured, stepping towards him, 'but may I speak with you a moment, Lieutenant?'

His gaze flicked across hers, but he shrugged. 'Aren't you afraid of your father? I believe it isn't proper for a lady to be in the company of a soldier.'

She ignored his mocking tone. She knew well enough that what she was doing was highly improper. 'I must ask you if you've seen my necklace. I've lost it, you see, and—'

'You think I took it.'

His posture had changed, and she wished she hadn't spoken. Just like her father, he was a man of pride. Soldiers valued their honour above all else, and she'd just insulted his.

Hannah chose her words carefully. 'The clasp may have slipped when you—when you touched my neck. I thought it dropped where I was standing.'

That sounded reasonable enough, didn't it? Surely he wouldn't take offence—

'I stole nothing from you.' A hard edge accompanied his remark. 'And there's nothing of yours that I want.'

His harsh words stabbed her pride. He wasn't merely speaking of the necklace any more. Hannah forced herself to nod, though her cheeks were burning. 'I didn't mean to imply anything.'

'Yes, you did. I'm the only man here who would need diamonds. A man without a fortune.'

'You aren't the only one,' she argued. 'But that's neither here nor there. You don't have the necklace, and that's that.'

She gathered her skirts and strode towards the rose garden without bidding him goodbye. Rude, yes, but she had no desire to speak to him any longer. It was possible that his wayward fingers had loosened the clasp, and the necklace had fallen on to the ground when she'd walked outside.

The idea of the Lieutenant being a thief didn't sit well with her. He was her brother's friend, and she wanted to believe that there was honour in him.

Her headache had intensified to an unbearable level, as though someone were bashing rocks against her temples. The sooner she found the necklace, the sooner she could rest.

Hurrying towards the rose canes, Hannah dashed back to where she'd spoken with her father last. She retraced her footsteps, searching everywhere. But there was nothing. She turned the corner, only to stumble into the Baron of Belgrave.

'Oh! I'm sorry. I didn't expect to see you here,' she apologised. The moonlight spilled a faint light over his face, and his gloved fingers withdrew something glittering from his pocket.

'Were you looking for these?'

Belgrave held out the diamonds in his palm, and Hannah breathed a sigh of relief. 'Yes, thank you.'

She reached for them, but he pulled his hand back. 'I saw them lying on the ground after your father escorted you back to the house.' He returned the necklace to his pocket and held out his arm for her to accompany him. 'I thought you might come back for them.'

Hannah didn't take his elbow, for she had no desire to walk alone with the baron. Her instincts prickled, for she had once again crossed the line of what was proper. If anyone saw them unchaperoned, the gossip tales would spread faster than a house fire.

But he had her necklace, and she needed it back. Reluctantly, she placed her hand upon his arm. Perhaps if she gave him a moment, he would return the jewels.

The baron led her away from the house, and with each step, her headache worsened. When they neared the stables, Hannah had endured enough. 'Lord Belgrave, give me my diamond necklace, if you please.'

And go away. Where were her father and brothers when she needed them most?

Belgrave's hawkish face appeared fierce in the moonlight. Diamonds or not, she'd made a terrible mistake in approaching him. She took a step back-wards, wondering if she dared flee.

The baron retrieved the necklace from his pocket and held the diamonds in his hand, stroking the gems. 'I overheard you speaking to your father about me.'

Hannah's heartbeat quickened, and she cast a glance around the garden, searching for another escape. 'Wh-what did you overhear?'

'You lied to me.' Cold anger edged his voice. 'You led me to believe you wanted my courtship.'

'I didn't want to hurt your feelings,' she ex-plained. His anger made her uncomfortable, and she was ready to get away from him. The necklace be hanged. Her safety was far more important than a strand of diamonds. With an apologetic look, she added, 'I'll send a servant to collect my necklace from you.'

'What's the matter? Are you afraid of me?' he murmured.

Hannah ignored the question and picked up her skirts, striding towards the house. Before she could reach the terrace, a firm hand clamped over her upper arm.

'I haven't finished our conversation.'

'We weren't having one,' she corrected. 'And I'll ask you to remove your hand from my arm.'

'You think you're better than me, don't you? Because your father is a Marquess and I a mere baron.' He bent closer, and her stomach wrenched, the pressure in her head rising higher.

Dear heaven, she felt like fainting. The headache was like a dagger grinding into her skull.

She opened her mouth to call for help, but Lord Belgrave cut off her scream. She struggled against his grip, but he pinched her nose. With the lack of air, the headache roared into a fury. Dizzy and sick, she stopped fighting, and he dragged her across the gravel. Nausea gripped her, and the agony in her head was so intense, it nearly brought her to her knees. It couldn't have come at a worse time.

The baron lowered his voice. 'You said that any woman would be fortunate to wed me.' He drew so close, Hannah could see the vengeance in his eyes. 'It looks like you're about to become very fortunate indeed.'

Chapter Two

Michael returned to the ballroom, his posture stiff with anger. Lady Hannah had all but accused him of stealing her diamonds. He might be poor, but he wasn't a thief. Yet she wouldn't believe that, would she? Her blush had revealed how she viewed him: as a lowborn man, a soldier who wouldn't hesitate to take advantage of a lady.

True, he had a weakness for beautiful women. But never if they were unwilling. And that was the curious part, wasn't it? He'd dared to touch Lady Hannah…and she hadn't protested. The aristocrat with impeccable manners hadn't slapped him with her fan, nor called out for help. She'd leaned into his touch, as though she were thirsty for it.

God, she'd smelled good. Like seductive jasmine, haunting and sweet. He hadn't been able to resist her. He'd wanted to run his mouth over her neck, sliding the ivory gown over those bare shoulders until he revealed more of her delicate skin, but then her brother would murder him where he stood.

Normally, Michael had no interest in husband-seeking innocents, but Lady Hannah captivated him. He didn't for a moment believe she would cast him a second glance. Not only because of her suspicions about the necklace, but also because of his status. As a lieutenant, he wasn't worthy of a woman like her.

He had no title, unlike the other officers who had bought their commissions. He'd been granted his own commission within the British Army as a gift from the Earl of Whitmore, after he'd saved the Earl's life five years ago. And last October he'd learned what it meant to give a command, knowing that men would die because of it.

He'd tried to save whatever men he could, after his Captain had died at Balaclava. But he'd failed to protect the vast majority of his company. Of the six hundred, less than two hundred had returned. He'd been one of them.

Even now, he could still hear the bullets ripping through flesh, the moans that preceded death. He couldn't erase the nightmares, no matter how hard he'd tried. A lump tightened in the back of his throat, and he went to get another drink. As he passed the entrance to the terrace, he wondered if he should check on Lady Hannah.

Though she wanted to find her diamonds, she was far too lovely to be venturing out alone. She needed someone to protect her from unsavoury men.

Before he could follow her, a gentleman stepped into his line of sight, clearing his throat. He was accompanied by Hannah's brother Stephen Chesterfield, the Earl of Whitmore.

'Forgive me, Thorpe, but there is someone whom I'd like you to meet.'

The older man wore a black cloth tailcoat, expertly tailored to his form. His salt-and-pepper beard and mustache were neatly groomed, while the rest of his head was bald. Gold glinted upon the handle of his cane, and every inch of the gentleman spoke of money. Idly, Michael wondered if the man wanted a personal guard.

'This is a friend of my father's,' Stephen said. 'Graf Heinrich von Reischor, the Lohenberg ambassador to England.'

Lohenberg. Uneasiness slipped over him like a gust of cold air. The mention of the country provoked a distant memory he couldn't quite grasp. His mouth tightened, and he forced himself to concentrate on the gentleman standing in front of him.

Whitmore finished the introduction, and Michael wondered if he was expected to bow before an ambassador. He settled upon a polite nod.

Graf von Reischor leaned upon his cane. 'Thank you, Lord Whitmore. I am most grateful for the introduction. If you will excuse us?' The Earl nodded to both of them and departed.

Now what was this all about? Michael wondered.

The Lohenberg Graf fixed his gaze upon him in an open stare, as though he were intrigued by what he saw. Then the man lowered his voice and spoke an unfamiliar language, one that sounded like a blend of German and Danish.

Michael wondered if he was supposed to understand the words, but he could do nothing but shake his head in ignorance.

Graf von Reischor's interest never wavered. 'Forgive me, Lieutenant Thorpe. I thought you might be from Lohenberg, given your appearance.'

'My appearance?'

'Yes.' The man's gaze was unrelenting, though there was a trace of surprise beneath it. 'You look a great deal like someone I know. Enough that you could be his son.'

'My father was a fishmonger. He lived in London all his life.'

The Graf didn't appear convinced. 'And your parents…they were both English?'

'Yes.' It didn't sit well with him that the Graf von Reischor was implying anything about his parentage. He had been their only son, and though it had been four years since they'd died of cholera, he hadn't forgotten Mary Thorpe dying in his arms. She'd been a saint, his mother. It shamed him that he'd never been able to provide more for them, though he'd done his best.

Graf von Reischor didn't appear convinced. 'It

may be a coincidence. But I don't know what to believe. You have no idea how strong the resemblance is.'

It was difficult to keep his anger in check. 'Paul Thorpe was my father. No other man. You have no right to suggest otherwise.'

'We should discuss this more in private,' the Graf said. 'Call upon me tomorrow at my private apartment at Number Fourteen, St James's Street.'

'I have no intention of calling upon you,' Michael retorted. 'I know who I am and where I come from.' He started to leave, but a gold-handled cane blocked his path.

'I'm not certain you understand, Lieutenant Thorpe,' the Graf said quietly. 'The man you resemble is our king.'

Michael pushed his way past the Graf, refusing to even acknowledge the man's words. He had no desire to be the brunt of a nobleman's joke. A Prince? Hardly. Von Reischor was trying to make sport of him; he wasn't foolish enough to fall prey to such nonsense.

As he made his way through the room of people, his anger heated up. Who did the Graf think he was, implying that a common soldier could be royalty? It was ridiculous to even consider.

A coldness bled through his veins, for the encounter had opened up the dreams that sometimes haunted him. Dreams of a long journey, voices shouting at him and a woman's tears.

He gripped his fists. It wasn't real. None of it was. And he refused to believe false visions of a life that wasn't his.

To take his mind off the ludicrous proposition, he decided to find Lady Hannah. She'd been gone a long time, and he hadn't seen her return to the terrace.

He retraced her path toward the roses. She'd been wearing a white gown, so it shouldn't be difficult to find her amidst the greenery. But after an extensive search of the shrubbery and rose beds, there was no sign of her.

She'd been here. He'd swear it on his life. Michael thought back to the direction she'd gone, and he knelt down near the walkway. It was an easy matter to slip back into his military training.

Light footprints had left an imprint upon the gravel. Michael tracked her path around the side of the house, when abruptly the footprints were joined by a heavier set. Then something…no, someone, had been dragged off.

His instincts slammed a warning into him—especially when he spied Lady Hannah's diamond necklace lying in the grass.

Michael raced toward the stables, cursing that he hadn't followed Lady Hannah immediately. There was no sign of her anywhere.

Michael clutched the diamonds, and near the end of the walkway, he spied a single landau and driver. Surely the driver would have seen anyone coming from the stables.

'Lady Hannah Chesterfield,' he demanded. 'Where did she go?'

The man shrugged, his hands buried in his pockets. 'Ain't seen nothing.'

He was lying. Michael grabbed the driver by his coat and hauled him off the carriage. A handful of sovereigns spilled onto the ground, and the driver scuttled to pick them up.

A haze of red fury spread over him as he pressed the man up against the iron frame of the carriage. 'Who took her?'

When the driver stubbornly kept silent, Michael tightened his grip on the man's throat. 'I'm not one of those titled gentlemen you're used to,' he warned. 'I'm a soldier. They pay me to kill enemies of the Crown. And right now, I see you as one of my enemies.' Holding fast, he waited long enough until the man started to choke.

Michael loosened his fingers, and the driver sputtered and coughed. 'The—the B-Baron of Belgrave. Said they was runnin' off t'be together. Paid me not to talk.'

'What does his carriage look like?'

The driver described an elaborate black brougham

with the baron's crest. Michael stepped aboard the carriage. 'I'll be needing this.'

'But—but you can't steal his lordship's landau! I'll lose me post!'

Michael took the reins and nodded to the man. 'And what do you think will happen when you explain to the Marquess of Rothburne that you allowed his daughter to be abducted for a few sovereigns? You had best alert him immediately, or you'll face much worse than dismissal.' Snapping the reins, Michael drew the landau around the circle and toward the London streets.

There were a thousand different places Belgrave might have taken her. As he struggled to make his way through the London traffic, Michael went through the possibilities. Was the baron trying to compromise her or wed her?

If the intent was to compromise her, then likely he would take Lady Hannah back to his town house where they would be caught together. Michael's fist curled into the diamond necklace. No innocent young lady deserved this. By God, he wanted to kill the baron for what he'd done.

Luck was on his side, for when he reached a side street past Grosvenor Square, he spotted the baron's brougham, which had pulled to a stop by the side of the road. *Thank God.*

Michael raced forward, urging the horses towards

the vehicle. He barely waited for the landau to stop before he ran to Belgrave's carriage and jerked the door open.

Lady Hannah was lying on the floor of the carriage, moaning with her eyes closed. Lord Belgrave appeared slightly panicked, his face pale.

Michael wasted no time and dragged the baron out, pushing him up against the black brougham. 'I should kill you right now.'

Belgrave blanched, and Michael punched him hard, taking satisfaction when he broke the baron's nose.

Blood streamed from the wound, and Belgrave snarled, trying to fight back. 'I'll see you hanged for assaulting me.'

Michael leaned in close, his grip closing over Belgrave's throat. 'I haven't yet decided if I'm going to let you live. I'm sure Lady Hannah's brother wouldn't mind at all if I rid London of an insect such as yourself.'

He clipped the baron across the jaw, following it up with another punch to the man's ear. The blow sent Belgrave reeling before he lost consciousness and slid to the ground. Michael glared at Belgrave's driver, who hadn't lifted a finger to help defend his master.

'My lord, I had no choice,' the driver apologised. 'The baron insisted—'

Michael cut him off. 'Take Belgrave back to Roth-burne House in this landau. Tell the Marquess what happened, and I'll bring Lady Hannah home.'

The driver didn't argue, but took possession of the landau immediately, loading Belgrave's slumped form inside. Michael waited until he'd gone, then climbed inside the brougham to Lady Hannah.

'Are you all right? Did he harm you?'

Lady Hannah clutched her head, tears streaming down her face. 'No. But my head hurts. The pain—it's awful.'

Her eyes were closed, and she was holding her-self so tightly, as if trying to block out the torment.

'Just try to hold on, and I'll bring you home to your father's house.' Gently, Michael placed her back into the carriage seat and closed the door. Taking control of the reins, he turned them back towards Rothburne House. The other driver had already departed with the Baron of Belgrave.

It had been tempting to leave Belgrave in the streets for thieves or cut-throats to find. A man like the baron didn't deserve mercy.

Michael increased the pace, turning towards Hyde Park, when he heard Hannah call out, 'Lieutenant Thorpe! Please, I need you to stop.'

Damn it. If she were ill, he needed to get her home. Get her a doctor. Stopping the carriage would only blemish her reputation even more.

He slowed the pace of the carriage and asked, 'Can you hold on a little longer?'

'I can't. I'm sorry,' she pleaded. 'I'm going to be sick.'

Michael expelled another curse and pulled the brougham toward a more isolated part of the park. With any luck, no one would see them or ask what they were doing.

He opened the carriage door and found Hannah curled up into a ball, her face deathly pale. 'What can I do to help you?'

'Just…let me stay here for a bit. You don't have any laudanum, do you?'

He shook his head. 'I'm sorry. Do you want me to go and fetch some?' But even as he offered, he knew it was a foolish thing to say. He couldn't leave her here alone, not in this condition.

'No.' She kept her eyes closed, resting her face against the side of the carriage. 'Just give me a few moments.'

'Let me help you lie down,' he suggested.

'It hurts worse if I lean back.' Her breathing was shaky, and Michael sat across from her. A gas lamp cast an amber glow across the carriage, and she winced. 'The light hurts.'

He'd never felt so helpless, so unable to help her through this nightmare. She was fighting to breathe, her face grey with exertion.

And suddenly, his worry about her family and

her reputation seemed ridiculous in light of her illness. This was about helping her to endure pain, and that was something he understood. He'd watched men suffering from bullet wounds, crying out in torment. On the battlefield, he'd done what he could to ease them. It was all he could do for her now.

Michael closed the carriage door, making it as dark as possible. He removed his jacket and covered up the window to keep out the light.

'I can't...can't breathe.' Her shoulders were hunched, her eyes turning glassy.

He didn't ask permission, but unbuttoned the back of her gown in order to loosen her stays. Hannah didn't protest, and she seemed to breathe easier once it was done. He held her upright in his arms, keeping silent.

An hour passed, and in time, he felt her body begin to relax. She slept in his arms, but Michael couldn't release his own tension. Her father would be looking for them. He needed to get her out of here, take her home. But he was afraid of causing her more pain.

Her hair had fallen loose from its pins, and the dark honey locks rested against his cheek, smelling sweetly of jasmine. He'd heard that some women suffered from headaches as excruciating as this one, but he'd never witnessed it before.

Nonetheless, her unexpected illness had probably saved her from Belgrave's unwanted attentions. It was a blessing in that sense.

The night air was cold, but Hannah's body heat kept him warm. His neck and shoulders were stiff, but that didn't bother him. She was no longer in pain, and he was grateful for it.

It had been a gruelling experience, one he didn't care to repeat. He was unbearably alert, attuned to Hannah in a way he'd never expected. Against his chest, he could feel the rise and fall of her breathing.

There would be hellish consequences. And yet he wouldn't have changed what he'd done. He'd rescued her from that bastard Belgrave and protected her innocence. She could go into her future marriage as an untouched bride, the way she should. That is, if he could get her home without anyone realising where she'd spent the last hour or two.

He had his doubts.

Michael watched her sleeping, the strands of hair twining around her throat and spilling over the curve of her breasts. Her beauty stole his breath away.

Innocence and purity. Everything he didn't deserve.

From his pocket, he withdrew the strand of diamonds and fastened them around her throat. Bare skin peeped from the open back of her dress where he'd loosened her corset. He wanted to kiss her, to run his mouth over that silken skin. Like forbidden fruit, she tempted him to taste.

Only a few hours ago, he'd touched her back, indulging himself in a bit of wickedness. She'd allowed him liberties he never should have taken.

Not for you, his brain warned.

An honourable man would leave her alone to sleep, taking the reins and driving her home again. He wouldn't run his palms over her arms, watching her skin tighten with gooseflesh. A good man would ignore the seductive glimpses of female skin and set his baser urges under control.

But he wasn't good. He wasn't honourable. Right now, he'd been given a few stolen moments with this woman. And he intended to take them.

Michael lowered his mouth to her shoulder blade, tracing the fragile skin up to her nape. Hannah shivered, lifting her face towards his as she awakened from sleep. He took possession of her softened mouth, not asking for permission.

Hannah awoke with her body temperature rising, as though she were suffering from a fever. The Lieutenant was kissing her, and she was sitting in his lap.

She couldn't move from the shock of feelings coursing through her. No man had ever kissed her before, and she trembled beneath the onslaught. It was as though he were starving for her, his mouth hot and hungry.

His tongue slid inside her mouth, caressing her intimately. Hannah had never imagined such a thing, and desire poured through her, making her skin hotter.

Push him away. Beg for him to stop.

But her mind was disconnected from her body, once again. She felt herself arching towards him, needing to be closer. His hands slipped beneath the open back of her gown, and dimly she remembered the Lieutenant unlacing her, to help her breathe easier.

The touch of his bare hands on her skin made her cry out, 'No! Stop, please.'

The remnants of her headache pressed into her, and tears spilled out. Not because of his unexpected kiss, but because of her guilt. He'd evoked shameful feelings inside of her, arousing her. And though she wanted to lay the blame at his feet, she knew in her heart that she couldn't. She'd allowed him to kiss her, to touch her in ways that no good girl would allow.

'I'm not going to apologise for that.' His voice was low and deep, a man who had seized what he'd wanted. 'You kissed me back.'

'I didn't want to.'

Liar. An aching throbbed within her womb. She felt damp, restless. The touch of his hard body against her pliant flesh was almost too much to bear.

'Yes, you did.' The the Lieutenant broke away, his breathing harsh. He moved to the opposite side of the carriage, resting his wrists on his knees. His head hung down, dark hair shadowing his face. He looked as though he'd been in a fist fight. 'I need to drive you home.'

'Please.' She tried to hold the back of her gown together, but the edges wouldn't hold. Exposed to him, she wanted to die of embarrassment.

'I'll help you get dressed,' he said. 'You'll never manage by yourself.'

'I don't want you to touch me,' she snapped. 'Take me back.'

'What do you think your father will say when he sees you like this?'

'You should be more worried about yourself,' she countered. 'He'll want to kill you.'

The the Lieutenant sent her a patronising smile. 'For saving your virtue?'

'You're the one who tried to attack me just now.'

'Sweet, I'm not a man who has to attack anyone.' He pulled his coat from the carriage door, and Hannah winced at the flash of light from one of the street lamps.

She said nothing, her thoughts drifting back and forth, trying to decide whether he was a rogue or a man of honour. Yes, he'd kissed her when he shouldn't have. But he'd also taken care of her.

Though he should have brought her home immediately, he'd listened when she'd begged him to stop the carriage. The excruciating, jarring sensation from the horses had made each mile an unending torture.

Another man wouldn't have done the same. He'd have ignored her needs, riding as fast as he dared, back to Rothburne House. But not the Lieutenant.

So many questions gathered up, needing to be asked. Hannah traced her swollen lips, wondering what had driven him to do such a thing.

'You don't need to be afraid of me,' he said quietly. 'I'm not going to kiss you again.' His cravat was loosened from his collar, while he donned the ill-fitting jacket.

'I should hope not.'

He raised his gaze to hers, and she caught a glimpse of green eyes with flecks of brown. His cheeks held a light stubble, and for a moment, she wondered why the texture hadn't scratched her skin.

'You really are an innocent, aren't you?' He glanced over her ivory silk gown, and the remark didn't sound like a compliment.

'I suppose. You speak of it as though it's a bad thing.'

He glanced outside the carriage window, as if searching for someone. 'It's what most men want.'

'But not you.'

A dark laugh escaped him. 'I'm not a good man at all.'

She didn't entirely believe that. 'Please take me home,' she reminded him. 'My family will be worried.'

'Turn around,' he ordered.

She knew what he needed to do, but she hesitated to let him touch her corset. It didn't matter that he'd already done so; she'd been half out of her mind with pain. 'No, it isn't proper.'

The Lieutenant didn't listen to her argument, but forced her to turn around. His hands fumbled with the stays, pulling them tight before tying them. 'Proper or not, I won't let your father think I ravaged you in a carriage.'

He was right. Her father would be angry enough at both of them, without him drawing the wrong conclusions.

'How long have we been gone, do you think?' Her stomach didn't feel right, and her head still ached.

'Longer than an hour. Two or three, perhaps. It isn't dawn yet.' His large hands struggled with the tiny buttons, and she couldn't help but be even more aware of him. He muttered, 'I'm better at taking these off than buttoning them up.'

Hannah didn't doubt that at all. When he'd

finished, she rested her head against the side of the carriage, waiting for him to go back to the driver's seat.

'Are you feeling better?' he asked.

'I'll manage.' Thank heaven, it had been one of the shorter headaches, swift and furious. The after-effects would dwell with her for a while, but the worst was over.

'What are you going to tell my father?' she asked.

Michael opened the door to the carriage, leaving it slightly open. 'The truth. Neither of us has done anything wrong.'

I have, Hannah thought. The kiss might not mean a thing to him, but it had shaken her. The sensation of his mouth upon hers had been the most sinful thing she'd ever experienced. She'd fallen under his spell, wanting to know his touch in a way she shouldn't.

Michael opened the carriage door the rest of the way, about to disembark, when they heard the sounds of men shouting and the rumble of another carriage approaching. Her father's voice broke through the stillness, and within moments, he was standing in front of the door.

'Are you all right?' the Marquess demanded of Hannah.

Hannah gripped her hands together, cold fear icing through her. For she suspected the truth was not going to be enough to pacify her father.

Chapter Three

'Get away from my daughter,' the Marquess of Rothburne ordered.

Hannah tried to rise from her seat, but the Lieutenant motioned her back. With a horrifying clarity, she realised what her father must think. With a pleading look she insisted, 'Papa, this isn't what it looks like. Lieutenant Thorpe rescued me from Lord Belgrave.'

Though she tried to find the right explanation, her father looked more interested in murder than the truth.

Hannah continued talking, though she knew how unlikely it must sound. 'Lieutenant Thorpe tried to bring me home but…I had one of my headaches. I didn't have any laudanum, and the pain was unbearable. He obeyed me when I ordered him to stop the carriage.'

Her father gave no indication that he'd even heard her speaking, but gave a nod to one of his footmen. The large servant reached to seize hold of the Lieutenant, but Michael's hand shot out and stopped him. With a twist to the man's wrist, the footman had no choice but to release him.

'Enough.' The Lieutenant climbed down from the carriage and regarded the Marquess. 'Instead of having this conversation here in the park, I suggest we return to Rothburne House. Take Lady Hannah home with you, and see to her health. I will follow in this carriage.'

'I should have the police drag you off to Newgate right now,' the Marquess countered.

'He didn't dishonour me, Papa.' Hannah moved forward, but when she exited the carriage, the world tipped. A rushing sound filled her ears, and Michael caught her elbow, steadying her. 'I swear it. He protected me while I was ill.'

'Because of him, you may be ruined.' Her father stared at her as though she'd just run off with a chimney sweep. 'You just spent the night with a common soldier.'

But she hadn't. Not really. Heated tears sprung up in her eyes, for she didn't know how to respond to her father's accusations. Never could she have imagined he'd be this unreasonable.

A defence leapt to her lips, but Lieutenant Thorpe shook his head. 'As I said before, this is not the place to talk. Take Lady Hannah home.'

Hannah had never heard anyone issue an order to

her father before, but the Lieutenant didn't appear intimidated by the Marquess.

'No one knows about this,' she whispered. 'My reputation is still safe.'

'Is it?' Her father's face was iron-cast. 'The Baron of Belgrave knows all about what happened to you. Nonetheless, he has graciously offered to wed you.'

She'd rather die than wed Belgrave. 'Papa, it isn't as bad as all that. Lieutenant Thorpe did nothing wrong.'

'Belgrave informed me that Thorpe assaulted him and took you away in a stolen carriage.'

'That lying blackguard,' Hannah blurted out, then clamped her hand over her mouth. Insults wouldn't help her cause.

Horrified, she met her father's infuriated expression, hoping he wouldn't believe the lies. Surely he would trust her, after all the years she'd been an obedient daughter. One mistake wouldn't eradicate everything, would it?

Thoughts of the Lieutenant's forbidden kiss flayed her conscience. She could have fought him off, but instead, she'd kissed him back. It had been curiosity and shock, mingled together with the first stirrings of desire. She'd wanted to know what a real kiss would be like. But not at this terrible cost.

'Harrison, take my daughter home,' the Marquess

commanded to his footman. 'I will accompany Lieutenant Thorpe in this carriage.'

The Lieutenant gave an abrupt nod, and Hannah tried to fathom the man's thoughts. His hazel eyes were shielded, his face expressionless.

She prayed that they could undo the mistake that had been made. Surely they could keep matters quiet. She'd been a victim and didn't deserve to be punished like this. If anyone deserved to be drawn and quartered, it was Lord Belgrave.

As the footman closed the carriage door, Hannah twisted her hands together. Thank goodness the Lieutenant possessed no title. Were he an earl or a viscount, no doubt her father would demand that he marry her.

As a common officer in the British Army, that would never happen. She should feel relieved, but her nerves wound tighter. Her father was so angry right now, he might do something rash.

And she didn't know what that might be.

'You should know that the only thing that prevents me from killing you where you stand is the fact that I don't want your blood staining my carpet.' The Marquess of Rothburne pointed to a wingback chair in his study. 'Sit.'

'I am not your dog,' Michael responded. He was well aware that he was only tossing oil upon the fire of James Chesterfield's rage, but he refused to behave as if he'd seduced Lady Hannah.

Kissed her, yes. But that wasn't a crime.

Michael rested his forearms upon the back of the chair and met the Marquess's gaze squarely. 'I don't regret rescuing Lady Hannah from the Baron of Belgrave. You know as well as I that the man isn't worthy of her.'

'And neither are you.'

'You're right.' There was no reason to take offence at the truth. He possessed enough to live comfortably on his army salary, but it wasn't enough to support a Marquess's daughter. He didn't want a wife, or any family who would rely upon him.

'Because of you, her reputation is destroyed.'

'No.' Michael drew closer to the desk, resting his hands upon the carved wood. 'Because of Belgrave. Were it not for him, she'd never have been taken from Rothburne House.'

'You should have brought her home immediately!' The Marquess's face was purple with wrath.

He knew it. But she'd been in such pain, he hadn't wanted to make it worse. At the time, he'd thought it would only be for a short while—not hours. Perhaps he should have driven her home, despite the agony she would have endured. Still, it did no good to dwell upon events he couldn't change.

'She's had headaches like that one before, hasn't

she?' Michael said softly. 'She told me she keeps laudanum in her reticule.'

'That is beside the point.'

'Is it? I presume you've seen how much she suffers? That any form of light or sound gives her pain beyond all understanding? I've seen men take a bullet through their shoulder and suffer less than what I saw her endure.'

He didn't add that there were moments when he'd wondered if she was going to die. She'd been so pale, in such agony.

'Even if what you say is true, it doesn't change the fact that you stayed with her alone for hours.' James reached out for a letter opener, running his finger along the edge. 'She is my only daughter. My youngest child.'

'This wasn't her fault.' Yet, Michael didn't see a clear solution. It wasn't fair for Hannah to endure the sly gossip of the society matrons, nor to be shunned if word got out.

'No, it's yours.' The Marquess folded his arms, adding, 'Don't think that I would allow a man like you to wed her. You won't touch a penny of her inheritance.'

Michael stepped back, his anger barely controlled. Keeping his voice steady, he said, 'I don't want anything from either of you. She was in trouble, and I went to help her. Nothing more.'

The Marquess set his pen down. 'I want you to

leave England. I don't want her to ever set eyes upon you again.' Picking up his pen, he began writing. 'I am going to ask your commanding officer to see to it. I'll contribute enough funds to the Army to make sure you stay far away from London.'

Michael didn't doubt that the Marquess's money would accomplish anything the man wanted. 'And what will happen to Lady Hannah?'

The Marquess set down his pen. 'Belgrave has offered to wed her.'

'No. Not him.' Michael clenched his fist. 'You would offer her up to a man like that?'

'There is nothing wrong with Belgrave. He's going to keep Hannah's reputation safe.'

'You mean he's going to reveal the scandal to everyone if she doesn't wed him,' Michael guessed.

The Marquess didn't deny it. 'I won't let my daughter be hurt. Not if I can prevent it from happening.'

Hannah had seen her mother cry before, but never like this. Usually Christine Chesterfield used her tears to dramatic effect, whenever her husband wouldn't let her opinion sway him.

This time, Christine simply covered her mouth with her hand while the tears ran down her cheeks. Hannah sat across from her, while two cups of tea went cold. The grandfather clock in the parlour chimed eight o'clock. Eight hours was all it had taken to change her life completely.

'I promise you, Mother, I am fine,' Hannah murmured. 'Neither of them compromised me.' She refused to cry, for the shock was still with her. 'I don't know what else to say, when you won't accept the truth.'

'This isn't about truth.' Christine dabbed her eyes with a handkerchief. 'It's about appearances.'

'It will be all right,' Hannah insisted. 'My friends will believe me, if they hear rumours. They know I would never do anything of that nature.' She stood up, pacing across the carpet. 'I don't see why we cannot simply tell everyone what happened.'

Christine blew her nose. 'You are far too naïve, my dear. We can't risk any of this scandal leaking to anyone.'

'I am not ruined.'

'You are. Your only hope of salvaging what's left of your honour is to marry Lord Belgrave and to do so quickly.'

'I will not marry that horrid man. He's the reason all of this happened!' Hannah arranged her skirts, tucking her feet beneath them. 'He kidnapped me from my own home, Mother! Why won't you believe me?'

Her mother only shook her head sadly. 'I believe you, Hannah. But the greater problem is that you spent hours alone in a carriage with a soldier. Lord

Belgrave is right: nothing will cover up that scandal, if it gets out.'

But no one knew about it, except...

'He's threatening you,' Hannah predicted, suddenly realising the truth. 'Belgrave plans to tell everyone about the scandal unless I wed him. Is that it?'

Her mother's face turned scarlet. 'We won't let that happen.'

Hannah couldn't believe what she was hearing. Her parents were allowing themselves to be manipulated for her sake.

Christine avoided looking at her. 'You have nothing to fear from the baron, Hannah. I believe him when he says he has nothing but remorse for his actions. He wants to start again, and I think you should give him a second chance.'

'I'd rather kiss a toad.'

'He is coming to pay a call on you tomorrow. And you *will* see him and listen to what he has to say.'

Without meeting Hannah's incredulous gaze, Christine retrieved a sheet of paper from a writing desk and chose a pen. Hannah clenched her fingers together, for she knew her mother was composing another list.

'Mother, no,' she pleaded. 'There has to be another way. Perhaps I could go to Falkirk with Stephen and Emily.' Her brother would offer her the sanctuary of his home without question.

'They have already left, early this morning,' her mother said. 'And your brother has enough to worry about with Emily due to give birth in a few weeks. He doesn't know what happened last night, and we are not going to tell him until it's all sorted out.'

Her mother handed her the list, and walked her to the door. 'Now. Go to your room and rest until eleven o'clock. When you rise, wear your rose silk gown with the high neck and pagoda sleeves. We will discuss your future over luncheon. The baron will come to call upon you tomorrow to discuss the arrangements.'

'I don't want to see that man again, much less marry him,' Hannah insisted.

'You no longer have a choice. You'd best get used to the idea, for your father is making the arrangements now. You'll be married within a week.'

After her mother's door closed, Hannah stormed down the stairs, her shawl falling loose from her shoulders. There was no hope of finding sleep, not now.

With a brief glance at the list, she saw her mother's orders.

1. Rest until eleven o'clock.
2. Wear the rose silk gown.

3. Drink a cup of tea with cream, no sugar, to calm your nerves.

Hannah read the list three times, her hands shaking. Her entire life, she'd done everything her parents had asked. She had studied her lessons, listened to her governesses and done everything she could to please her family.

It made her stomach twist to see them turn against her this way. Her parents no longer cared about her future happiness—only their reputations.

Though she was supposed to return to her room, she kept moving towards the gardens. Tears of rage burned down her cheeks. All her years of being good meant nothing if she had to wed a man like Belgrave.

The list no longer held the familiarity of a mother's love, helping her to remember the tasks at hand. Instead, it was a chain, tightening around her neck.

Hannah crumpled up the paper and threw it into the shrubbery. Rules, rules and more rules. Once, she'd thought that, by obeying the rules, her reward would come.

Did her mother truly expect her to wed the man who had caused her such misery? She'd sooner drown herself in the Thames than marry Belgrave.

She stumbled through the garden, the remnants of her headache rising up again. Why? Why did this have to happen to her? Only yesterday, she'd had so many choices before her. Now, she had nothing at all.

Hannah wrapped her arms around her waist, as if holding the pieces of herself together. With each step forward, she released the sobs, letting herself have a good cry. She wandered down the gravel pathway, to the place where she had lost her necklace last night.

Unexpectedly, her hand rose to her throat. The diamonds were there. The Lieutenant must have returned the necklace to her early this morning. She didn't remember him wrapping the strand around her neck, for most of the night had been a blur of pain.

After she'd been abducted, the baron had grown flustered at her illness, demanding that she cease her tears. He'd cursed at her, but she'd been unable to stop weeping.

Then the Lieutenant had rescued her. He'd covered up all light, keeping her warm. Not speaking a sound. Holding her in the darkness.

Hannah pulled her shawl around her shoulders. She didn't know what to think of him. One minute, he'd been her saving grace, and the next, he'd stolen a kiss.

Shielding her eyes against the morning sun, she saw him standing near the stables while a groom readied his horse. Almost against her will,

Hannah's feet moved forward, drawing her closer to the Lieutenant. She didn't have the faintest idea what to say, or why she was even planning to speak to him.

The Lieutenant's hazel eyes were tired, his cheeks covered in dark stubble. The white cravat hung open at his throat, and he held his hat in his hands.

Hannah dipped her head in greeting, and out of deference, the groom stepped away to let them talk. She kept her voice low, so the servant wouldn't over-hear their conversation. 'I'm glad my father didn't murder you.'

Michael shrugged and put on one of his riding gloves. 'I'm a difficult man to kill.'

Hannah found her attention caught by his long fingers, and she remembered his bare hand caress-ing her nape. No one had ever made her feel that way before, her skin sparking with unfamiliar sen-sations.

She closed her eyes, clearing her thoughts. Then she reached for what she truly needed to say. 'I never thanked you for rescuing me. It means a great deal to me. Even despite all of this.'

The Lieutenant gave a slight nod, as though he didn't know how to respond. He didn't acknowledge the words of gratitude, but instead glanced over at the house. 'Lord Rothburne said you're going to marry Belgrave.'

Hannah tensed. 'My father is ready to marry me

off to the next titled gentleman who walks through the gate.' She stared him in the eyes. 'I won't do it. He'll have to drag me to the altar.'

'I thought you were the obedient sort.'

'Not about this.' She could hardly believe the words coming out of her mouth. It wasn't like her, not at all, but then she felt like someone had taken a club to her life, smashing it into a thousand glass pieces.

Obedience had brought her nothing. And right now she wanted to voice her frustrations to someone who understood.

'Why is this happening?' she whispered. 'What did I do that was so wrong?'

'Nothing,' the Lieutenant said. His hand started to reach for hers, but he drew back, as if remembering that it wasn't proper. 'Your only fault is being the daughter of a Marquess.'

'I wish I weren't.' Hannah lowered her head. 'I wish I were nothing but an ordinary woman. I would have more freedom.'

No lists, no rules to follow. She could make her own decisions and be mistress of her life.

'You wouldn't want that at all.' The Lieutenant gestured toward her father's house. 'You were born to live in a world such as this.'

'It's a prison.'

'A gilded prison.'

'A prison, nonetheless.' She raised her eyes to his.

'And now I'll be sentenced to marriage with Lord Belgrave. Unless I can find a way out.'

He didn't respond, but she saw the way his mouth tightened, the sudden darkness in his eyes. 'You will.'

'And what about you?' She realised she'd never asked what had happened to him. Surely the Lieutenant had faced his own lion's den, courtesy of the Marquess. 'What happened between you and my father?'

He hesitated before answering, 'My commanding officer will see to it that I stay on the Crimean Peninsula.'

'What exactly...does that mean?' A shiver of foreboding passed through her.

'I'll be sent to fight. Possibly on the front lines.' He shrugged, as if it were to be expected. But she understood what he wouldn't say. Men who fought on the front lines had essentially been issued a death sentence without a court-martial. Certainly it was no place for an officer.

She stared at him, her skin growing cold. Though he might be an unmannered rogue who had taken unfair advantage of her, he didn't deserve to die.

This is your fault. Her conscience drove the truth home like an arrow striking its target. If it weren't for her, he'd be returning to his former duties.

'You were wounded before,' she said slowly. 'With the Light Brigade.'

He gave a nod. 'I would have been returning to duty anyway. I've made a full recovery.' He spoke as if it didn't matter, that this was of no concern.

She looked into his eyes, her heart suddenly trembling. 'It's not right for you to be sent away again.'

'I've no ties to London, sweet. I always expected to return. It doesn't matter.' He started towards his horse, but Hannah stopped him.

He was going to lose everything because of her. Because he'd rescued her and taken care of her that night.

'It matters.' She touched the sleeve of his coat, feeling obligated to do something for him. There had to be some way she could intervene with her father's unnecessary punishment.

'Stop looking at me like that,' he murmured, his eyes centering directly on hers.

'What do you mean?'

'Like you're trying to rescue me.'

'I'm not.' She lifted her face to his, studying those deep hazel eyes. He was a soldier, trained to strike down his enemies. Right now, he looked tired, but no less dangerous.

'Trust me, sweet. I'm not a man worth saving.' He took her hand in his and, despite the gloves, she felt the heat of his skin. 'You'd do well to stay away from me.'

The evocative memory of his stolen kiss conjured gooseflesh on her arms. The Lieutenant never took his eyes from her, and Hannah held herself motionless.

It went against everything she'd been taught, to hold an unmarried man's hand while standing in the garden where anyone could see. He was so close, the barest breath hung between them.

Something wanton and unbidden unfurled from within her, making her understand that Michael Thorpe was no ordinary man. He fascinated her. Tempted her.

And the daughter of a Marquess could never, never be with a man like him. He was right.

At last, she took her hand from his, ignoring the pang of disappointment. It was better for her to stay away from him. He was entirely the wrong sort of man.

Yet he was the only man who had noticed her absence at the ball. He hadn't stopped to notify her father and brothers, but had come after her straight away. An unexpected hero.

The Lieutenant's ill-fitting coat had a tear in the elbow. Shabby and worn, he didn't fit into the polished world in which she lived. But beneath his rebellious air was a man who had fought to save her.

Would he do so again, if she asked it of him?

'Lieutenant Thorpe, I have a favour to ask.'

He eyed her with wariness. 'What is it?'

It felt so awkward to ask this of him. She dug her nails into her palms, gathering up her courage.

'If I am forced into marriage with Lord Belgrave, would you…put a stop to the wedding?'

A lazy smile perked at his mouth. 'You're asking me to kidnap you from your own wedding?'

'If it comes to that—yes.' She squared her shoulders, pretending as though she hadn't voiced an inappropriate request. 'I shall try to avoid it, of course. You would be my last resort.'

He expelled a harsh laugh and went over to his horse, bringing the animal between them. Grasping the reins in one hand, he tilted his head to study her. 'You're serious.'

'Nothing could be more serious.' It was an arrangement, a practical way of preventing the worst tragedy of her life. And though it might cause an even greater scandal, she would do anything to escape marriage to Belgrave.

'I have to report to duty,' the Lieutenant warned. 'It's likely I would be gone within the week.'

She gave a brisk nod, well aware of that. 'Believe me, my parents want to see me married as soon as possible. It's likely a wedding will be arranged in a few days. I simply refuse to wed Belgrave. Any other man will do.'

'Even me?' He sent her a sidelong smile, as though he, too, couldn't believe what she was asking.

'Well, no.' She pinched her lips together, realising that she'd led him to believe something she'd never intended. 'I couldn't possibly—'

'Don't worry, sweet.' His voice grew low, tempting her once again. 'I'll stop your wedding, if it's in my power.'

She breathed once again, her shoulders falling in relief. 'I would be most grateful.' Knowing that he would be there in the background, to steal her away from an unwanted wedding, gave her the sense that somehow everything would be all right. She held out her gloved palm, intending to shake his hand on the bargain.

The Lieutenant took her gloved hand in his. Instead of a firm handshake, he raised her palm to his face. 'If I steal the bride away,' he murmured, pressing his lips to her hand, 'what will I get in return?'

Chapter Four

'What do you want?'

Michael's response was a slow smile, letting her imagine all the things he might do to a stolen bride, if they were alone.

Hannah's expression appeared shocked. 'I would never do such a thing. This is an arrangement, nothing more.'

Her face had gone pale, and Michael pulled back, putting physical distance between them. 'Don't you recognise teasing when you hear it, sweet?'

She looked bewildered, but shook her head. 'Don't make fun of me, please. This is about Belgrave. I simply can't marry him.'

'Then don't.'

'It's not that simple. Already my mother has decided it would be the best future for me.' Hannah rubbed at her temples absently. 'I don't know what I can do to convince her otherwise.'

'It's very simple. Tell her no.'

She was already shaking her head, making excuses to herself. 'I can't. She won't listen to a thing I say.'

'You've never disobeyed them, have you?'

'No.' She seemed lost, so vulnerable that he half-wished there was someone who could take care of her. Not him. There was no hope of that. She was far better off away from a man like himself.

'No one can force you to marry. Not even your father.' He adjusted her shawl so it fully covered her shoulders. 'Hold your ground and endure what you must.'

Visions flooded his mind, of the battle at Balaclava where his men had obeyed that same command. They'd tried valiantly to stand firm before the enemy. A hailstorm of enemy bullets had rained down upon them, men dying by the hundreds.

Was he asking her to do the same? To stand up to her father, knowing that the Marquess would strike her down? Perhaps it was the wrong course of action.

'I don't think I can,' Hannah confessed. She tugged at a finger of her glove, worrying the fabric. 'Papa can make my life a misery. And I'll be ruined if I don't marry.'

Though she was undoubtedly right, he could not allow himself to think about her future. They were worlds apart from one another. She would have to live with whatever choices she made.

'Time to make your own fortune. If you're already ruined, you've nothing left to lose. Do as you please.'

Hannah stared at him, as though she hadn't the faintest idea of how a ruined woman should behave. 'I don't know. I've always...done what I should.'

She took a step towards the house, away from him. He suddenly understood that she'd asked him to rescue her, not because of her parents, but because the need to obey was so deeply ingrained in her. If he kidnapped her from the wedding, she could lay the blame at his feet, not hers.

She's not your concern, his brain reminded him. *Let her make her own choices. Tell her no.*

But he didn't. Though he shouldn't interfere, neither would he let her marry a man like Belgrave. He let out a breath, and said, 'Send word to me if anything changes. Your brothers know where I can be found.'

'Will you be all right?' she asked in a small voice. 'What if my father—?'

'He can do nothing to me,' Michael interrupted. Within a week or two, there would be hundreds of miles between them. He'd be back with the Army, fighting the enemy and obeying orders until he met his own end. Men like him weren't good for much else.

The troubled expression on her face hadn't dimmed. Instead, a bright flush warmed her cheeks. 'Thank you for agreeing to help me.' Hannah reached up to her neck and unfastened the diamond necklace. 'I want you to have this.'

'Keep it.' He closed her fingers back over the glittering stones. An innocent like her could never conceive of the consequences, if he were to accept. Her father would accuse him of stealing, no matter that it had been a gift.

'If you're planning to keep watch over me, then you'll need a reason to return.' She placed it back in his palm.

He hadn't considered it in that light. 'You're right.' The necklace did give him a legitimate reason to return, and so he hid the jewellery within his pocket.

'Return in a day or two,' she ordered. 'And I'll see to it that you're rewarded for your assistance, whether or not it's needed.'

He wouldn't accept any compensation from her, though his funds were running out. 'It's not necessary.'

'It is.'

In her green eyes, Michael saw the loss of innocence, the devastating blow to her future. Yet beneath the pain, there was determination.

She crossed her arms, as if gathering her courage. 'I won't let my father destroy my future.' Her expression shifted into a stubborn set. 'And I won't let him destroy yours, either.'

* * *

The older woman wandered through the streets, her crimson bonnet vivid in the sea of dark brown and black. Michael pushed his way past the fishmongers and vendors, minding his step through Fleet Street.

Mrs Turner was lost again. He quickened his step, moving amid sailors, drovers and butchers. At last, he reached her side.

'Good morning,' he greeted her, tipping his hat.

No recognition dawned in her silver-grey eyes, but she offered a faint nod and continued on her path.

Damn. It wasn't going to be one of her better days. Mrs Turner had been his neighbour and friend for as long as he could remember, but recently she'd begun to suffer spells of forgetfulness from time to time.

He hadn't known about her condition until he'd returned to London last November. At first, the widow had brought him food and drink, looking after him while he recovered from the gunshot wounds. He'd broken the devastating news of her son Henry's death at Balaclava.

And as the weeks passed, she began to withdraw, her mind clouding over. There were times when she only remembered things from the past.

Today she didn't recognise him at all.

Michael tried to think of a way to break through

to her lost memory. 'You're Mrs Turner, aren't you?' he commented, keeping up with her pace. 'Of Number Eight, Newton Street?'

She stopped walking, fear rising on her face. 'I don't know you.'

'No, no, you probably don't remember me,' he said quickly. 'But I'm a friend of Henry's.'

The mention of her son's name made her eyes narrow. 'I've never seen you before.'

'Henry sent me to fetch you home,' he said gently. 'Will you let me walk with you? I'm certain he's left a pot of whisky and tea for you. Perhaps some marmalade and bread.'

The mention of her favourite foods made her lower lip tremble. Wrinkles edged her eyes, and tears spilled over them. 'I'm lost, aren't I?'

He took her hand in his, leading her in the proper direction. 'No, Mrs Turner.'

As he guided her through the busy streets, her frail hand gripped his with a surprising strength. They drew closer to her home at Peabody Square, and her face began to relax. Whether or not she recognised her surroundings, she seemed more at ease.

Michael helped her inside, and saw that she was out of coal. 'I'll just be a moment getting a fire started for you.' Handing her a crocheted blanket, he settled her upon a rocking chair to wait.

* * *

After purchasing a bucket of coal for her, he returned to her dwelling and soon had a fire burning.

Mrs Turner huddled close to it, still wearing her bright red bonnet. He'd given it to her this Christmas, both from her love of the outrageous colour, and because it made it easier to locate her within a crowd of people.

'Why, Michael,' she said suddenly, her mouth curving in a warm smile. 'I didn't realise you'd come to visit. Make a pot of tea for us, won't you?'

He exhaled, glad to see that she was starting to remember him. When he brought out the kettle, he saw that she had hardly any water remaining. There was enough to make a pot of tea, though, and he put the kettle on to boil.

'You're looking devilishly handsome, I must say.' She beamed. 'Where did you get those clothes?'

He didn't tell her that she'd loaned them to him last night, from her son's clothing. Bringing up the memory of Henry's death would only make her cry again.

'A good friend let me borrow them,' was all he said. When her tea was ready, he brought her the cup, lacing it heavily with whisky.

She drank heartily, smacking her lips. 'Ah, now you're a fine lad, Michael. Tell me about the ball last night. Did you meet any young ladies to marry?'

'I might have.' The vision of Lady Hannah's lovely face came to mind. 'But they tossed me out on my ear.'

She gave a loud laugh. 'Oh, they did no such thing, you wretch.' She drained the mug, and he refilled it with more tea. 'I'm certain you made all the women swoon. Now, tell me what they were wearing.' She wrapped the blanket around herself, moving the rocking chair closer to the fire.

While he answered her questions about the Marquess and his vague memory of the women's gowns, he tried to locate food for her. Scouring her cupboards, he found only a stale loaf of bread. Beside it, he saw a candle, a glove and all of the spoons.

He searched everywhere for marmalade, finally locating it among her undergarments in a drawer. He was afraid to look any further, for fear of what else he might find. Ever since she'd begun having the spells, he'd found all manner of disorganisation in her home.

He cut her a thick slice of bread and slathered it with marmalade. God only knew when she'd eaten last.

Mrs Turner bit into it, sighing happily. 'Now, then. Who else did you meet at the ball, Michael?' She lifted her tea up and took another hearty swallow.

'A foreign gentleman was there,' he added. 'Someone from Lohenberg.'

The cup slid from Mrs Turner's hand, shattering on the floor. Tea spilled everywhere, and her face had gone white.

Michael grabbed a rag and soaked up the spill, cleaning up the broken pieces. 'It's all right. I'll take care of it.'

But when he looked into Mrs Turner's grey eyes, he saw consummate fear. 'Who—who was he?'

'Graf von Reischor,' he said. 'The ambassador, I believe. It was nothing.'

He said not a word about the man's impossible claim, that he looked like their king. But Mrs Turner gripped his hand, her face bone white. 'No. Oh, no.'

'What is the matter?' He stared into her silver eyes, wondering why the mention of Lohenberg would frighten her so. Neither of them had ever left England before.

A few minutes later, Mrs Turner's face turned distant. She whispered to herself about her son Henry, as though he were a young child toddling toward her.

It was useless to ask her anything now. The madness had descended once more.

Hannah wasn't entirely certain what a ruined woman should wear, but she felt confident that it wouldn't be a gown the colour of cream. This morning, Christine Chesterfield had inspected every inch of her attire, fussing over her as if she were about to meet the Queen.

'Now remember,' her mother warned, 'be on your very best behaviour. Pretend that nothing happened the other night.'

Nothing did happen, she wanted to retort, but she feigned subservience. 'Yes, Mother.'

Christine reached out and adjusted a hairpin, ensuring that not a single strand was out of place. 'Did you read my list?'

'Of course.' Hannah offered the slip of paper, and her mother found a pen, hastily scratching notes.

'I've made changes for tonight. At dinner, you are to wear the white silk gown with the rose embroidery and your pearls. Estelle will fix your hair, and you should be there by eight o'clock.'

Her mother handed her the new list. 'I have advised Manning not to serve you any blanc mange or pudding. And no wine. You have been indulging far more than you should, my dear. Estelle tells me that your figure is a half-inch larger than it should be.'

Her throat clenched, but Hannah said nothing. She stared down at the list, the words blurring upon the page. Never before had she questioned her mother's orders. If she couldn't have sweets, then that was because Christine wanted her to have an excellent figure. It was love, not control. Wasn't it?

But she felt herself straining against the invisible

bonds, wanting to escape. Her mother was worried about the size of her waistline, when her entire future had been turned upside down? It seemed ridiculous, in light of the scandal.

With each passing moment, Hannah's discomfort worsened. 'Mother, honestly, I don't feel up to receiving visitors. I'd rather wait a few days.' She hadn't slept well last night, and her mind was preoccupied with the uncertain future.

'You will do as you're told, Hannah. The sooner you are married, the sooner you can put this nightmare behind you.' Her mother stood and guided her to the parlour. 'Now wait here until Lord Belgrave arrives. He told your father he would come to call at two o'clock.'

Hannah realised she might as well have been speaking to a stone wall. In her mind, she envisioned her parents chaining her ankle to the church pew, her mouth stuffed with a handkerchief while they wedded her off to Belgrave.

At least she had an hour left, before the true torment began. She contemplated escaping the house, but what good would it do to run away? Nothing, except make her parents angrier than they already were.

No, if she had to face Lord Belgrave again, she would tell him exactly what she thought of him. Perhaps he would call off his plans.

Her father, the Marquess, stood beside the fireplace, his pocket watch in his hands. Disappointment and sadness cloaked his features as he put the watch in his waistcoat. He paced towards the sofa and sat down, his wrists resting upon his knees.

Hannah went and sat down beside her father. She reached out and took his hand. Anger would never win a battle against her father. But he had a soft spot for obedience.

'I know that you are trying to protect me,' she said gently. 'And as your only daughter, I know that you want someone to take care of me.'

His grey eyes were stormy with unspoken fury, but he was listening.

'I beg of you, Papa, don't ask me to marry Lord Belgrave,' she pleaded. 'I don't care if he reveals the scandal to everyone.'

'I do.' Her father's grip tightened around her knuckles. 'I won't allow our family name to be degraded, simply because you lost your judgement one night.'

Hannah pulled her hand away. 'I will marry no one.' Rising to her feet, she added, 'Most especially not the Baron of Belgrave.'

'It won't be Michael Thorpe. God help me, you will *not* wed a soldier.'

The thought had never entered her mind, but at the reminder of the Lieutenant, a caress of heat erupted over her body. Sensual and rebellious, a man like Michael Thorpe would never treat her with the polite distance so typical of marriage. No, she suspected he was the sort of man who would possess her, stealing her breath away in forbidden pleasure.

Hannah shook her head. 'Of course not.'

Plunging forward, she revealed an alternate plan. 'Send me somewhere far away from London until the talk dies down. We have cousins elsewhere in Europe, don't we?'

'Germany,' he admitted. His countenance turned grim, but she though she detected a softening in his demeanour. *Please, God, let him listen to me,* she prayed.

At that moment, the footman Phillips gave a quiet knock. 'Forgive me, my lord, but the Baron of Belgrave has come to call upon Lady Hannah.'

The Marquess hesitated a moment before speaking. Hannah gripped her fingers together so hard, her knuckles turned white. She shook her head, pleading with her father.

'Give him another chance, Hannah,' the Marquess said quietly. 'Despite his reproachable actions, the man does come from an excellent family. He can provide you with anything you'd ever need.'

She couldn't believe the words had come from her father's mouth. She'd known that he cared about appearances, that upholding model behaviour was important to him. But she'd never thought it was more important than her own well-being.

'Papa, please,' she whispered again. 'Don't ask this of me.'

Her father's face tensed, but his tone was unyielding when he spoke. 'Tell the baron my daughter will await him in the drawing room.'

Chapter Five

Michael stood at attention when Colonel Hammond entered the room. He'd been summoned to the War Office this morning, but it wasn't the commander-in-chief who'd prepared his new orders. Instead, he'd been shown into a smaller sitting room. 'Colonel, you asked to see me?'

'Yes. I'm afraid there's been a change in your assignment,' the Colonel admitted. The senior officer's red jacket gleamed with brass buttons, the gold epaulettes resting upon his shoulders. Michael felt ill at ease in his own slate-blue uniform, which still bore the bloodstains he hadn't been able to wash clean.

The Colonel gestured towards a wooden chair, and Michael took a seat. 'You won't be returning to the front, after all.'

'I've made a full recovery,' Michael felt compelled to point out. 'I'm ready to fight again.'

Colonel Hammond looked uncomfortable. 'That

will have to wait, I'm afraid. Though I should like to see you return to battle as well—we can always use men of your fortitude—I'm afraid the Army has other plans for you.'

An uncomfortable suspicion settled in his gut. Had the Marquess used his powers of influence so soon? He'd known that he would probably be sent away from England, but he'd expected to return to duty.

'What are my orders?'

The Colonel sat across from him, a large mahogany desk as a barrier between them. 'You will accompany the ambassador from Lohenberg, the Graf von Reischor, to his homeland. He has proposed to send supplies to the Crimean Peninsula, offering aid from their country to our troops. You will assist the Commissariat by choosing what is most needed for the men.'

Michael's hand clenched into a fist. He didn't believe for a moment that the Graf was acting out of concern for the British troops. This was nothing but a stranger meddling in his military career, all because he'd ignored the summons. Why should he care whether or not he resembled the King of some tiny, forgotten country?

He'd given years of service to the Army, obeying orders and doing his best to keep his men alive. And with a single stroke of the pen, the Lohenberg

Graf had turned his military career from a soldier into an errand boy.

'You honour me, Colonel,' he lied, 'but I'm nothing but a lieutenant. Why not one of my commanding officers?'

'The ambassador requested you. I suggested another officer as a liaison, but he insisted that it must be you, or he would reconsider the offer.' There was a questioning note in the Colonel's voice, but Michael gave no response. He couldn't tell his commander why the Graf wanted him to travel to Lohenberg, when he didn't know the man's intent.

'I'd rather be back with my men,' he said quietly. 'I owe it to them, after what happened at Balaclava.' He'd tried to save whatever lives he could until he'd fallen, shot and bleeding on the field.

'I understand Nolan spoke well of you and your bravery before the battle.' The Colonel's voice was also quiet, as though remembering those soldiers who had not returned.

He turned his attention to pouring a cup of tea. 'While we would welcome you back on the Peninsula, Lieutenant Thorpe, this alliance is far too important. I'm afraid your orders are clear. The Graf has requested you, and it is our hope that you can convince the Lohenberg Army to join in our cause.'

Bitter silence permeated the room, and Michael rose from his seat. Damned if he was going to allow the Graf to ruin everything he'd worked for. He would go and try to convince the man to choose another officer. Then, perhaps he could rejoin what was left of the 17th Lancers.

Michael bowed and offered a polite farewell to Colonel Hammond, who shook his hand afterwards and wished him well.

'I will give your regards to the men, upon my return to Balaclava, Lieutenant. You will report to Graf von Reischor at eight o'clock tomorrow morning.'

His heart filled with anger; numb to all else, Michael gripped the Colonel's hand and murmured another farewell.

It was becoming quite clear that Graf von Reischor believed himself to be a puppet master, jerking his strings toward a path that was not his.

As he left the War Office, Michael shoved his hands inside his pockets, only to find the tangled strand of diamonds Hannah had given him.

He slid his hands over the hard stones, feeling the chain warm beneath his fingertips. Although Hannah believed the diamonds would grant him an excuse to return to Rothburne House, that wasn't a wise idea. The Marquess would murder him if he so much as set foot upon a blade of Rothburne grass.

It's not your battle to fight.

He knew he shouldn't be involved. Their lives

were too distant from one another, and despite the night they'd spent in the carriage, she was better off if he left her alone. Most likely Hannah would be all right, with her father and brothers to protect her.

The way they had on the night Belgrave took her? his conscience reminded him. His trouble instincts were rising up again.

He expelled a foul curse and continued walking through the streets. An hour. He could spend that much time ensuring for himself that she hadn't been dragged off by Belgrave.

Hackney cab drivers called out, offering to drive him, but he ignored them. It wasn't such a long walk, and he didn't have the money for it anyway.

The thin soles of his shoes were worn down, and as he continued on the walk to Rothburne House, he felt the cobbled stones more than he'd have liked. He hadn't broken his fast this morning, and the thought of food made his stomach hurt. It didn't help matters to see a vendor selling meat pies and iced raisin buns.

After half an hour, he finally reached Rothburne House. He recognised Lord Belgrave's carriage waiting outside. A grim resolution took root inside him, to get rid of Belgrave.

He couldn't approach the front entrance, however. Rothburne's footmen would throw him out.

His military uniform also made it impossible to reconnoitre without being easily noticed.

Quickly, Michael stripped off his jacket and shako, hiding the plumed military cap and outer coat beneath a trimmed boxwood hedge. Beside it, he placed his officer's sword. He removed Hannah's necklace from the jacket and placed it in his pocket.

Traversing the perimeter of the house, he spied an open window on the first floor. Time to discover exactly what Belgrave was up to.

Lord Belgrave's hardened face transformed into a smile when he saw her. 'Lady Hannah, you look lovely, as always. Well worth the wait.' The baron bowed in greeting, and Hannah felt an unladylike sense of satisfaction at the bruises darkening his cheek and the bandage across his nose. No doubt the wounds were from his brawl with Lieutenant Thorpe.

Only years of training made her dip into a curtsy. She'd changed her gown three times in an effort to delay the inevitable. Only when her mother had arrived to escort her in person did she finally enter the drawing room.

Lady Rothburne sent the baron a blinding smile, gripping Hannah's wrist so hard that the skin turned white. 'Lord Belgrave, it was kind of you to pay a call under these…circumstances.'

'It was my pleasure, Lady Rothburne.'

Another jerk of the wrist, and Hannah understood her mother's silent rebuke. All right. If she had to endure this charade, so be it.

'Lord Belgrave.' She didn't care how icy her tone was; the sooner she could get rid of him, the better.

'Lady Hannah, I believe you know why I have come.' He patted the seat beside him in an obvious invitation.

'And I believe you know what my answer is.' Hannah remained standing, her arms crossed. 'Your visit was a waste of time, I am afraid.'

'Hannah—' Lady Rothburne implored. 'Do be kind enough to at least listen to Lord Belgrave.'

Though she wanted to fight back, to lash out at her mother, Hannah found herself sinking into a chair. Out of habit, she fell silent, as if a shroud had fallen over her. Choking off any hint of defiance, she listened to Belgrave speak.

'I offer my apologies for what happened the other evening,' the baron began. 'But, Lady Hannah, I believe it would be in your best interest to consider my offer.' He went on to describe his different estates, both in London and Yorkshire. And of course, how much of an honour it would be to join their families together.

Hannah didn't listen to a word of it. Did Belgrave honestly believe that she would consider him, after the abduction? And were her parents so swept up in his money and family name that they would ignore what he'd done?

'We are pleased that you would still consider our daughter,' Lady Rothburne said. 'I am sure Hannah understands the necessity of protecting her reputation.' Brightening her smile, the Marchioness offered, 'I have ordered a picnic basket from Cook, and you both may wish to discuss wedding plans outside in the garden. It is a lovely day, and it would allow you to become better acquainted.'

'I would welcome the opportunity,' Belgrave answered.

'But, Mother, I—'

'Would next Tuesday morning suit, for the wedding?' the Marchioness interrupted.

'I am certain I can procure a special licence in time,' Belgrave reassured her mother. 'The archbishop will understand the need for haste.'

Say it. Tell them you'll never marry a man like him.

Hannah gripped the edge of her chair, and finally broke in. 'No.'

Her word came out too softly, and neither her mother, nor Lord Belgrave, seemed to notice.

'A quiet wedding would be best,' Belgrave suggested. 'Don't you think?'

'No,' Hannah tried again, this time louder and filled with all of her frustration. 'I don't think so.'

Lord Belgrave rose from his seat and came to stand beside her chair. His large fingers reached out to rest upon her shoulder. The weight of his palm was a firm reminder, not an act of comfort.

And suddenly, her mother's discussions of how a husband would have full dominion over her body made Hannah jerk away. She couldn't lie on her back and let a man like Belgrave do what he wished. Good wives were supposed to submit to their husbands, but, God help her, she could never let him touch her.

She didn't know where the words came from, only that she couldn't bear it any longer. 'There will not be a wedding.' Her voice shook with nerves, sounding more uncertain than she'd intended. 'I won't agree to it. And if you will excuse me, I intend to retire to my room.'

Her mother scurried forward to try to stop her, but Belgrave lifted his hand. 'Forgive me, Lady Rothburne, but perhaps if I had a moment in private with Lady Hannah, I could reassure her that I have only the best of intentions.'

The Marchioness hesitated, and Hannah prayed that her mother wouldn't dare allow such a thing.

'Wait in Lord Rothburne's study,' her mother advised the baron. 'I will speak with my daughter first.' She gestured for Hannah to sit down, and Lord Belgrave followed a servant into her father's study.

The grim expression on her mother's face was not at all encouraging. Christine sat across from her, and her face held nothing but disappointment.

'Hannah, you must know how much your father and I want what's best for you,' Christine began. With a tremulous smile, her mother wiped at her eyes with a handkerchief. 'We want you to have a wonderful marriage with every comfort you could possibly want.'

'Not with him,' Hannah insisted. 'Mother, I won't do it.'

'Is he really as awful as all that?' her mother asked softly. 'He's handsome and wealthy. You got off to a terrible start, I'll grant you that much. But couldn't you possibly give him a chance? This isn't only about your future. The scandal will darken your father's good name.'

'There must be another way.'

The Marchioness rose and drew close, putting her arms around her. 'Talk to him, Hannah. That's all I ask. If, after this, you still don't wish to wed him—' Her mother broke off, tears glistening in her eyes.

I don't, Hannah wanted to say. But she kept silent, knowing that to pacify her mother was the easiest way to get rid of Belgrave. 'Very well. I'll talk to him.'

Christine embraced her again, wiping her eyes. 'Thank you, my dear. It won't be so bad. You'll see.' Her mother took her by the hand and escorted her into the study. 'I'll be right here in the hall,' she offered. With an encouraging squeeze of the hand, she stepped back into the hallway, leaving the door wide open.

It was dark inside her father's study, with the curtains pulled shut. Hannah waited for Lord Belgrave to speak. Instead, he approached the door and closed it. Seconds later, he turned the key in the lock.

She stood immobile, stunned at his actions. What was he doing? Did he plan to assault her in her own home? Hannah's paralysing fear suddenly transformed into rage.

'Be thankful that I will forgive this defiance,' Belgrave murmured. 'You seem to be under the delusion that you have a choice in whom you wed. No other man will marry a woman who was defiled by a soldier.'

'Lieutenant Thorpe did nothing wrong. And I'd rather be a spinster than wed you.'

She wouldn't simply stand here and become Belgrave's victim. Good manners weren't going to protect her virtue, only actions.

Hannah eyed the contents of the study, dismissing the books or the large globe in one corner. Where was a medieval sword when she needed one? Or, better yet, a chastity belt.

He sent her a thin smile. 'Once you and I are married, no one will worry about the hours you spent with the Lieutenant.'

'It was your fault,' she shot back. 'All of this. And I know you've threatened to spread gossip about me.'

'Only the truth,' he said, with a shrug. 'But if you marry me, I'll forget all about it.'

'Do you honestly believe I would forgive you for threatening my family's name?'

'How else am I to wed the daughter of a Marquess?' he asked, his hand moving to her cheek. 'The ends justify the means. Perhaps tomorrow you and your mother might begin shopping for your trousseau.'

That was it. Just being in the same room with Belgrave made her feel like insects were crawling over her skin. When his mouth lowered to kiss her nape, Hannah reached for the gleaming brass candlestick. Swinging hard, she struck Belgrave across the skull, while another attacker hit him with a dictionary.

The baron crumpled to the floor.

'That was well done,' Lieutenant Thorpe complimented her, emerging from the shadows. He wore only part of his slate-blue military uniform, while his jacket, shako and sabre were missing.

Dear God, where had he come from? Not that she wasn't grateful, but he'd scared the life out of her.

Hannah choked back her shock and stared down at the fallen body of Belgrave. Her heart was still pounding with horror at what she'd done. 'Did we kill him?'

That was all she needed now. To be hanged for murder.

'I doubt it.'

She slumped into a leather chair, resting her forehead on her palm. Relief poured through her. 'What are you doing here? I thought you'd wait a few days at least.'

Michael pulled a chair across from her and sat. 'A soldier's instincts. You asked me to prevent a marriage between you and Belgrave. I saw his carriage when I passed by the house.'

It was a mild way to state that he'd been spying on her. And yet, she was grateful. Knowing that he'd kept his promise to watch over her made her feel safe. 'How did you get in here without anyone seeing you?'

The Lieutenant pointed towards the window. 'It's not difficult. I thought I'd sneak in, see that you were all right and leave.'

Her breath caught for just a moment. He'd planned to rescue her with a dictionary. A choked laugh bubbled in her throat, but Hannah tamped it down as she studied Belgrave's unconscious form. 'I should probably get some smelling salts.'

'Leave him. He looks good on the floor, after what he did to you the other night.'

She agreed with the Lieutenant, but didn't say so.

'No, it's really not a polite thing to do. I shouldn't have struck him with the candlestick. My mother would faint if she learned of it.'

He turned serious, resting his forearms on his knees as he regarded her. 'If you hadn't done so, he would have forced his attentions on you.' The Lieutenant's words were brutally blunt. 'And your parents could not have stopped him.'

Hannah's hands started to shake. It was cold in the study, and she gripped her arms to try to warm them.

A squeaking noise caught her attention—the Lieutenant was occupied with pushing the curtains aside and raising the window. 'Come on. We'll leave him here while you make your escape.'

'Not out there.' Anyone might see her, and it was impossible in her skirts. 'I'll just go back through the study door.'

'Do you plan to rummage through his pockets for the key?' he enquired. 'Or will you shout for one of the servants to break down the door?'

Hannah winced at the thought of touching Belgrave. 'There's no other way, Lieutenant Thorpe. Even if I wanted to go out the window, my skirts wouldn't fit.'

'You could remove some of your petticoats.'

'Never.' The thought made her ill. He might catch a glimpse of her ankle. Or worse, part of her stocking-clad leg. 'It's a terrible, ridiculous idea.'

He sat on the window sill, one leg in, one leg out. 'I never said it was a good idea. It's simply one of your options.' He shrugged. 'Either way, I am leaving through this window.' He disappeared from the sill, and Hannah stared at the study door.

Outside, she heard the voices of servants and her mother. She was about to approach the locked door, when Belgrave suddenly stirred.

His eyes snapped open, and he groaned, rubbing his head. When he staggered to his knees, Hannah didn't wait any longer. There wasn't time to get the key.

She raced towards the window and saw that it was about a six-foot drop. Not as bad as she'd expected. Below, the Lieutenant was waiting.

'Did you change your mind?'

'Don't let me fall,' Hannah ordered. She had a fleeting image of flying into the shrubbery, with her skirts over her head. The vision made her stomach lurch. Ladies did not jump from the window into an unmarried man's arms.

But her alternative was to face Belgrave again.

Why in the name of heaven did this have to happen to her? Hannah bemoaned the indignity of it all as she sat upon the window sill. Her tiered skirts fluffed around the window, the petticoats amassing in a large pile before her.

'I'll catch you,' came his voice. Glancing down, she saw the Lieutenant standing with his arms outstretched. His face was confident, his arms strong. He looked as though he would never let anything happen to her. 'Trust me.'

With a backwards glance, she saw Belgrave stumbling towards her. Squeezing her eyes shut, Hannah let herself tip backwards. Though she longed to release a scream as she fell, only a muffled 'oomph' left her lips as she landed in his embrace.

Sure enough, every petticoat remained in place. The Lieutenant lowered her down, and as they stood outside the servants' entrance, she marvelled that she'd done such a thing.

'To the garden,' she ordered. 'Quickly, before anyone sees us.'

He didn't argue, but led her towards the tall hedge, ducking around the corner. A crooked grin creased his mouth. 'I suppose that's the first time you've ever thrown yourself out a window.'

She flushed. 'I had no choice. Belgrave woke up.'

His smile faded into a tight line. 'You're safe from him now. You can go back through the front door and tell your mother what happened. I doubt if they'll force you to marry him now.'

'I should think not.' Hannah brushed at her gown, to give herself a way of avoiding his gaze. He was looking at her as though he wanted to kiss her again, and her nerves tightened. The boxwood hedge dug into her neck as she pressed herself against it. 'Thank you, Lieutenant.'

He acknowledged her thanks with a nod, but didn't leave immediately. She noticed the way his attention shifted towards the kitchen. His features grew tight, and she understood suddenly that he was hungry.

Though she wanted to send the Lieutenant to the kitchen for a hot meal as a reward, she didn't dare, for fear her father would discover his presence.

'Go to the gardener's shed, and wait for me. I'll be right back.'

The Lieutenant shook his head. 'Lady Hannah, I have to leave.'

'You're hungry,' she said quietly. When he was about to protest, she held up her hand. 'I can see it. I'll get a basket of food for you from the kitchen. You'll have a meal as repayment for rescuing me.'

He took another step away from her. 'It's not a good idea for you to be seen with me again.'

'It sounds as though you're afraid of my father.'

He grimaced at her implication, and Hannah moved in for the kill. 'Don't worry, Lieutenant.'

She stepped towards the kitchen, her mood improving. 'If Papa dares to try to kill you, I promise to defend your honour, just as you did mine. I'm quite good with a candlestick.'

Chapter Six

When Hannah opened the back door to the kitchen, she saw the servants busy chopping vegetables at the long table on the far side of the room. Their backs were to her, and they were busy talking amongst themselves. Near the wall beside her, she saw a tea tray with the picnic basket her mother had ordered earlier. Perfect.

Holding fast to her skirts, Hannah slipped inside and snatched the basket. She didn't wait to find out if anyone had seen her, but hastened back outside, ducking behind the arborvitae hedge. Within a few minutes more, she reached the gardener's shed.

The Lieutenant sat on the floor of the shed, but he'd spread out a few burlap sacks for her to sit upon. She handed him the basket. 'It's not much, but it's the only reward I could think of on such short notice. Thank you for rescuing me.'

He didn't take the basket immediately. 'No reward

was necessary. I wasn't about to let Belgrave raise a hand against you.'

The words were spoken with a casual air, as though it were nothing. But even as he rested with one knee up, she saw his wrist hanging down, she saw a caged alertness. This was a man who would defend someone to the death. A ruthless soldier, one who showed no mercy to his enemies.

'A dictionary,' she remarked. 'Not a weapon I'd have expected. It seems you are a man of more words than I'd thought.'

A hint of a smile twitched at his lips, and she avoided further discussion by opening the basket. She found a china plate and began loading it with slices of ham, bread and creamed spinach.

Concentrating on the food made it easier to forget that she was alone in a gardener's shed with a man who was far too handsome. Her nape prickled with awareness of him, and she tried to ignore his scrutiny.

Her hand reached up to straighten a strand of hair, and she felt completely improper without a bonnet or gloves.

'Aren't you going to eat?' he asked, after he'd made a sandwich out of the bread and ham. He ate slowly, but from the flash of relief on his face, Hannah knew she'd made the right decision to offer food.

'I'm not hungry.' She'd lost her appetite after the

ordeal with Belgrave. Her emotions were bottled up so tightly with the knowledge that her family's reputation was about to be destroyed.

The awful pressure was building in her chest, and she clenched her skirts, staring down at them. A tear dripped down on her palm, and she struggled to keep herself together.

'Lady Hannah,' came the Lieutenant's deep voice. 'What is it?'

'Shh.' She raised a hand, unable to look at him. 'I just need a moment to…fall apart before I collect myself. It's been a most difficult morning.'

'Go ahead and cry,' he said. 'You deserve it, after the way he threatened you.'

Hannah couldn't stop the sobs from breaking forth, her shoulders huddled forward as she released the anger and disappointment.

'He's going to ruin me, after this,' she cried. 'All because I refused to marry him.'

Strong arms enveloped her in an embrace, but there was no judgement, only comfort. He said nothing, but she sensed his anger toward Belgrave.

'What am I supposed to do now?' Hannah whispered, feeling ashamed that her tears were dampening his shirt.

He held her against his chest, gently patting her back. 'I think you should leave London.'

'I agree.' A change in her surroundings was

the only thing that would allow the gossip to die down.

She dried her tears, extricating herself from his arms. Though she'd expected to feel abashed at being in his embrace, strangely, she didn't.

Afterwards, she sat down upon one of the sacks, keeping a respectful, proper distance. Across from him, she felt small, almost fragile. He remained alert, as though he expected to leave at any moment.

'I am grateful for your help today. Tell me, did anyone else see you?'

'I don't think so.' His eyes held a glint of mischief. 'It's a good thing your father opened the window earlier.'

Smoothing her skirts, she straightened her posture. 'I do appreciate your help.'

'I suspect, after you struck Belgrave with the candlestick, Lord Rothburne will be less likely to force you into marriage.'

Hannah nodded, hoping that was true. 'When do you have to leave for the Crimean Peninsula?'

The Lieutenant tensed, and he busied himself with finishing the ham sandwich. After a moment, he replied, 'My orders were changed. I've been asked to go to Lohenberg instead.'

Lohenberg? Hannah frowned, wondering what the Army would possibly want with the tiny country, nestled between Germany and Denmark. In school, she'd learned Lohenisch, among her studies of European languages, but it was hardly an important principality.

Hannah stared at him, unable to comprehend what he'd just informed her. 'Do you mean you're not going to fight any more?' Before he could answer, she plunged on. 'This is my fault, isn't it? My father—'

'—had nothing to do with it,' he finished. 'Another man is involved.'

'Who?'

'The Graf von Reischor.' He shook his head, stabbing at a bite of creamed spinach. 'It's a long story.'

'He was at Papa's ball the other night, wasn't he?' Hannah mused. Her father was good friends with the Lohenberg ambassador, but she'd hardly spoken with the man beyond an introduction, over a year ago. 'What would the Graf want with you?'

She bit her tongue as soon as she spoke, for it sounded as though she'd denigrated the Lieutenant's rank. 'I mean, why would he interfere with your orders?'

'I presume he will tell me that tomorrow morning.' His stiff posture made it clear he had no desire to discuss it further.

He was about to leave, but Hannah stopped him with a hand. 'Wait. You haven't finished everything.'

She removed a covered container and offered it

to him, along with a spoon. 'It's Cook's newest dessert. She copied it after the Sacher Torte, which my parents tasted in Vienna. You'll want to try it.'

She'd never been allowed to partake of the rich dessert, but there was no reason why the Lieutenant should not enjoy the rare delicacy. Setting the container into his hands, she made him accept it.

Hannah lifted the lid, and against her will, her mouth watered. Rich chocolate covered the cake, while the inner layers were filled with apricot jam. What would it be like to taste such decadence?

The Lieutenant dipped his fork into the cake, and Hannah stared at the forbidden dessert.

Was it as good as it appeared to be? The soft icing looked so tempting, she forced herself to look away.

'You look as though you're ready to snatch my cake away,' he observed. 'Did you want some?'

'No, that's all right.' Lies. All lies. She breathed in the scent, wishing for just the tiniest taste. 'I'm not allowed to have sweets very often,' she admitted. 'Mother has my waist measured every day.'

The Lieutenant set his fork down, studying her as though she were a foreign creature. 'What do you do when you attend the dinner parties and balls? Surely you would offend the hostess if you refused to eat the dessert.'

She gave a reluctant smile. 'There are ways to play with your food, so it appears that you've eaten it. Don't tell me you never tried it, when you were a boy.'

'I ate everything my parents gave me. I was glad if it wasn't rancid.'

Hannah rested her hands in her lap. She'd never worried about where her food came from. It was always there, in endless variety. Only the best cuisine would meet her mother's impossible standards.

It was sobering to remember that most people worried about whether or not they had enough to eat. She should be grateful for her circumstances, despite the lack of freedom.

'Close your eyes,' the Lieutenant said suddenly.

'Why?'

'Do it.'

She obeyed, wondering what he intended. A moment later, she felt the light brush of metal tines against her lips. His thumb urged her mouth to open, and the fork slid inside.

The sweetness hit her tongue first, then the bittersweet chocolate icing of the cake. Hannah breathed in as she held the unbelievable flavours against the roof of her mouth. She almost didn't want to swallow, it tasted so good.

When at last she did, she opened her eyes. The Lieutenant was staring at her, his gaze filled with heat. 'Don't ever look at a man like that,' he murmured. 'Else you'll find yourself in his bed.' There was wickedness in his tone, as if he wanted to be that man.

She returned the fork to him, suddenly conscious of the intimacy of sharing it. Michael set the plate aside, rising to his feet. 'I'm going to go now. Thank you for the food.'

'You're welcome.' She held the taste of the torte against the roof of her mouth, savouring the last remnants. And despite the terrible temptation, she would *not* lick the plate after he'd gone away.

'Wait here for a few moments, then go and sit in the garden,' he suggested. 'They'll find Belgrave and come looking for you.'

'Heaven help me when I'm found.'

He took her shoulders, looking her straight in the eye. 'You were brave enough to defeat Belgrave once before. You'll manage it again.'

She wished she felt the same confidence. Even so, it wasn't as if she had any choice. Lifting her gaze to his, she saw the faith in his eyes. And suddenly, she grew aware that he hadn't pulled his hands back.

His palms dominated her narrow shoulders, while hazel eyes bore into hers. He seemed to struggle with an invisible decision, but his hands remained where they were. She was caught by the memory of his fingers caressing her skin, and the unexpected brush of his mouth on her nape. The stolen kiss in the carriage…all of it made Hannah's sensibilities drift away.

If it had been the Lieutenant whom her parents wanted her to marry, she might have had a very different response. There was something forbidden about him. Something tempting.

'I'm not brave at all,' she whispered. 'I'm nothing but a foolish girl.' She lifted her hands to his shoulders, knowing that she was provoking him. Knowing that he wasn't safe at all, nor was he a gentleman.

The effect of her hands upon him was instantaneous. His hands stilled, and he leaned in, his cheek resting against hers. 'Tell me to stop.'

But she didn't. She had broken so many rules today, shaming her family and behaving like the worst sort of daughter.

'Push me away, Hannah. Take a damned spade and strike me over the head.' His gaze was heated, his eyes burning with a warning she couldn't possibly heed.

She couldn't have moved if she'd wanted to. Something about this man drew her in, tantalising her with the promise of physical pleasure.

'Don't stop. I need this...for a moment.' She didn't even understand what she was asking for.

'So innocent.' His mouth moved over her skin, caressing her with his warm breath. Like before, her body came alive, needing him to touch. To taste.

No matter how many books she'd read or how many languages she spoke, in physical matters she was completely ignorant. A secret part of her thirsted for the knowledge.

Michael pulled her against the shed, though he didn't hold her tight. 'This is your last chance to run away. I'm not above taking what's offered.'

'Show me what it's supposed to be like,' she murmured.

The words were all the encouragement he needed. He trapped her against the wood, covering her breathless mouth with his own. Instinct took over, and Hannah kissed him back, ignoring every warning that flew into her mind. She didn't care. Soon enough, she'd never see him again.

And, by heaven, if she was going to be ruined after today, she might as well have a memory to show for it.

His tongue slid inside her mouth, evoking a shocking sensation. Her breasts ached against the fabric of her gown, her nipples rising. Michael slipped his hands around her waist, his wide palms resting upon her ribs. His kiss grew more fierce, his mouth conquering hers. She opened to him, and raw desire pummelled her senses, making it impossible to stop, even if she'd wanted him to.

And God help her, she didn't. He pulled her close and she felt the hard length of his body nestled against her. Something unexpected blossomed inside, and she shifted her thighs, not understanding what was happening.

His mouth moved over her throat in a forbidden caress. 'You shouldn't have started this. I was going to let you go untouched.'

'I know.' She shuddered as his tongue flicked over her pulse. The secret longings made it impossible to think clearly, and she couldn't bring herself to pull away. 'But there's no harm in a kiss, is there?' When he didn't answer, she prompted, 'Lieutenant?'

'Michael,' he corrected. 'And you're wrong, if you think that's all I want from you.' His hands moved over her bodice, resting just beneath her breasts. Hannah grew feverish, her skin blazing with wanton needs.

'I don't know what you want.' *Or what I want,* she thought.

With his thumbs, he stroked her nipples, tantalising her. His breathing had grown harsh, and she cradled his head, kissing him deeply.

'Are you trying to punish yourself?' he asked, his lips resting upon her skin. 'By kissing a man like me?'

'You're not a punishment,' she whispered. 'It's just that—I wanted to know what it was like. To be desired.' She lowered her head. 'Not for my fortune, not for my hand in marriage. But for me.'

He took her lips again, this time softly. A lover's kiss, one that made her tremble. Michael broke away, resting his face against hers. 'I should never have come here. You're a complication I don't need right now.'

Her throat was burning, but she managed an apology. 'I'm sorry.'

He cupped her cheek then pulled away. 'Be well, Lady Hannah.' The door clattered shut behind him.

Hannah stayed inside the shed, the privacy cooling her unexpected desire. Regardless of what he said about himself, Michael was no ordinary soldier. He didn't let any man intimidate or threaten him. Instead, he carried himself with self-assurance, a man accustomed to guarding others.

And yet, there was no one protecting him. Her spirits dimmed at the thought of the Lieutenant enduring hardships he'd never admit. Like hunger.

Her mother had always cautioned her to think of the poor, to put others before her own needs. The Lieutenant needed someone to look after him.

But it could never be her.

Chapter Seven

The following morning, Michael stood in front of Number Fourteen, St James's Street, the Graf von Reischor's residence. All night, he'd thought of Lady Hannah.

He'd never intended to kiss her again. It had been a monumental mistake, and one he wouldn't repeat. She'd been distraught after the events of the afternoon, and he'd taken unfair advantage. Again.

But when she'd clung to him, kissing him back, he hadn't been able to stop the rush of desire. Like a train, crashing through him with unstoppable force, he'd touched her the way he'd wanted to. Like the bastard he was.

She was well rid of him. Though he intended to keep his promise of ensuring that she didn't have to wed Belgrave, the sooner he was free of Lady Hannah, the better.

He had his own mess to unravel. The Lohenberg ambassador had left him no other choice but to see this through. Michael intended to get his answers today, no matter how long it took.

A sense of uneasiness rippled inside. Last night, he'd had the nightmare again. In his dream, he'd seen pieces of images, one after the other. Falling from a high distance, wounding his leg. A hand gripping his, dragging him down the street. Frigid waves, striking against a ship's hull. He'd woken up shaking, his body cold with fear. But whenever he tried to recall the details, the dreams faded into nothingness.

Though he wanted to pretend that this was nothing but a distorted trick, that these were nothing but idle visions, he wasn't convinced. As he stood before the door, he quelled the anxiety in his stomach, steeling himself for whatever confrontation lay ahead.

Michael removed his shako when the footman led him into the drawing room, tucking the hat beneath one arm. The ambassador's residence held a deceptive opulence. At first glance, the room appeared no different than the others he'd been inside. But the mahogany side table was polished to a sheen, the wood almost warm in its deep color. Inlaid wood formed a geometric pattern of shapes, like a fine mosaic.

The silver tea service was polished and gleaming, and the tray probably cost more than his yearly salary. Two porcelain cups painted with blue flowers rested upon the tray. The butler offered to pour him a cup, but Michael refused.

He waited for a full half-hour in the drawing room, ignoring the refreshments. His frustration mounted with each passing minute, until finally, he rose from his seat.

'I see you've had enough of waiting,' a cultured voice spoke. The Graf von Reischor entered the drawing room, leaning upon his gold-handled cane. The man's bald head gleamed, his salt-and-pepper beard framing a gnarled face. 'Have you finally decided to confront your past?'

'No. Only the present.' Michael strode forward, standing directly in front of the Graf. At the sight of the ambassador's smug expression, his anger sparked. 'You had no right to interfere with my orders.'

A faint smile tipped at the Graf's mouth. 'You enjoyed being shot, did you?'

'I need to return to my men and finish the campaign. I owe it to them.'

The Graf's expression grew solemn. 'Yes, I suppose you must feel an obligation. I apologise for that, but it couldn't be helped.' He gestured for Michael to sit, and withdrew a cloth-wrapped parcel.

'I made some enquiries, after you refused my initial invitation to come and discuss this mysterious resemblance. I learned from your commanding officer that you had an anonymous benefactor who ordered you brought back from Malta.'

Michael's gaze narrowed, not understanding what the Graf meant. 'I was sent back because of my gunshot wounds.'

'Did you never wonder why your return to service was delayed for so long? Or why none of the others were brought back to London?'

He hadn't, not really. But then, he'd been in and out of consciousness, fighting for his life. He doubted if he'd have been aware of anything, not after nearly losing his leg. 'I thought other soldiers had returned with me.'

'None but you.' The Graf held out the cloth-wrapped package. 'I find that rather curious, don't you? It must have cost a great deal, both to locate your whereabouts and to bring you back to London. Someone obviously wanted to keep you alive. But who?'

Michael took the cloth package and unwrapped an oval miniature. He didn't know what he expected to see in the painting, but it wasn't an aged version of himself. The resemblance was so strong, he couldn't find any words to respond.

'You see?' The Graf held out his palm, and Michael returned the miniature to him.

Right now, he felt as if the ground had cracked open beneath him, sending him into a darkened chasm of uncertainty. Though he'd successfully ignored the frequent nightmares, now he could no longer be sure.

'It could be a coincidence.' But even as he spoke the words, he knew it wasn't.

The ambassador levelled a piercing stare at him. 'That, Lieutenant Thorpe, is what we must find out.' He poured two cups of tea, but Michael refused the hot drink. The ambassador added milk and sugar to his own cup.

'There is a legend in Lohenberg. One that has persisted for nearly twenty-three years, of a Changeling Prince.'

'Changeling?'

'Only a fairy tale, perhaps. You know how rumours spread.'

Michael waited for the Graf to continue. The ambassador rubbed his beard, lost in thought. 'Some believe the true Prince was stolen away, switched with another child on All Hallows Eve.'

'Wouldn't the King or Queen have noticed, if the boy was different?'

'The King saw the child for himself and proclaimed that Karl was indeed his son. He silenced the rumours.' The Graf sipped his tea.

'Do you think the King was telling the truth?'

'I don't know. But I want to be sure that the right man is crowned.' The Graf finished his tea and set down the cup. 'Forgive me for interfering with your orders, but I saw no other choice.'

Michael preferred to face enemy bullets, rather than unlock a past that might or might not belong to him. He knew, deep down, that he was the very last sort of man capable of leading a country.

'If I am wrong,' the Graf offered, 'you may return to the Army with no further interference from me. I will repay you handsomely for your co-operation, and I will see to it that Lohenberg provides several ships full of supplies and clothing for your fighting men.'

'In the meantime,' Reischor continued, 'you'll want to pack. I've arranged for your passage upon a steam packet, and we sail for Lohenberg at the end of the week.'

A full day passed before Hannah's parents addressed the subject of Lord Belgrave. She heard not a word of gossip from the servants, only that the baron had returned home with a headache.

An understatement, that.

After dinner, her parents awaited her in the parlour. The silence was so grim, Hannah wondered if they could see the guilt she was feeling right now. Did they know she had kissed the Lieutenant in the shed yesterday? Had any of the servants seen her after she'd gone out the window?

Already, she'd chastised herself for her act of rebellion with the Lieutenant. The kiss had gone too far, but he'd warned her, hadn't he? She could blame no one but herself.

Just thinking of it made her body go warm, her shame multiplying. All she needed was a scarlet letter to brand upon her gown to make her sins complete.

'Lord Belgrave has withdrawn his offer of marriage,' her father began. His tone was flat, his face careworn. 'I imagine you are not surprised.'

'No,' she managed. Few men would appreciate being bashed upon the head. Twice.

'Your mother has something she wishes to say to you.' The Marquess sat back in his chair, nodding to Lady Rothburne.

Her mother paled, her gloved hands twisting a handkerchief. 'Your father…was unaware that I allowed Lord Belgrave to speak with you privately.'

From the dark look on her father's face, she realized with shock that he was on her side. A frail flame of hope burned within her.

'I never dreamed Lord Belgrave would lock himself inside with you.' Her mother's face appeared sickly, and suddenly, she began to weep. 'Hannah, I am so sorry. I was naïve to think he would behave like a gentleman. You were right about him.'

'Then you're not…angry that I struck Lord Belgrave with the candlestick? Or—' she thought wildly for an explanation '—or the dictionary?' She directed her query towards her father, who cleared his throat, looking uncomfortable.

'There were other ways to handle the matter, but, no, I do not blame you. Hannah, I must ask you this—how on earth did you get out of the study? It took us nearly half an hour to find the other key. I was so worried, I nearly ordered Phillips to break down the door.'

'Belgrave was starting to wake up, so I went out the window.' There. Best to tell as much of the truth as she could.

'You could have broken your ankle,' her mother protested. 'I can't believe you risked such a fall.'

Hannah shrugged. 'Better an ankle than my virtue.'

Her mother's expression was incredulous. 'Why didn't you cry out to us for help?'

'What good would it have done?' she shot back. 'You didn't believe me when I told you what sort of man he was.'

Her mother blanched, staring down at her handkerchief. The Marquess regarded Hannah with a solemn face. 'We needn't discuss Belgrave any further. That matter is closed.'

And thank heaven. Hannah let out a sigh of relief. But there was no satisfaction on her parents' faces, only worry. It led her to wonder what they intended to do next.

Her father stood, answering the unspoken question. 'I have decided to send you away for a time. No doubt Belgrave will spread whatever rumours he can. Your mother and I will weather his accusations and do what we can to discredit the stories. In the meantime, I will arrange for your passage to Bremerhaven, Germany. You'll stay with our cousins Dietrich and Ingeborg von Kreimeln.'

Hannah had never heard of the cousins, and uneasiness threaded through her mind. Being sent away was what she'd hoped for, but she hadn't expected it to be half a continent away.

'When must I leave?'

'In three days' time.'

Three days? Though her father continued to explain his plans for her temporary exile, she hardly comprehended a word of it.

He cleared his throat, adding, 'I sent your cousins a letter yesterday, explaining what has happened. I've promised to provide a stipend for your care. No doubt they will be glad to take you in.'

'For how long?'

When her father didn't answer at first, Hannah suspected that he wasn't certain either. An unexpected loneliness spread inside her stomach at the thought of spending years away from her family. London had been her home all her life, and she couldn't imagine being away for an extended time.

'Until talk has ceased,' her father acceded. 'Or until you find another gentleman to wed. Perhaps someone from Germany or Denmark, who doesn't know of the scandal.'

He wanted her to hide the truth, then. The dishonesty didn't sit well with her, and Hannah decided that if she did meet a possible husband, she would tell him exactly what had happened.

'I've ordered the servants to pack your trunks in the morning,' the Marquess added. 'Quentin will escort you to the ship, and after that, the Graf von Reischor has promised to take you the remainder of the journey.'

The ambassador? She recalled Lieutenant Thorpe's confession that he was accompanying the Graf to Lohenberg. Most certainly her father knew nothing of this.

And neither did Lieutenant Thorpe. Hannah suppressed a shiver, wondering if she dared to travel with them. Even with an army of servants to chaperone her, she was afraid of falling prey to her own weakness. The Lieutenant had awakened something inside her, and she feared that the more time she spent with him, the easier it would be to let go of her strict rules of proper conduct.

The Marquess crossed the room and opened the door. 'We will speak more about your journey in the morning.'

It was a dismissal, and Hannah bid her parents good night. Once she left the parlour, she returned

to her room, where she found another list of reminders from her mother.

1. Wear the rose silk gown tomorrow morning
   with the cream gloves.
2. Supervise the packing for Germany.
3. Send farewell notes to your friends.

The last reminder was one she hadn't thought
about. She didn't know when she would see her
friends again. It hurt to think of them getting married and going on with their lives, without her there
to see it. She would miss Bernadette, her dearest
friend from boarding school. And Nicole.

She couldn't possibly explain everything in a
note. No, tomorrow she would pay a few calls and
bid them farewell in person.

Her maid Estelle began unlacing Hannah's dress,
helping her into a nightgown. 'Lady Hannah, I am
so dreadfully sorry about what happened yesterday
afternoon. I can't think of the ordeal you must have
endured.'

'Yes, well, it's over now. I won't have to see
Belgrave again.' She didn't want to dwell upon the
past, not any more.

Hannah dismissed her maid and sat down upon
her bed, drawing her legs beneath the covers and
reaching for a book. Though she tried to read a bit
of Goethe, practising her German, she couldn't con-

centrate on the words. Her mind kept returning to the Lieutenant. They would spend two nights upon the ship, and several days more by coach, until she reached her cousins' home in Germany.

It would be all too easy to ignore the years of proper comportment, letting herself explore the strange yearnings she felt. But, in spite of the forthcoming scandal, she was still untouched. There was no reason to let go of that.

Fluffing her pillow, Hannah rolled over. Beneath it, her fingers brushed against something cold and hard. She lifted up the glittering strand of diamonds, and her heartbeat quickened. The Lieutenant had been here, in her room. He'd touched her bed, and no one had seen him. Not even her.

An invisible phantom, keeping her safe, just as he'd promised.

Hannah returned the diamonds to her jewellery chest, wondering how and when he had managed to enter her room. He'd given the necklace back, successfully avoiding her. Once, she'd offered him the jewels as an excuse to return. Now, that reason was gone.

A slight disappointment filled up the crevices of her heart. But then, what had she been expecting? He was a soldier and she a lady. There was no possible future for them, except an illicit affair.

She'd never consider such a thing. Michael Thorpe was not the man for her. It didn't matter what he'd made her feel when he'd kissed her. Like a decadent chocolate torte, he'd provided nothing but forbidden temptation.

And no matter how badly he provoked her, she would not allow herself to fall beneath his spell. They would be acquaintances, nothing more. On the ship, she simply had to avoid him at all costs.

That night, she had dreamed of the Lieutenant. Of his mouth, arousing such feelings within her. Hannah awoke in the early morning darkness, her skin alive with unspoken needs. Her cotton nightgown was gathered up around her thighs, and she tried to still the rapid beating of her heart.

A beam of moonlight rested upon her coverlet, the silvery light reminding her of the hours she'd spent in the Lieutenant's arms, only a few nights ago. She rested her hands upon her waist, calming her breathing.

Her hand crept up to her throat, her elbow grazing against her breasts. Instantly, the nipples hardened, provoking the memory of his kiss. She let her hand fall to the curve of her breast, touching herself. The nipples were hard nubs, and the sensation was painfully delicious.

Michael had touched her there, making her body desire so much more. A swell of arousal filled her up inside, and she drew her legs together, her breath quickening. She squeezed the tips of her breasts, and the aching sensation made her damp between her thighs. Never had she felt this way before. She twisted the sheets against her core, craving something she didn't understand.

God help her, she wanted to know more. Michael had given her a taste of sin, leaving her unsatisfied and curious.

But it was wrong. She knew that, and in time, she would learn to forget about him. There was no alternative.

Chapter Eight

Michael stood on board the ship *Orpheus*, staring out at the brown waters. The ships he'd sailed on earlier had been far smaller, perhaps 150 feet in length. In contrast, this one was nearly 600 feet long.

A large central funnel released a light steam, while six more masts rose high above them. The sails were tied up, and the wooden decking shone new. The rigging ropes were as thick as his wrist, the ratlines stretching up to the top mast.

As he looked aft, he saw the wheelhouse enclosed within glass windows. The *Orpheus* had made its first voyage only a month ago, and the ship was in prime condition.

It felt strange, being a first-class passenger.

Michael tugged at the tight sleeves of his new double-breasted black cloth frockcoat. Though it was a fine cut, he felt conspicuous in the expensive clothing. The shawl collar and cravat abraded his neck, and he felt stiff. His attire had cost more than three years' salary, and he longed for the familiarity of his own worn clothing.

He hadn't wanted to transform his appearance, but the Graf had insisted. 'If you are, in fact, related to the royal family, then you must dress as such. No one will accept your rank unless you appear as the King's son.'

'I may not be his son.'

But he'd succumbed to the changes because his only other attire was his military uniform. The Graf insisted that he travel under the guise of a nobleman, reminding him that his co-operation would help improve the living conditions of the soldiers.

Hundreds of men on the Crimean Peninsula had starved to death, due to lack of rations. It made him sick to think about the shipments of vegetables and meat left to rot because there was no one to transport the supplies to the soldiers' camp.

There would be changes when he returned to the front; he would see to it.

Michael gripped the cuffs of his coat, the guilt erasing any enjoyment he might have had from this journey. He didn't deserve fine clothing or luxurious accommodations upon a steamship bound for Bremerhaven.

His gaze drifted downward to the gleaming buttons on the coat. *Bide your time,* he warned himself. Already the Graf had given him two new suits of clothing that he could sell. He'd loaned hundreds of pounds in spending money, meant for a new wardrobe, once they arrived in Lohenberg. Michael didn't intend to touch a penny, if at all possible.

Behind him, he heard the conversational noises of more passengers boarding the ship. He'd made arrangements for Mrs Turner to be brought with the servants, not trusting anyone to look after her welfare. She'd be lost within a week and forget to eat.

The Graf had protested, but Michael's insistence had won over. No doubt Mrs Turner was pestering the servants about her trunk, making sure no one bumped it or put a scratch upon the wood.

He heard the tones of her voice, anxious and excited, while she inspected the ship. With a quick glance, he saw that today would be one of her more lucid moments. She stared up at the tall masts and funnels, shielding her eyes from the sun while a broad smile creased her cheeks.

God help him, he hadn't told her their true destination. He'd let her believe that it was a trip to Germany, and had ordered the other servants not to reveal their true destination. There was no reason to upset her.

Other passengers boarded the ship, pretending as if they didn't see the elderly woman. He could guess their ranks, without knowing a single name. Dukes and viscounts, ladies and lords. Those who believed themselves too good to mingle with the public.

Michael kept an eye upon Mrs Turner, watching to ensure that no one bothered her. A few of the men cast quizzical looks towards him, as though trying to decide whether or not they were acquainted.

He pretended as though he didn't see, for he didn't belong among them. He'd learned that on the night he'd dared to accept Whitmore's ball invitation.

There was no use in attempting a conversation with London's elite. What could he say, after all? *Have you shot any men recently?* No, he couldn't mingle with them. Far better to stay away.

But then, he heard the soft tones of another woman's voice. He knew her voice, knew the timbre and the familiar way it rose and fell.

Lady Hannah Chesterfield. What in the name of God was she doing upon this ship? Had she followed him?

Michael spun around, intending to confront her. When her gaze met his, she blushed and nodded in greeting.

Clearly, she'd known they would be traveling upon the same ship. Why hadn't she mentioned it the last time he'd seen her?

She wore a grey cashmere pelisse trimmed with a fringe, and beneath the outer garment, he caught a glimpse of a dark blue gown. Her grey bonnet was adorned with lace, ribbons and cream roses. Impeccably attired, she held herself like a queen.

From the vast quantity of trunks and luggage

brought on to the ship by her servants, it appeared she was travelling for an extended period. He saw her brother Quentin bringing up the last of the servants, and he spoke softly to his sister, offering an embrace. It was a farewell.

What was going on? Michael didn't believe for a moment that her presence upon the ship was a mere coincidence, even if the *Orpheus* was one of the most luxurious passenger steamers.

His question was answered a moment later, when the Graf brought Lady Hannah towards him. 'Lieutenant Thorpe, there will be an addition to our travelling party,' he said. 'The Marquess of Rothburne asked me to escort his daughter, Lady Hannah Chesterfield, to their cousins' estate in Germany, after he learned I was returning home.'

There was no doubt in his mind that the Lohenberg Graf had arranged this little detail for a reason—most probably as a means of manipulating him. Michael wouldn't allow any harm to come to Lady Hannah, and the Graf knew it.

'Lady Hannah,' Michael greeted her. He let nothing betray his emotions, for he didn't want her caught in the middle of his disagreement with Reischor.

Like him, Hannah kept her reaction cool and veiled. 'Lieutenant Thorpe.' It was as if an icy wall had gone up between them. If Michael hadn't been there himself, he'd have doubted that their kiss had ever taken place. The prim and proper Lady Hannah was back, with no glimpse of the woman who had struck down her last suitor with a candlestick.

Graf von Reischor cleared his throat to interrupt them. 'Lieutenant Thorpe has agreed to accompany me to Lohenberg, conducting business on behalf of the British Army.'

'I am glad to hear that you have been tasked with something so important.' Although she had already known of his orders, he suspected Lady Hannah was itching to ask more questions. Nonetheless, he didn't want her to know anything about the Graf's theory with regard to his heritage.

'When did your father make the decision about this journey?' he enquired, directing the conversation back to her.

'A few days ago.' Hannah twisted at one of her gloves, and the conversation fell flat between them.

Exile was a better word for it. The Princess locked away in a tower, away from those who might scorn her.

'Forgive me,' Graf von Reischor excused himself. 'I must speak with the Captain about our cabin arrangements. I shall return shortly.' He gestured for one of Hannah's maids to remain nearby, as a chaperone.

As soon as he was out of earshot, Michael lowered his voice. 'Why would your father choose Reischor for an escort? Has he lost his wits?'

Hannah seemed taken aback, but a moment later,

she raised her chin. 'Papa wants me to wed a foreign count or duke, and Graf von Reischor has many acquaintances.'

That didn't surprise him at all. Lady Hannah was the sort of woman who belonged among high society, her blue blood too good for anything less. If the London suitors wouldn't have her, certainly her father's money would pave the way for a foreign wedding.

'So long as he has the proper title and enough money, not much else matters, does it?' The words came out before he could stop them. He felt like a bastard for voicing them.

But proper to a fault, Hannah didn't let any hurt feelings show. 'I am not allowed to marry a man who does not possess the means to take care of a family.'

'Your father wouldn't let you wed a merchant, sweet. Not even if he possessed a million pounds.' Men like the Marquess were only interested in bettering the family name. 'The higher the title, the more likely you'll gain his permission.'

'There are titled gentlemen who are good men,' she pointed out. 'Not all of them are like Belgrave. Many would value a virtuous woman who wants to provide a comfortable home for him.'

'Like you?'

She turned crimson, and he wished he'd kept his mouth shut. None of this had been her fault. He ought to reassure her that nothing had changed, that she was still the same woman as before. But that was a lie. She would never be the same, not with a scandal shadowing her.

Then, too, he hadn't behaved with honourable intentions, either. He'd taken full advantage of Hannah's innocence, claiming stolen embraces and touching her in a way that was forbidden.

Right now, she was perfectly composed, every button fastened, every hair in its proper place. She looked nothing like the woman who had clung to him in the shed, kissing him as though time were running out.

The high-collared pelisse hid her neck, and he asked, 'Did you receive your necklace back?'

'I did. You could have returned it yourself.' There was a hint of scolding in her tone.

'I thought it best not to see you again.' His voice came out rougher than he'd intended.

The wind buffeted Hannah's bonnet, and she kept her gaze fastened upon a seagull circling the boat. Her green eyes were almost grey this morning, mirroring the darkness of the water.

'You're right, of course.' She drew the edges of her pelisse tighter against her body. 'We've caused enough scandal. It's better for us to stay away from one another.'

She said it so firmly, he wondered whom she was trying to convince. Her face held a lonely cast to it, her eyes glimmering with unshed tears. She watched the shoreline, as though she didn't know when she would see England again. And from the way Hannah was glancing over her shoulder, he suspected she didn't want to keep his company any longer.

Sailors began releasing the ropes from the dock. The steam engines rumbled as they began to take the vessel away from its landing and down the river.

Michael wanted to offer her words of comfort, but he suspected it would only make her feel worse about her exile. He rested his wrists on the side of the boat, staring out at the water. Waiting for her to leave.

But long moments passed, and she stood a short distance away, resting her own gloved hands upon the wood. He ventured a glance at her, and she kept her eyes averted. Her lips were pressed together, her cheeks pale from the cool sea air. He remembered just what her mouth tasted like, as sweet as a succulent berry.

'Why are you watching me?' she whispered. Her hands came together, and she rubbed her palms.

He didn't tear his gaze away. Instead, he looked his fill, memorising her green eyes and flushed cheeks, down to the prim-and-proper body he wanted to touch.

'Don't you want to retire to your cabin?' he prompted.

It was a veiled dare, to see if she truly wanted to be rid of him. He waited for her to march off, sweeping her skirts clear of a man like him.

Her face reddened, but she held her ground. 'I don't want to just yet.' Taking a deep breath, she confronted him. 'I think we are both capable of being civil to one another. We've agreed that there will be nothing improper at all about our behaviour.'

They had? He raised an eyebrow, but she seemed completely unaware of it.

'As travelling companions, we have no other choice, if we wish to avoid future gossip.' She squared her shoulders. 'If we attempt to avoid one another, that may cause further talk. Instead, I suggest that we behave with politeness and decorum.'

It was with great difficulty that he held back his own opinions. Instead, he studied the other passengers on board the ship.

'Well?' she prompted. 'Is that acceptable to you?'

His gaze fixed upon Mrs Turner at that moment. It occurred to him that he could not watch over the widow at night. He needed someone to protect her, in case she suffered from one of her spells.

Facing Lady Hannah, he said, 'You want to pretend as though we're strangers. As though I never kissed you.'

A slight shiver passed over her, but she nodded.

'Then I want a favour in return.' Before she could

protest, he continued, 'There is…an elderly woman I've known for many years. Abigail Turner is her name, and she has joined our travelling party.'

Though he could have found another place for Mrs Turner, he didn't trust anyone else to handle the widow's welfare. Others wouldn't understand her condition, nor would they sympathise. He didn't want Mrs Turner sent to an asylum if she suffered from one of her spells.

Hannah didn't answer, and he wasn't certain she'd heard him until at last she said, 'Go on.'

He stepped in front of her line of sight, forcing her to look upon him. 'Mrs Turner is starting to grow forgetful. Sometimes she doesn't remember her name or where she lives.

'She needs someone to look after her,' he continued, in all seriousness. Staring directly at Hannah, he added, 'She tends to find trouble when she isn't looking for it.'

Hannah shielded her eyes as she stared behind him at the tall funnel. 'What is it you want from me?'

He raised his voice above the din of the engines. 'Would you allow Mrs Turner to join your maids? I cannot watch over her at night, and there are no other female servants travelling with us.'

'She may join us.' Then Hannah studied him, searching his expression. 'Why is she so important to you?'

He had never been asked the question, and he didn't really want to explain it. Abigail Turner had lived near his family all his life. She was the woman who had slipped him sweets when his mother wasn't looking, allowing Henry and him to build fortresses in the bedroom out of sheets and old pillows. As long as he could remember, she'd been like an aunt or a godmother, watching out for him.

'She saved my life,' he admitted. 'After I was shot at Balaclava, I was sent back to London. Mrs Turner nursed me back to health.' He pointed out the widow to Hannah as the woman strolled around the deck.

'How badly were you hurt?'

He sobered. 'I'm alive. Which is more than I can say for most of my men.' He thought of Henry Turner, whose body he'd lain beneath. There wasn't a day that went by when he didn't wish he'd been the one to die instead of Abigail's son.

'I should be glad to look after her for you,' Hannah offered, holding out her hand for him to shake.

He stared down at her gloved hand, and she snatched it back, caught off guard by what she'd done. But he reached forward, taking her palm in his. The sudden touch seared his consciousness.

He took a step forward, and in turn, she stepped back, her shoulder brushing against one of the ratlines. Interesting.

He hadn't truly intended to start this game of cat

and mouse, but her reaction was intriguing. She appeared flustered, as though she didn't know what to do about his sudden attention.

But her eyes held no fear. No, there was anticipation in them.

Michael reached up and took hold of two of the ropes. Though he didn't touch her at all, it was the hint of an embrace. Hannah coloured, but held her ground as though it were the most natural place to be, with her back against the ratlines. She glanced around, to see if anyone saw them, but they were further back on the ship, with no one nearby.

'Why would your father force you to travel with strangers?' he asked.

'The Graf isn't a stranger. He's Papa's friend. They've known each other for years.'

Michael took a step closer, lowering his voice. 'How well do *you* know him?'

'Not well.' Stiffening at his comment, she added, 'But Papa would never place me in harm's way.' She glanced at his arms pointedly, but he refused to move them. He wanted to see what she would do. Would she push him aside? Or surrender, waiting for him to let her go?

Right now, he wanted to take her below the deck, away from everyone else. To kiss her until she could no longer stand. To feel her naked skin beneath his.

'And there's you,' she said softly. 'You would protect me, if I needed it.'

'Don't try to put me on a pedestal, Hannah.' The more time he spent near her, the more he desired her. Michael let his hand brush against hers, and she started at the contact. She truly had no idea of the sort of danger she was in. Twice, he'd kissed her. And though he possessed a slight bit of honour, even that was beginning to unravel.

'You're trying to intimidate me,' she accused. 'And I know none of this is real. You wouldn't dare hurt me.'

Michael leaned closer so that his breath was against her cheek. 'Sweet, you don't know me at all, do you?'

'You—you don't know me, either.' She squared her shoulders, lifting her chin until her mouth lay only inches from his.

'I know enough about ladies such as you.'

'And what is that supposed to mean?'

'You live your life bound by a strict set of rules. I'm the sort of man who breaks those rules.'

'Do you truly believe I enjoy living that way?' she asked. 'I'm not allowed to choose my own clothing or decide what to eat.' Her eyes held frustration, and she stared down at the wooden decking, her face pale.

'I can't go back to the life I had,' she murmured. 'It's gone forever. This time, I want to make my own choices.' She pushed his hands aside and broke free of him.

'I want to eat whatever I want and wear a gown of my own choosing.' She calmed herself, taking a deep breath. 'I want my freedom.'

He saw the desperate need within her, and knew he could do nothing to destroy that hope. 'You have two days before we reach Germany. Perhaps less.'

Staring hard at him, she whispered, 'Then I'll have to make the most of my voyage.'

God help him, he hoped she would.

Chapter Nine

Hannah spent a good part of the afternoon exploring the ladies' saloon and the promenade deck with her maid Estelle. She'd met several of the other ladies travelling in first class, and most seemed friendly enough. One had urged her to explore the ship further, and Hannah was delighted at what she'd found. She'd expected this passage to be gruelling, but instead the ship was designed for luxury at every turn.

She spied *portières* of crimson velvet at each of the doorways, while the maroon carpet was thick and comfortable. Within the saloon, the sofas were made of Utrecht velvet, while the walnut buffets were covered with green marble tops. Grand chandeliers hung throughout the saloons, giving them the appearance of ballrooms.

In one corner, a string quartet was rehearsing their set of music. Standing with his back to her was Lieutenant Thorpe. He looked ill at ease, pacing slightly as he appeared to stroll through the saloon.

Hannah almost turned on her heel and walked away. He hadn't seen her, so there was no need to greet him. She could leave right now, and he'd never know differently.

But then, that was the coward's way, wasn't it? He'd cornered her this morning, intimidating her without actually laying a finger upon her. She pressed a hand to her heart, trying to calm the rhythm. Just thinking of it made her even more aware of him.

He was intensely handsome, in an uncivilised manner. Although his new clothing fit him perfectly, it didn't change the man he was. Unpredictable. And…not at all safe. He'd been right about that.

Without warning, he turned around and saw her. His gaze held none of the polite greeting that most men would have offered. No, he looked as though he wanted to cross the room and take her away with him.

Her senses grew weak just thinking about it.

Gesturing for Estelle to remain a short distance behind her, Hannah braved a polite smile. Best to say hello and leave as quickly as possible. But as soon as she reached his side, he turned away.

The ship's funnel casings were enclosed with mirrors, and a rich pattern of gold and white covered the wall surfaces. 'Are you studying the wallpaper?' Hannah asked. 'It's lovely enough but a bit boring, I'd imagine.'

'Listening to the music,' he corrected. 'And trying to remain unnoticed.'

That much was doubtful. A man like the Lieutenant could never escape attention. His height and handsome demeanour made that impossible, not to mention he walked like a man in command.

'You're not a very good wallflower,' she said.

He shot her a sidelong glance. 'I was doing quite well before you arrived. No one approached me or spoke to me.'

'They were afraid you'd wrestle them to the ground or throw them into the mirror.' She took a discreet step away from him.

'It's possible,' he admitted. His mouth turned up at the corners, and Hannah relaxed, glad that she'd made peace with him. 'What do you want, Lady Hannah?'

'Nothing, really. I thought it would be rude to leave without saying hello.'

'You've said it. Duty accomplished.'

She refused to be put off by his abrupt air. 'You don't feel comfortable here, do you? Amidst all this.' She gestured toward the opulent decorations.

'I'd rather be on a battlefield. Shooting enemies.' A wicked look of amusement lit up his eyes. He glanced over at a group of matrons talking in a corner.

'Target practice?' she suggested.

'You're tempting me.' His gaze flickered toward

two gentlemen, whom she just now noticed were staring at them. 'I don't think you should be standing here, speaking to me alone.'

'My maid is here.' Hannah glanced over at Estelle. 'And we're already acquainted. For all those guests know, you could be my brother.'

He sent her a lazy smile that made her skin turn to gooseflesh. 'I'm most definitely not your brother, sweet.'

She stared down at the floor, uncertain of how to respond. 'Well. What happened between us is all in the past. Right now, we are travelling companions, nothing more.'

'Really?' The dangerous glint in his eyes sent a blush through her cheeks.

'Of course.' She took another step back, pretending everything was fine.

At that moment, the two gentlemen strolled forward. They looked as though they were about to ask for an introduction, but Michael sent them a dark glare. Hastily, they tipped their hats and continued on their way.

'Now what was that about?' Hannah demanded. 'You looked as though you were about to tear them apart with your bare hands.'

'I was acting like any brother would.' Michael's gaze fixed on the doorway as though he expected the two gentlemen to return. 'Keeping you safe, just as you asked.'

If he'd had a firearm at that moment, Hannah had no doubt it would be aimed at the gentlemen. His behaviour bordered on barbaric, with a hint of jealousy.

'If a gentleman asks me to dance this evening after supper, I have no choice but to accept,' Hannah pointed out. 'You can hardly prevent it from happening.'

'Can't I?'

She ignored the remark, continuing, 'I suspect you don't dance at all, do you?'

'Do I look like the sort who enjoys dancing?' he gritted out.

'No, you look like the sort who enjoys glowering at others.' She tilted her head to study him. 'I would wager that you don't know how to dance.'

He took a glance around the saloon. Except for her maid Estelle, there was no one else in sight. Even the matrons had already strolled away.

The musicians were still practising a set; without warning, Michael took her in his arms. He didn't ask but began dancing with her. His hand pressed against the curve of her waist, guiding her masterfully through the steps.

She couldn't have been more surprised. When had a soldier learned how to dance like this?

He took her through the steps of a waltz, spinning her around without a single misstep.

'In school,' he replied, answering her unspoken

question. 'Every last one of us learned to dance. I hated every minute.'

'But you're good,' she whispered. 'Better than I thought you'd be.'

He whirled her around, bringing her against one of the mirrors. The cool glass pressed into her back, and he stopped short.

'I'm good at many things, sweet.' His voice held the undertones of a forbidden liaison. Caught in his embrace, he kept his hands at her waist, looking into her eyes. She saw the rise and fall of his breathing, the desire that he held back.

'And what is something you're not good at?' she asked softly.

'Letting go of something I want badly.'

Without a single word of farewell, he left the saloon. Hannah leaned back, resting her head against the mirrored panel. *Neither am I.*

Hannah lifted out a sage-green dress with a high collar and fitted long sleeves. She was grateful for the new travelling clothes in other colours besides rose and yellow. Though the gown covered every inch of her body, at least the colour complimented her light brown hair.

'Lady Hannah, this is not the gown your mother selected for this evening's dinner,' her maid Estelle protested.

'No, it isn't.' And she didn't care. The midnight-blue gown Christine Chesterfield preferred reminded Hannah of mourning garb. 'I prefer this one,' she added, handing it to Estelle so she could dress her.

As soon as she arrived in Germany, she would visit a dressmaker to order new gowns that were more flattering. Perhaps she would even cut her hair shorter. Hannah smiled at the thought, fingering the long strands.

While Estelle finished styling her hair, she thought back to what Lieutenant Thorpe had said—*I'm not safe at all.*

It was a warning to stay away. To guard her virtue at all costs. And she should, no doubt. Yet there was a part of her that wanted to know more about the man behind the soldier. He intrigued her, awakening the rebellious side of herself. What would it be like to live her life, not caring what others thought?

Or was it merely a façade, a means of keeping people away from him? He isolated himself from others, and it troubled her.

A knock sounded at the door, and Estelle went to open it. Hannah caught a glimpse of Mrs Turner, the elderly woman whom Michael had asked her to watch over.

The woman appeared nervous, twisting a red bonnet in her hands. 'Lieutenant Thorpe sent me here to assist you, Lady Hannah. I am Abigail Turner.'

'Come in.' Hannah gestured toward a chair. 'Would you care to sit down?'

'No, thank you, my lady.' The woman stood near the door, as though trying to fade into the papered walls. The small cabin held three berths, one for each of them. Against the far wall were two chairs and an end table. On the wall adjacent to the berths, stood a large chest of drawers.

Estelle began helping Hannah into the sage-green gown, and a moment later, signalled to Mrs Turner. 'You, there. Fetch Lady Hannah's silk fan from inside that trunk.' Without waiting for a response, the maid began fastening a pearl necklace around Hannah's throat.

'Emeralds would look better,' Mrs Turner suggested.

Estelle sent the widow a tight smile. 'I do not believe you are responsible for Lady Hannah's wardrobe. Her mother has taken great pains to organise each of her gowns with the appropriate matching fan, jewels, stockings and gloves, and has made lists of what outfit should be worn upon which occasion. Your help is not needed.' With a flourish, Estelle produced a small handful of papers.

'Estelle, Mrs Turner is here at my request,' Hannah corrected.

Mrs Turner did not react to the maid's arrogant

tone, but instead, a light appeared in her eyes as though she were squaring off for battle.

Estelle pressed the lists into Hannah's hand, and she glanced at them before setting them down on the table. Orders of what to wear, what not to eat, how to greet the other first-class passengers…the reminders went on and on.

Her mother was *still* trying to give orders, even while they were miles apart.

Enough. Balling up the lists into a crumpled heap of paper, Hannah tossed them in the wastebasket. Her maid gave a cry of dismay, but left the lists alone.

'Did you pack the emeralds, Estelle?' she enquired.

'Yes, my lady, but your mother's orders were—'

'I beg your pardon.' Mrs Turner cleared her throat and turned a sharp eye upon Estelle. 'Are you arguing with your mistress?'

'Do you dare to criticise me?' The maid puffed up with anger. 'Lady Rothburne is one of the greatest ladies in all of London. I take pride in following her explicit orders.'

Mrs Turner frowned and began looking around the cabin. She lifted a cushion, spying beneath it. 'Well, I don't see Lady Rothburne here, do you?'

Hannah had difficulty concealing her smile.

'If your lady wishes to wear emeralds instead of pearls, what does it matter?'

'Emeralds are not proper for a young lady.' The maid glared at Mrs Turner. 'And you should learn your place, if you expect to remain in Lady Rothburne's employ. I shall write to her about you, see if I don't.'

Hannah didn't like her maid's attitude. She'd considered getting rid of the woman even before now, but she'd had enough of this rudeness. 'Estelle, if you wish to stay, you will obey my orders.'

Mrs Turner drew close. 'May I help you with that clasp, Lady Hannah?'

Hannah turned, and Mrs Turner unfastened the pearls, replacing them with an emerald pendant Estelle grudgingly gave her.

'Go and find some refreshments for Lady Hannah,' the matron suggested to Estelle. 'A glass of lemonade, perhaps, or a bit of cake.'

'Chocolate cake,' Hannah breathed, like a prayer.

'Chocolate, then.'

'But Lady Rothburne has strictly forbidden—'

Mrs Turner shut the cabin door in the maid's face. Dusting off her hands as though they were well rid of her, the widow offered a broad smile. 'I've been wanting to thank you for granting me a place to sleep.'

'It's no trouble.' Hannah struggled with her stockings, and Mrs Turner helped her to adjust them.

The widow added, 'If you don't mind my saying

so, I think you should get a lady's maid who is a bit more loyal to you than to your mother.'

'You may be right.'

Mrs Turner fussed over her, helped her finish dressing, and exclaimed over the gown. When Hannah was ready, the older woman smiled. 'He really does like you, you know. My Michael. He spoke of meeting you at the ball that night. You made quite an impression upon him.'

Why a stranger's words would make her stomach flutter, Hannah didn't know. She picked up her fan, feeling like an awkward fifteen-year-old girl once again. She resisted the urge to ask what he'd said about her. It didn't matter.

And if she told herself that a hundred times, she might actually start to believe it.

A knock sounded at the door, and Hannah saw the Graf von Reischor waiting to escort her to dinner. He murmured a compliment in his native language. Before Hannah could respond with her thanks, Mrs Turner followed behind them, adding, 'Yes, she does look lovely, doesn't she?'

The Graf turned, staring at the widow. 'Do you speak Lohenisch, Mrs Turner?'

'No, of course not.' A curious smile rested upon her lips. 'Why ever would you think that?'

The dining room was exquisite and could hold nearly four hundred first-class passengers. Long tables set with white linen tablecloths gleamed with silver and bone-china plates. Above, an ornate brass chandelier provided lighting while potted tropical plants added a splash of greenery to the tables.

Several guests were already seated, and the gentlemen rose at the sight of her, Michael among them. He wore black evening clothes and a white cravat. His dark hair was sleek and combed back. Even with his grooming, there was an air of impatience about him, as though he were uneasy about being here. He looked like he'd rather be dining in steerage than among the elite.

Hannah nodded politely to the other women after the Graf von Reischor introduced her. One of the ship's butlers poured her a glass of water and another of wine.

She'd never been allowed to taste spirits before, and she wondered what it would taste like. Would it lure her into a life of sin and greed, the way her mother insisted?

But when she saw that no one else had touched theirs, Hannah restrained herself.

The Graf began introducing her to their dinner companions. 'The Marquess of Rothburne is a close friend of mine,' the Graf explained. 'He asked me to escort Lady Hannah to her cousins' home in Germany. She received so many offers of marriage, her father thought it best that she take some time away from London to make up her mind.'

Hannah nearly choked on her soup. It wasn't at all what she'd expected him to say. After a few more introductions to those seated around her, one of the gentlemen offered her a warm smile, then nodded to the Graf. 'I hope she has not made a decision as of yet, Graf von Reischor.'

'She hasn't,' came a clipped voice. The Lieutenant sent the would-be suitor a warning look, and Hannah's fingers curled over the stem of her wine glass. What gave him the right to be so rude? He was behaving as though he had some sort of claim over her. The glare in his eyes held a shadow she didn't recognise. Not exactly jealousy, but something that made her skin prickle against the fabric of her gown.

The first course was served shortly thereafter, a bowl of turtle soup. Hannah noticed the Lieutenant subtly observing her and the other gentlemen before lifting his own spoon. Surely he must have attended formal dinners before? But then, her father's ball was the first time she'd ever seen him among her social peers.

Michael sat across from her, and she felt his gaze, like a forbidden caress. There was also a sense of reluctance, as though she were a temptation he didn't want.

Hannah reached for her glass of white wine, taking a first sip. It held a slight tang, a sweetness that didn't taste sinful at all. When she glanced over at Michael, he lifted his own glass, and she found herself watching his mouth, remembering his kiss.

The memory pooled through her skin, past her breasts and between her legs. He was staring at her as though he didn't care who was watching. In a ship such as this, there were a hundred different places to hold a secret liaison. And no one would know.

Across the table, he didn't take his eyes from her. She recalled the warmth of his lips, wondering if she would taste the sweetness of wine upon his mouth.

'Lady Hannah?' the Graf prompted her. She hadn't heard a word of his questioning. She took another sip, and managed a smile.

'I'm sorry. What was it you were saying?'

'I was introducing the Lieutenant to our dinner companions,' he replied. 'This is Lieutenant Michael Thorpe, an officer in the British Army,' the Graf said to the others.

A spoon clattered from a woman's hand into the soup tureen. Hannah turned in curiosity and saw a dark-haired woman with a large ruby necklace and matching rings upon her fingers. She covered her blunder by pretending as though someone else had dropped the utensil.

'You said you are travelling to Lohenberg?' a stout English gentleman enquired. 'My wife is from that country.' He offered a nod toward the woman who had dropped the spoon, then raised a quizzing glass to one eye. 'You look familiar to me, somehow. Have we met before?'

'He looks like the King of Lohenberg,' his wife answered. Though she kept a smile fixed upon her face, her answer held a cold tone.

Lieutenant Thorpe's knuckles clenched upon the spoon. He looked as though he'd rather take a bullet through his forehead than endure this dinner. But he didn't rebut the woman's claim.

What was that about? Hannah tried to catch Michael's attention, but he kept his gaze averted, almost as if he were hiding something.

'Why, you're right, m'dear.' The stout man beamed and speared a bite of asparagus. To his companions, he added, 'I was privileged to have met His Majesty, King Sweyn, when he was visiting Bavaria last summer. Splendid mountains there, I must say.'

The Graf introduced them. 'Lady Hannah and Lieutenant Thorpe, may I present the Viscount Brentford?'

Lord Brentford greeted her heartily and presented his wife Ernestine and his daughter, Miss Ophelia Nelson.

'I am glad to make your acquaintance, Lady Brentford,' Hannah said. Offering a smile of friendship to the younger woman, she continued, 'And yours, Miss Nelson.'

'Delighted, of course,' the matron said, though she didn't look at Hannah when she spoke. Her wide smile emphasised a double chin, and she added, 'Ophelia has just been presented to the Queen and will enjoy her first Season after we return to London.'

Michael didn't respond, and Hannah kicked him under the table to get him to look at the young woman. He sent her a nod of acknowledgement, but a moment later, Hannah felt his shoe nudge against her stockinged calf.

Mortified, she reached for her water glass and took a deep swallow. Only to find out that it was wine she'd drunk instead. She clamped her mouth shut to keep from coughing, and the spirits burned the back of her throat.

Though the Lieutenant didn't look at her, his foot moved against hers once again. Though it was nothing more than a casual touch, the caress distracted her from the dinner conversation. Like a silent admonition, he touched her the way a secret lover might.

Hannah kept her knees clamped together, pushing her ankles as far beneath the chair as she could. He seemed to sense the effect he had on her, and his lips curved upwards.

The Viscount nodded towards his daughter, sending the Lieutenant a knowing look. 'Ophelia is quite talented and has the voice of an angel.' Hannah supposed the Viscount was waiting for someone to suggest that Miss Nelson offer entertainment later that evening.

When neither the Graf nor the Lieutenant responded, Lord Brentford continued, 'Perhaps she might sing for the King of Lohenberg, if the opportunity presented itself on our journey. If someone were to…suggest it.' The Viscount gave a pointed look toward the ambassador.

Miss Nelson turned to the Graf and offered a shy smile.

'I have no doubt that Ophelia will have her opportunity one day,' Lady Brentford interjected. She patted the young girl's hand and discreetly slid the wine glass away from Miss Nelson's place setting. 'It is my country, after all.'

Without an invitation, the Viscountess launched into a dissertation describing the principality. 'And of course, the winters are simply enchanting.'

'No, it's quite cold in the winter,' the Lieutenant interrupted. His eyes were distant, as though he'd spoken without thought.

The Viscountess stopped short, waiting for him to elaborate. When he didn't, she continued, pretending that he hadn't spoken at all.

Hannah caught the Graf's discerning gaze, and he shook his head discreetly. More and more, she was curious about their journey. She suspected the military orders did not reveal the entire story.

'Forgive me, Graf von Reischor,' Viscount Brentford interrupted, 'but I've heard rumours, and I wonder if you could verify them. Is it true that Fürst Karl is going to be crowned king within the next few weeks?'

The Graf set down his fork and regarded Lord Brentford.

'King Sweyn has been ill, but we do not know for certain whether or not a new king will be crowned.'

'How exciting,' Miss Nelson breathed. 'I suppose there must be many men in line for the throne, even for so small a country.'

'There is only one Crown Prince,' the Graf admitted. His gaze turned to Michael, and Hannah felt an icy chill shiver through her. 'And one true heir.'

Chapter Ten

Michael endured the remaining hour of dinner, hating every moment of it. He watched the other guests to determine which forks to use, how much of the food to eat, and whether or not he was supposed to drink the contents of a bowl or wash his hands in it.

What bothered him most was the sheer waste. The ladies picked delicately at their plates, tasting a bite of fish or a spoonful of soup before the course was taken away. It was as if eating were out of fashion.

The men adjourned with brandy and cigars, the ladies retreating to their own saloon after the dinner was concluded. Michael took his moment to escape, though the Graf had ordered him to return for the parlour games.

He had no intention of letting the Lohenberg ambassador dictate what he would or would not do. He wasn't a trained animal to be led about on a leash.

With each moment, his resentment rose. The eyes

of everyone at dinner had bored into him, and when Lady Brentford had mentioned his resemblance to the King, no doubt they thought he was a bastard son. Michael hated being the centre of attention, much less the subject of gossiping tongues.

Outside, the sky was black, the white sails taut with wind while the paddle wheel churned through the water. The promenade deck was partially shielded from the winds, but the rocking of the ship sent several guests falling over. Raucous laughter accompanied one poor woman's misfortune as her skirts went flying.

Michael gripped one of the ropes leading to the foresail. Though the sea had turned rough, his mind was in greater turmoil. He didn't want to believe that his childhood had been a lie, that his parents were not whom they seemed to be. Surely the strange, fleeting memories that caught him from time to time were nothing but dreams. They had to be.

He caught a glimpse of Mrs Turner strolling around the deck, and he took a step towards her. It wasn't good for her to be alone. But before he could reach her side, Lady Hannah appeared, followed by her maid. She wore no outer wrap, only her sage-green gown. In the frigid air, she rubbed her arms for warmth.

'Lieutenant Thorpe,' she asked quietly, 'I want to know what's going on.'

'About what?'

'Your resemblance to the King of Lohenberg. I saw the way the Graf was watching you.'

'It's nothing. Merely a coincidence.'

She stepped in front of him, preventing him from going any further. 'He thinks it's true, doesn't he? The Graf believes you're connected to the royal house of Lohenberg.'

'It doesn't matter what he thinks. I've never set foot in the country.' He strode past her, but Hannah dogged his footsteps.

'You said it was cold there, in the winter.'

He had no idea what she was talking about. 'As I said, I've never been to the country before.'

'Are you lying to me? Or to yourself?' She touched his arm lightly.

'I'm a soldier, nothing more.'

'Are you certain?'

No, he wasn't certain of anything. Nothing except the way she made him feel. Michael inhaled the light citrus scent she wore. Lemon and jasmine mingled together, seductive and sweet.

'Go back to your cabin, Hannah,' he ordered. It was all he could do not to kiss her again. This time, if he touched her, he wouldn't hesitate to try to seduce her.

'The evening isn't over yet,' she said. 'The entertainment will begin shortly. And whether or not you're too afraid to join us, I intend to participate.'

'Hoping to find a husband, are you?'

She shot him a dark look. 'Whether I am or not doesn't matter to you at all, does it?'

'It matters.' His palm cupped her cheek, his gloved hand sliding against her skin. Ripples of desire erupted all over her skin. She wanted him to kiss her. He tempted her in all the wrong ways. Or perhaps, all the right ways.

It took all of her willpower to break free of him. 'Run away, if you're too afraid,' she taunted. 'Or join us. The choice is yours.'

Hannah had played a few parlour games during boarding school. Blind Man's Buff and charades were quite popular. But as these games involved men and women, she supposed they must be rather different.

A group of twenty gentlemen and women met in the Grand Saloon. The ship's waiters had arranged several chairs in a circle, and a small table stood at the front. Hannah spied a pocket watch and a slipper upon the table, while other guests were rummaging through their belongings. They would be playing Forfeit, she realised.

Each player would surrender a personal item to be auctioned. In order to get it back, he or she had to perform a forfeit, such as singing or dancing. Viscount Brentford had claimed the role of auctioneer, and from his amused expression, it seemed he was looking forward to the position of power.

A moment later, the waiters brought a large screen to shield the contents of the table, allowing guests to walk behind it, one at a time, to deposit their forfeited item. Reaching into her reticule, Hannah chose an embroidered handkerchief, keeping it hidden in her hand. After she passed behind the screen, she added it to the pile of gloves, shoes, jewellery and cravats.

She took her seat among the other ladies, hoping to see the Lieutenant. A glass of sherry was passed to her, and she sipped at the drink. It was smooth and sweet, and she felt herself beginning to relax. It wasn't nearly as wicked as her mother made it sound. She set it down on a table beside her, feeling her skin flush.

Two of the gentlemen moved the screen away, revealing a large pile of personal belongings.

'My friends, I know many of you are familiar with the game of Forfeit,' the Viscount began. 'However, tonight, I am suggesting that we use this game to raise money for an appropriate charity rather than strictly for amusement.'

He exchanged a glance with his wife and daughter. 'Ladies may bid to win a forfeit from the gentlemen, and gentlemen may bid on the ladies' items. The winning bidder shall send the promised amount to the poor and orphaned children of London. The owner of the item shall perform a forfeit of the bidder's choice.'

It was a scandalous game, one that could involve public humiliation or even a kiss. From the way the sherry, wine and brandy continued to be passed around, Hannah suspected things might indeed get out of hand.

'The winner of the auction will return the item to its owner, after the forfeit is paid.' Viscount Brentford reached behind the screen and picked up a black cravat. He cast a wicked look toward the ladies. 'Shall we start the bidding?'

Poor Henry Vanderkind, the owner of the cravat, was forced to crawl about on all fours while singing 'Woodman Spare That Tree'. Lady Howard, a widow nearing the age of sixty, howled with laughter and promised to send fifty pounds to the orphan fund.

As revenge, Henry Vanderkind bid thirty pounds on Lady Howard's quizzing glass and made her bleat like a goat in order to get it back again.

As each item was auctioned off, Hannah found herself wiping her own tears of laughter. She'd lost count of how much sherry she'd drunk, for a waiter kept all of the glasses full.

The room seemed to tilt, the voices buzzing in a haze. She pushed the glass aside, hoping that another headache would not come upon her. Someone passed a plate of cheeses, and she took a slice, thankful for the food to settle her stomach.

At that moment, she caught a glimpse of the

Lieutenant. He didn't look at all entertained by the revelry.

But when he caught Hannah looking at him, his hazel eyes narrowed with interest. He rested his hands upon the back of a carved dining-room chair, and for a moment, she felt like the only woman in the room. The rest of the crowd seemed to melt away, and her body grew warmer as she met his gaze.

It was improper, certainly, but she couldn't stop herself from staring back. Her dress felt too tight, her heartbeat quickening. Though she finally looked away, she was aware of him taking a glass of wine. His mouth pressed against the crystal in a sip, and she again imagined his lips upon hers.

The Lieutenant crossed the room to stand at the other side, effectively distancing them. Hannah noticed that only two items remained on the table: her own handkerchief and a man's pocket watch.

The Viscount gave a silent nod to his daughter and lifted the watch. From the tension emanating from the Lieutenant, she supposed it must be his.

'The last gentleman's item is this pocket watch. It's quite heavy, I must say—no doubt made of the finest gold. Shall we start the bidding at five pounds?'

A flurry of female hands rose into the air, and Hannah saw Michael's discomfort rising. He held his posture stiff, his eyes staring off into the distance. He had loosened his cravat, while his black cloth jacket was unbuttoned to reveal a bright blue waist-coat. The pocket watch he'd worn was missing.

The bidding rose higher, the women laughing at the thought of the forfeit they would ask.

'With a handsome one like that, I'd ask for a kiss,' one woman remarked.

Another giggled. 'I'd kiss him without the auction, if he asked me to.'

Hannah didn't join in, but neither did she want Michael to pay a forfeit that would embarrass him. From the way he eyed the doorway, it wouldn't surprise her if he left the room. He didn't seem to care whether or not the watch was returned to him. It probably belonged to the Graf von Reischor.

When Miss Nelson held the highest bid of eighty pounds, the Viscountess shook her head sharply, whispering in her daughter's ear. Hannah didn't like the look of it. They were plotting against Michael, she was sure. It angered her, for she didn't want him to be the target of anyone's humour.

'One hundred pounds,' she heard herself saying. If nothing else, she might prevent the Lieutenant from being made into a fool.

A ripple of gasps resounded through the crowd of ladies. One woman sent her a dark look, as though she wanted to stab Hannah with a hat pin.

'One hundred and ten pounds,' Miss Nelson countered.

'Two hundred pounds.' Hannah didn't know

whether the sherry had loosened her tongue or where this daring feeling had come from. All she knew was that she didn't want to lose the bidding war.

You can't have him, she wanted to say to Miss Nelson. But it seemed her bid of two hundred pounds had silenced the young woman. Viscount Brentford asked for any final bids, but none was forthcoming. Hannah rose from her seat, grasping the arms of the chair for support. With a determination she didn't quite feel, she moved towards the watch.

'What forfeit will you ask from Lieutenant Thorpe?' the Viscount asked.

Hannah looked into Michael's face. His hazel eyes held a rigid expression, his hands clenched at his sides. He didn't know why she'd bid upon him, and the tension in his stance suggested he had no intention of doing her will.

'No forfeit at all,' she whispered.

His eyes stared at her in disbelief for a long moment. When she brought the pocket watch to him, there was a barely perceptible acknowledgement.

'Now, now, Lady Hannah. That isn't playing by the rules,' another matron protested. 'He must pay his forfeit to get back his pocket watch. Perhaps you should have him sing. Or give a demonstration of his fighting skills.' The woman's gaze shifted to

Michael's muscled form beneath the tightly fitted jacket.

'I'll reserve the right to ask for my forfeit later,' she said. The ladies squealed in delight, and Hannah instantly regretted the scandalous remark. A moment later, their attention was turned to the last item— her handkerchief.

Viscount Brentford lifted up the handkerchief, sending her a mischievous smile. 'Gentlemen, should we start the bidding for this lovely embroidered handkerchief?'

Michael stood from his seat. 'A thousand pounds,' he said softly.

There was a flurry of discussion over the exorbitant amount.

'For what, Lieutenant?' Viscount Brentford asked.

'For Lady Hannah's handkerchief.' His eyes never left hers when he added, 'That is my bid.'

The room grew uncomfortably quiet, and Hannah wanted to sink beneath the table. Dear God. Did he realise what he'd done? Now, the entire room would believe they were having an affair. She was mortified to think of it.

There were no other bids. Michael took the handkerchief and pocketed it, leaving the guests behind as he exited the dining room. He asked for no forfeit, and Hannah knew she was expected to follow him.

The Graf silently shook his head in disapproval.

Hannah didn't know what to do. The game was not yet at an end, not to mention, Michael did not possess a thousand pounds.

Her embarrassment rose even higher as she overheard two ladies speculating about their relationship and whether or not Michael would offer for her. She knew, full well, that it would never happen.

Miss Nelson insinuated herself beside Hannah. 'Aren't you going to return Lieutenant Thorpe's pocket watch?'

It took Hannah a moment to realise she was still holding the watch. 'Oh. Eventually, I suppose.'

'Why did he bid a thousand pounds for your handkerchief?' Miss Nelson asked. 'Are you betrothed to one another?'

Hannah shook her head. 'I'm not certain why. I suppose it gave him an excuse to leave the game.'

Her explanation didn't appear to satisfy the young woman. 'Would you like me to return the watch to him?'

Hannah's fingers curled over the gold. It was a way out, a means for her not to see the Lieutenant again. She looked over and saw the hopeful light in her eyes. Miss Nelson honestly believed that Lieutenant Thorpe was a marriageable man, an officer from a noble family.

'No, thank you.' Hannah stood from her chair. 'I'll take care of this.'

The other ladies had begun a new game of Look

About, searching for a hidden item. After several minutes, Miss Nelson joined them, seemingly disappointed that Hannah had not accepted her offer.

Graf von Reischor caught her arm as Hannah reached the door to the staircase, warning beneath his breath, 'Don't, Lady Hannah. It would do your reputation no good.'

'Whatever was left of my reputation, Lieutenant Thorpe just destroyed with that bid. He's going to answer for it.' She tightened her lips and strode forward.

There were less than twenty-four hours where she would be permitted to make her own decisions. Escort or not, the Graf would not control her actions tonight.

'I'm going to return the watch,' she said.

The Graf opened the door for her, gesturing for her maid to accompany them. Lowering his voice, he asserted, 'Regardless of what there might have been between you once, do not compromise yourself. He cannot wed you.'

Marry Lieutenant Thorpe? A man who had said she was nothing but a complication he didn't want? Frustration poured through her, and Hannah clenched her fan tightly. 'You see things which are not there.'

'I see more clearly than you, it seems. And neither your mother, nor your father, would allow you to speak to a man alone.'

She took a calming breath. 'I will not be alone. And you insult me by implying that I am trying to seek out an affair.'

'An affair is all you could ever hope to have with him.'

'Why? Because you think he's related to the royal family of Lohenberg?'

The guess was an impulsive prediction, but the Graf's face paled. 'Keep such theories to yourself, Lady Hannah.'

She closed her mouth to keep from gaping. 'You're not serious.'

'I have eyes, Lady Hannah. Any Lohenberg native who encounters Lieutenant Thorpe would see it. He looks like König Sweyn, enough to be his son.'

'You have no proof of his birthright.'

'No. But I intend to find out the truth.' He rested his hand upon the stair banister. 'You should be aware that any contact with him bears a risk.'

She took the remaining steps and rested her hand upon the door leading to the promenade deck. 'I am returning a watch, nothing more. I see no reason to be afraid.'

As she left, she heard the Graf speaking softly. 'He has enemies you can't even comprehend.'

Michael tucked the handkerchief into his coat pocket, contemplating whether or not he dared ascend to the upper deck. The sea waves were still rough, the ship swaying in spite of the roaring steam engines and paddle wheel.

He wanted fresh air and the coolness of the night. As he entered the upper deck of the *Orpheus*, the rocking motion of the ship became more pronounced. Wind billowed through the sails, and he heard the groaning of ropes straining against their knots.

The game of Forfeit had taken a turn he hadn't intended. He'd been angry at becoming an object for ladies to bid on. Lord Brentford had practically offered his daughter's hand in marriage, when he'd only just met the girl. No doubt if she'd won the bid, Miss Nelson would have asked him for a kiss. He wouldn't have given it. He despised people staring at him with expectations he couldn't possibly fulfil.

But Lady Hannah had intervened, casting a bid to guard his privacy. She'd faced down the women, protecting him from having to make an idiot out of himself.

There wasn't a man at the dinner table who hadn't wanted her to pay their choice of a forfeit. The thought of any man touching her was enough to make him snap a silver fork in half.

She's not yours. Never will be.

He knew that. And he'd done his best to keep his hands off her. She was a woman of Quality, a diamond who needed a polished setting in order to shine.

But he wasn't a damned saint. He desired her, knowing exactly the way he wanted to worship her body. He wanted to taste her skin, to run his mouth over her flesh until she cried out with pleasure.

What did it matter whether or not a gentleman bid upon Lady Hannah's handkerchief? She deserved the opportunity to make a good marriage. Certainly, the gentlemen on board the ship had no idea of the scandal.

For so long, she'd been trapped in her father's cocoon. Now was her chance to rip away the rigid rules and gain her freedom. He was a selfish bastard, wanting her to surrender to him.

Michael rested his hand upon the wooden railing, staring out at the dark waters. What was it about her that drew him in, like a seedling to the sun? She wasn't anything like the women he'd known while he was in the Army. Kind-hearted, well-bred and beautiful, she belonged with an English lord who would sleep in a separate bedroom and let her plan the household menus and entertainment.

She didn't belong with a man like him. A man with baser urges, who would much rather unravel those sensibilities than uphold them.

When he'd made the ridiculous bid of a thousand pounds, it hadn't been a true charitable contribution. It had been a warning to the other men to stay away from Lady Hannah, or they would regret it. Like a beast marking his territory, he'd laid claim to her.

But now what was he supposed to do?

Footsteps sounded behind him. He didn't turn around, expecting Hannah to move beside him.

Instead, a rope slid around his neck. Stars glimmered in his consciousness, his lungs burning for air. Michael fought against the tight noose, throwing himself to the decking and knocking his assailant's feet beneath him.

Tearing the rope away, he reached for the man, intending to find out what in God's name was going on.

Chapter Eleven

A strong wave shook the ship, and Michael skidded backwards. His head struck one of the masts, and he grimaced at the impact. Salt water sprayed the deck, while in the distance, he heard the crew shouting orders to one another.

When he scrambled to the place where he'd been attacked, there was nothing. Not a trace of the man, as though his assailant had been a phantom. Only the raw abrasions on his throat gave any evidence that he'd very nearly been strangled.

'Lieutenant Thorpe?' Lady Hannah called out to him. She hadn't seen what had happened, from the questioning tone of her voice.

Michael didn't turn, his attention fully upon the shadows. He didn't want to endanger Hannah if his attacker returned.

'Is everything all right?' she enquired, drawing closer to stand beside him. 'You seem distracted.'

'I'm fine.' His voice came out hoarser than he'd

intended, and he coughed to disguise it. He withdrew her handkerchief from his waistcoat pocket and offered it back. She took it, handing him his watch. Her fingers lingered upon his palm.

Behind him, he heard a slight shuffling. He didn't know whether it was another passenger or the assailant, but he didn't intend to remain standing about.

'We need to get off the upper deck. Now.' Without waiting to find out who the intruder was, he grasped Hannah's hand and pulled her through a door. The stairs led to the private state rooms, and Michael continued through the maze of first-class rooms until he located hers. Thankfully, she didn't argue with him, but let him escort her back.

'Where is your maid?' he demanded. 'Why are you alone?'

'I dismissed her to our room a few moments ago. I didn't think—'

'It's not safe for you to be alone on this ship. Not ever.' Though he didn't mean to snap at her, he didn't want her risking her well-being on his behalf.

Before he could open the door to her room, Hannah reached up to his neck. 'Dear God, what happened to you? You're bleeding and the skin is raw.'

'Don't concern yourself over it.'

He was about to leave when she held up her hand. 'Wait over there while I send away my maid and

Mrs Turner. And if you disappear, so help me, I will seek you out. We are not finished talking.'

He didn't doubt that. She was stubborn, far more than was good for her. But once she had entered her room, he ducked behind the corner to wait.

Several minutes later, the cabin door opened, and he saw her maid Estelle leading the way down the hall, followed by Mrs Turner. Michael waited until the women reached the far end, and then approached Hannah's door.

She stood waiting for him, her expression hesitant. He knew, as she did, that it was entirely improper for him to even be near her cabin, much less inside it.

'You didn't need to send them away.'

'You wouldn't tell me the truth if they were here. And it's best if no one knows about our conversation.' Hannah steeled her posture, nodding. 'Come in and let me tend that for you.' Without waiting for a reply, she turned and went to her dressing table.

She poured water into a basin, dipping her handkerchief into the liquid. When she risked a glance at his neck, she gave a perceptible wince. Though her intentions were good, he doubted if she'd ever tended a wound before in her life. To avoid embarrassing her, he took the damp cloth from her and swabbed at his throat, surprised that there was more blood than he'd thought.

'Tell me what happened,' she demanded, keeping

her gaze firmly fixed upon his eyes and not the abrasions. 'I want the truth.'

'Someone tried to strangle me, just before you came.'

'Were they trying to rob you?'

'Trying to kill me, more like,' he admitted.

She froze, her hands falling away. Her complexion paled, and she clenched her fingertips. 'Do you really believe that?'

'It's not the first time someone has tried to do so,' he admitted. 'Usually it was someone on the opposite side of the battlefield.' Reaching out for one of her hands, he asked, 'Are you afraid he'll come after you as well?'

Her hand was cool within his, and she swallowed, as if trying to find her courage. 'Would you protect me if he did?'

His lips curved slightly. 'What do you think?'

She didn't answer, but tried to pull her hand back. He retrieved the damp handkerchief and touched the raw skin at his throat again.

Hannah stopped him, her hand bumping against his. 'Wait. You're missing it.'

Without asking permission, she loosened his collar, untying his cravat to reveal his skin.

Though the water was probably cold, he hardly felt the temperature. Instead, he was intensely aware of Hannah standing between his legs, her hands upon his skin. He was growing aroused, just being near her. The green gown she wore accentuated the swell of her breasts, the curve of her waist. But it was her innocence that was even more alluring. She didn't seem to understand what her simple touch was doing to him.

Awkwardly, she dabbed at his flesh, her lower lip caught between her teeth as though trying to overcome her distaste for blood. He held himself motionless, willing himself not to respond.

'Why would anyone want to kill you?' she asked. A slight shiver crossed over her before she studied his skin, searching for any other wounds.

He didn't answer, offering a shrug.

'Someone believes it's true,' she murmured. 'That you have royal blood.'

Michael didn't acknowledge her guess, though he agreed with her prediction. There was no other reason for anyone to kill him.

'Fairy tales aren't true, Hannah. A common soldier doesn't simply become a Prince.'

He could smell the faint scent of jasmine, and when she'd finished washing his throat, she kept her hands upon his shoulders. 'Unless he already was a Prince. And didn't know it.'

Catching her wrists, Michael drew her hands away. 'Don't do this, Hannah.'

Confusion clouded her gaze. Then abruptly, she seemed to grasp his meaning. Her face coloured, first with embarrassment, then anger.

'Were you trying to make a fool of me?' she demanded. 'Bidding a thousand pounds for a handkerchief?'

He kept his mouth shut, with no intention of explaining himself.

'You made them believe that we were lovers. That I'd given myself to you.'

'Is that what you're doing?' He stood up so suddenly that her hands fell away.

He needed her to realise that she was tempting the devil, whether or not she intended to do so. Possibly frighten her a little, so she wouldn't risk coming too close.

'You had no right to blemish my reputation before all of those people,' she whispered. 'I left London to start over again. And now they are talking about us.' She stepped backwards, her hands clenched.

He stared hard at her, willing her to see the truth. 'You don't want your freedom as much as you think you do. You like the rules you pretend to despise.'

She held still, like a wild animal about to flee. 'You don't understand.'

'I understand perfectly.' He closed the distance, resting his hands on the wall behind her. 'You want it both ways, don't you? You want them to believe you're a lady, when you secretly desire something else.'

'No. That's not it.' She shielded herself with her arms, hugging them to her chest.

He let his hands slide down to her small waist, feeling the tightness of her corset beneath the gown. 'Why did you bid on the pocket watch?'

She looked guilty. 'Because I didn't want the women treating you that way. Like a piece of meat fought over by dogs.'

'I don't care about what other people think of me.'

'Perhaps you should.' Her breath hitched when his hands slid up her spine once more. 'You're not at all the man you pretend to be.'

'I'm the kind of man you shouldn't be alone with.' Lowering his mouth to her chin, he let his mouth nip the edge of her flesh. He tasted the light sweetness of sherry upon her mouth and waited for her to strike out at him. The kiss made her tremble, but again, she didn't order him to leave.

Instead, her eyes filled with indecision, almost as if she were considering letting him ruin her.

'You'd better find that candlestick,' he warned. 'Or I won't be responsible for what happens. I'm going to take that forfeit now.'

'You would never harm me,' she whispered. To emphasise her prediction, she rested her palms upon his heart. The slight touch made the muscle contract faster within his chest.

He wasn't quite so confident. Just being near her, touching her in this way, was making it difficult to concentrate.

Her scent was shredding his restraint, and he realized she was waiting for him to act. Her mouth was softened, slightly open in anticipation. But he didn't take her offering. Not yet.

He pressed his mouth to her throat, kissing a path down to her exposed collarbone. She shuddered in his arms, not offering a single protest.

The taste of her skin, the way her palms moved up to cup his neck…he wasn't certain he would be able to stop if she let things go much further.

Michael removed his gloves, letting them fall to the floor. His hands moved to the back of her gown, unbuttoning the first few buttons. 'This isn't part of the forfeit any more.' He grazed her shoulder with his teeth, kissing the soft place and evoking a sigh from her throat. 'Order me to leave.'

One word, and he would go. She could lie in her nightdress tonight and imagine the things he wanted to do to her. But she would remain untouched.

'I'm going to take my forfeit, too,' she whispered. 'You're going to make me forget all the rules.'

Deliberately, she caressed his head, bringing her hands back down to his shoulders. Her touch made his body tighten with a greater frustration.

He unfastened another three buttons, baring more silken skin, before tilting her face to look at him. Her body had been touched by no other man, he was certain. Only him.

He didn't know why she was letting him take

such liberties, but he suspected she wasn't thinking clearly. 'Do you want another kiss as your forfeit from me?'

She inhaled sharply when his bare palm touched her back. 'Yes.'

He smiled against her mouth and guided her to sit down. He knelt down at her feet, reaching for her ankles.

'Wh-what are you doing?' She held down her skirts, her face pale.

'I'm going to kiss you, all right.' Michael slid his hands up her calves, his palms caressing the silken stockings. 'But you never said where.'

'No. That's not what I meant. I wasn't intending for you to—to ruin me.'

'I'm not going to ruin you, sweet. I'm going to pleasure you. Unless you're too afraid?'

She had gone so pale, her fingers dug into the arms of the chair. And though it was painful to stop this wicked game, he started to draw back. His desire for her was strained to the breaking point, so it was probably for the best.

She shocked him by bringing his mouth to hers. Against his lips, she whispered, 'I'm more terrified than I've ever been in my life. But I don't want you to stop.'

God forgive him for what he was about to do. Michael took her mouth hard, kissing her roughly. He pulled her body tightly to his, letting her legs fall open around his waist. Her shoulders rose and fell as she struggled to catch her breath. To ease her, he unlaced more of her corset.

'But what if someone comes—?'

He kissed another bit of revealed skin, swirling his tongue over it. 'The risk makes it more arousing.'

She shivered in his arms, and he could almost hear the second thoughts racing through her mind. 'I shouldn't let you do this. I know it's wrong.'

'But it feels good to you.'

She lowered her head, as if in surrender. 'Yes. And I'm beginning to wonder what I have left to lose.'

'You would lose far too much.' He took her hands, lifting them to her bodice. Her palms cupped her own breasts, and he held them in place, forcing her to touch herself the way he wanted to.

Though her nipples were beneath the heavy corset, he knew her mind was imagining the sensation.

'You're tempting me down a path I should never tread.'

'I'm a sinner. I live for temptation.'

Hannah leaned back against him, letting him guide her hands. It was hard to breathe, the room swimming in heady sensations.

She never should have let Michael enter her room. Her mother's warnings haunted her, but she couldn't bring herself to step away. Not yet.

This forbidden pleasure coursed through her, for

she'd never been touched like this before. She didn't even know such feelings existed. Her body was hot, the skin fiery and unbearably sensitive. Between her legs, she felt empty, swollen and aching. And yet she knew that, regardless of what he said, Michael would stop at any time she asked.

He might be a man who neglected the rules of propriety when it suited him, but beneath it all he possessed an unfailing honour.

With her last vestiges of control, she pushed him back, away from the chair. She stood, needing to know whether she was making the right choice to be with him tonight.

As she'd expected, he held back from her, his face expressionless. The black cloth jacket fitted his broad shoulders perfectly, the evening clothes making him even more handsome. In the lamplight, his hazel eyes were nearly black, heated with desire.

Someone had tried to kill him tonight, yet he gave no indication of being afraid. She supposed soldiers were accustomed to the risk of death. But if someone had just tried to murder her, she would be a sobbing mess.

His strong will and courage intrigued her. Tempted her in ways she didn't understand.

'Michael?' she whispered. She'd never used his first name before, always distancing him with his rank.

'What?'

Touch me again. Kiss me. She didn't say it, the words caught up in a trap of her own morals. And yet, she didn't want him to leave, as he surely would.

She didn't know what was coming over her. Perhaps it was the wine. Perhaps her desire to make her own decisions. All she knew was that she didn't want to be alone.

'What if…I asked you for more than a kiss?'

Michael held so very still, she wondered if she'd made a grave mistake. Her cheeks burned with embarrassment as the silence stretched longer.

'I'm not the right man for you, Hannah. I can't ever marry you.'

His honesty was meant to quell her desire. But she'd always known there could be no future for them. And he didn't love her, either.

'I know that,' she heard herself saying. 'It's not what I want from you.' She held her posture erect, as though it would keep her sensibilities from crumbling. What would it matter if she let him kiss her, let him show her the mysteries of a forbidden liaison? Her reputation was already in shambles.

She stood an arm's length from him, but an invitation rested in the space between them. Michael took a step closer, until she could feel the warmth of his breath upon her forehead. The physical closeness of him turned her thoughts erratic.

Her body tingled, imagining his body atop hers.

Never in her life had she known such an experience. The weight of her gown upon her breasts, the heavy skirts covering her legs… It made her uncomfortable, as if too many layers separated them.

He caught her palm and grazed it with a slight kiss. 'You're not yourself.'

'You're right.' She pulled his hand to her cheek, not caring that it was wrong. The need to rebel was rising higher with each moment. 'I have exactly fifteen hours to not be myself. Before we leave this ship.'

His hand drifted to her back, and she felt his bare palm upon her skin. He loosened a few more buttons, sliding his hand beneath the back of her gown.

This was her last chance to say no. Did she want to ruin herself with a soldier? With a man who had no future and could not take care of her? With a man who made her heart beat like the wings of a hummingbird?

Yes.

Hannah reached out and rested her hands upon his evening jacket, tracing the breadth of his shoulders. Before she could talk herself out of it, she lifted her mouth to his in a defiant kiss. He tasted of champagne and a hint of almonds.

That was the last thought in her mind before he took command. He pressed her against the wall, his hot kiss possessing her with no chance of escape.

She was aware of his hands unbuttoning the rest of her gown. In turn, she removed his jacket, untying the cravat.

'I loathe women's fashion,' Michael gritted out. Despite her layers of skirts, he managed to reach beneath them to untie a few of the petticoats, and divest her of the heavy crinoline. Without the weight to support her gown, the fabric hung down. She felt small, completely at his mercy. He undressed her, each piece falling away until she was standing in her undergarments.

The reality of her decision hit her like a bucket of freezing water. Why was she casting aside all of her inhibitions, everything she'd been taught, for a man who had already admitted he could give her no future?

He is nothing, her mind insisted.

He is everything, her body contradicted. Only hours ago, someone had tried to kill him. The thought of losing this man, when she'd only just begun to know him, crept into the spaces of her heart, making her ache. And tonight, he belonged to her.

The war between her body's needs and her mind's agonising control was growing even hotter.

His tongue slipped inside her mouth, and her breasts grew taut as though he'd kissed the nipples. Between her thighs, she grew moist, and Hannah shifted her legs together. No one had ever prepared her for this, and she was too afraid to ask him what was happening.

Michael extinguished the lamp, flooding the cabin in darkness. 'Come here,' he urged, taking her hand. He guided her towards him, and when she realised he was seated in the chair, he pulled her onto his lap.

Her womanhood was intimately pressed against the hard length of his arousal, with only her drawers and his trousers as a barrier. She clung to him, her fingers pressed against his hair.

In the darkness, her skin became even more sensitised. She didn't know what he would do next, and it both excited and terrified her.

Michael slid his hands into her hair once again, and the pins scattered across the wooden floor. His fingers spread through the silken locks while he kissed her.

Her hands rested upon his chest, and he sensed her desire to touch. He loosened his shirt, moving her hands beneath the cambric. His pectoral muscles were rigid, his pulse rapid. Bare skin warmed her fingertips, and her bravado was beginning to disappear.

'Are you certain you want this?' he murmured, kissing her deeply.

When he broke free, she couldn't answer, not knowing what she should say. Things had already progressed too far, hadn't they? Her silence weighed down upon his question.

She wanted him. But was the cost too great?

When his hand moved between her legs, she shivered. His fingers moved to the thin drawers, and she flushed, knowing that he could feel the wetness dampening the cloth. She didn't understand why, and it embarrassed her.

'I know you're afraid of me.' His voice was deep, the rich timbre making her quiver.

'A little,' she confessed. 'I don't know what to do.'

His hand moved against her woman's flesh, arousing her. 'Surrender to me, Hannah. And let me touch you the way I've dreamed.'

She didn't know what he meant by that until his thumb rubbed a small nub above her entrance. A harsh cry caught in the back of her throat, and she forced herself not to moan. With a soft rhythm, he nudged it, sending a shock of warmth spiralling into her womb.

Though she wanted to pull away, she couldn't bring herself to move.

'You're beautiful, Hannah.' He leaned her back, nuzzling her throat as he increased the rhythm. 'If I could, I'd be inside you right now.'

Was that what happened between a man and a woman? She could feel the hard length of his manhood against her inner thigh. The thought of him entering her body conjured a response that made her even wetter. He teased the moisture, using the fabric to abrade her sensitive node.

Hannah fought against the rising wave of pleasure that threatened to drown her. He dipped his finger slightly, caressing the opening of her womanhood.

'I don't understand,' she admitted, her face burning with discomfort. 'How could you be inside me?'

She'd never been taught anything about lovemaking, and she half-wondered if this touching was what husbands and wives did. Somehow, she suspected not. It felt like forbidden temptation, to experience such desire.

He brought her hand to his trousers, letting her feel the firm length straining beneath the cloth. She was startled at the thickness of him, the hard ridge of male flesh.

'This part of me would slide deep inside you,' he said gruffly. His hand moved beneath her drawers to her feminine centre. He dipped his hand against her sensitive flesh, inserting a single finger to demonstrate. 'When you're wet, it makes it easier for both of us.'

He captured her mouth again, using his fingers to stroke her. Before she could beg him to understand the unfamiliar longings, something unexpected began to break through. Her breathing quickened, her back arching out of instinct.

His hand rubbed faster without warning, crumbling away her inhibitions until a hot, piercing sensation pushed her closer to the edge. Then abruptly, he slowed the pace, deepening the pressure.

'Let go for me, Hannah.'

She was fighting against the maddening heat building up. Her inner thighs were silken, craving more.

Without warning, pleasure rammed into her, making her writhe against his hand. Never had she felt anything like this before. He rode his palm against her centre, until she was trembling with aftershocks.

Michael removed his palm, his own breath shaken. His mouth pressed light kisses over her temple, while she clung to him. Nothing could have prepared her for such unexpected ecstasy.

'Would it…have been like that if you'd…made love to me?' she panted.

'Better,' he swore. There was pain in his voice, as though he were fighting off his own frustration. A moment later, he lifted her to her feet, turning the lamp back on. The light speared her eyes, breaking through the spell.

She stood in her underclothes, feeling the shock of reality striking through her. She might as well have been naked before him. He didn't look at her, but reached for his fallen jacket.

Oh, dear God above, what had she done? Why

had she fallen into temptation this way? And what could she possibly say to him now?

When Michael turned to face her, all emotions were masked, as if they had done nothing but conversed. The back of her throat ached, while her cheeks burned with humiliation. To distract herself, she reached for her own fallen clothing.

'I'll help you dress, before I leave,' Michael said at last.

Hannah would have refused, if she could have managed it herself. She tied the layers of petticoats, unable to face him. Irrational tears stung her eyes, but she kept them at bay. Michael held up her dress and lifted it over her head and arms, helping her to rebutton it.

Despite the deep languor that permeated every inch of her skin, she felt like a piece of crystal teetering on the edge, ready to shatter.

'Are you all right?'

No. No, she wasn't all right. But she forced herself to nod. 'Of course. Why wouldn't I be?' Her voice came out too bright, and his hands caressed her shoulders.

His hazel eyes stared at her, gazing at her with such an intensity, she wondered what he wanted to say but couldn't. Instead, he held himself motionless.

'Be careful when you go back to your room,' she offered.

Michael inclined his head. 'Lock your door until Mrs Turner and your maid return.' There was a forced coolness to his voice, and the invisible mien of a soldier seemed to slide over his face.

Humiliation at succumbing to the liaison, without any future promises from him, made her throat go dry. But she'd known it. There would never be any sort of vow from Michael Thorpe.

'Don't trouble yourself about me.'

He took another step backwards, and a faint tinging noise resounded. Michael reached down to the floor to pick up the object. In his hand, he held a fork.

'How strange,' Hannah remarked. 'I didn't bring any silver into the room.'

Both of them stared at the interior of the state room, suddenly seeing pieces neither of them had noticed before. Pieces of silverware, hair pins, a strand of pearls…seemingly random items now were arranged in a pattern. A rectangle had been constructed around the room, framing the contents.

'How curious. What is it, do you think?' Hannah asked.

But Michael ignored the question, already opening the door. 'Where did you tell Mrs Turner to go?'

Hannah shrugged. 'I only told them to return in an hour. I assumed she stayed with my maid Estelle.'

He cursed, stepping into the hallway. 'I have to find her.'

Not we, she noticed. *I.*

Was he so eager to cast her aside now? Her disgruntled feelings pricked her like the numerous forks lying about the room.

But she didn't understand why a strange arrangement of utensils would cause him to worry so. 'What is it that you're not telling me?'

He pointed towards the perimeter of silver. 'She's having another of her spells. I need to find Mrs Turner before she harms herself.'

It would be easy enough to send him away, to wish him luck in finding her. But she felt responsible for the woman's disappearance. Were it not for her, Mrs Turner would still be inside her room, probably sleeping.

Hannah reached for her pelisse and pulled on a bonnet. 'I'm coming with you.'

Chapter Twelve

Outside on the upper deck, the ship rose and fell with the waves. The darkness was broken only by a handful of scattered oil lamps. Several deck hands adjusted the sails while the dull noise of the steam engine droned on.

Michael kept Hannah's hand firmly in his, wondering why he'd agreed to this. There was no reason to bring her with him, where her presence would be noticeably out of place. It was irrational and dangerous.

But he didn't want to leave her alone. Not after he'd been attacked tonight. And especially not after what had just happened between them.

It had taken an act of the greatest restraint not to seduce her. He didn't doubt for a moment that he could have. Her body responded to him with a passion he'd never expected. More than anything, he'd wanted to strip off her remaining undergarments, joining their bodies together.

The sensual image of her legs wrapped around his waist while he buried himself deep within was like a fire igniting his lust. She was a lady, not a woman to be trifled with. Softhearted, stubborn and highly intelligent, everything about her captivated him.

And yet he couldn't bring himself to dishonour her. If he took her innocence, she would pay the price. And he couldn't destroy her chance to make a strong marriage, no matter how much he might want her.

The thought of another man being intimate with Hannah made him clench his fists. At dinner tonight he'd seen the way the gentlemen watched her. He had no right to feel possessive towards her. Not then, and not now.

He gripped her hand, studying the area for any sign of Mrs Turner. When they passed by one of the sailors, he drew Hannah closer, both to protect her from the rocking of the ship and to send an unmistakable warning to the other sailors.

The bo'sun stepped forward and intercepted them. 'Pardon me, m'lord, but passengers aren't allowed on deck at this hour. Best be returnin' to your cabin. Captain's orders.'

Michael wasn't surprised to hear it, but he didn't give a damn what the Captain's orders were. Whenever Mrs Turner had one of her spells, there was no telling what she'd do. He didn't want her to fall into the sea and drown, if her madness tempted her to do something rash. Abigail Turner was the only family he had left, and he would keep her safe at all costs.

He faced the bo'sun and drew upon his officer's hauteur. Had they been in the Army, he would out-rank this man. 'One of Lady Hannah's servants has disappeared.' He nodded to the bo'sun, adding, 'We believe she may be lost.'

The bo'sun shrugged. 'Haven't seen her. She might've gone to meet someone.' His disrespect-ful leer suggested that he suspected Hannah and Michael had done exactly that.

Michael sent the man a blistering look. He was well aware of the implications of bringing Hannah with him, but he wasn't about to let anyone insult her. The sailor straightened, his smirk disappearing at once.

'She is a woman of about sixty-three years, with curling grey hair and light brown eyes,' Michael added. 'About this plump.' He held out his arms to show her girth, though Mrs Turner had lost a good deal of weight since he'd first known her. Too often she forgot to eat.

The bo'sun shook his head. 'Sorry, m'lord. I'm in charge of the rigging and the deck crew. But I'll send one of the hands to look for you, if y'like.'

'Do that.' And in the meantime, he and Hannah would continue searching. He gave a brusque nod before taking Hannah's hand. He intended to survey every inch of the upper deck, to ensure that they hadn't missed her.

Turning away, he pretended to escort Hannah to the stairs of the promenade deck, but at the last moment he guided her around the side of the boat, towards the forecastle.

Together, they traversed the upper deck, slipping into the shadows when any of the deck hands or officers came close. In the dim amber light of the oil lamps, it was nearly impossible to see.

Luck was with them; a few minutes later he spied a red bonnet rolling across the deck.

'She's here.' He kept Hannah's hand firmly gripped in his. 'Tell me if you see her.'

It took nearly a quarter of an hour before they both heard the singing at the same time. The quavering voice of Mrs Turner came from above them. Michael lifted his gaze and saw her holding onto the rigging, her body swaying as the ship rocked on the waves.

'Oh, dear heaven,' Hannah breathed when she spied her. 'What's she doing up there? She'll fall and break her neck.'

'Not if I can get to her first.' Michael removed his jacket and grasped the heavy rope, climbing up the ratline toward Mrs Turner. Calling out to her, he said, 'Mrs Turner, let me help you down.' It was so dark, he doubted if she could see his face. If she didn't recognise him, it would be a problem.

'Henry?' she cried out, asking for her son. 'Is that you?'

He thought about lying, if that would bring her to safety. But if she glimpsed his face, she might panic and fall.

Instead he admitted, 'No. It's Michael Thorpe.'

At first, she didn't reply, which gave him hope. Her skirts and petticoats billowed in the night air, while she held fast to the ropes.

'Will you let me help you down?'

'I don't know anyone named Michael. Now stay away from me while I wait on my Henry.' She began singing again, her voice high-pitched. 'Mad. She's gone mad, for her boy has gone away.' Her voice grew tighter, mingling with tears. 'My fault. It's my fault that it happened.' Sobbing harder, she moaned, 'I didn't want him to die, you see.'

'Shh—' Michael reached up take her by the waist, but she slapped his hands.

'You're not my Henry. I don't know you. Get away from me!' The wind whipped at the ratlines, and Mrs Turner's hand slipped. She shrieked as the line spun, making her swing downwards. Michael caught her hand and put it back to the rope, though she screamed at him.

Damn it. The precarious balancing point on the ratlines stretching up to the mast made it too dangerous to seize her against her will. Either of them could lose their grip and fall. Mrs Turner was nearly twenty feet up in the air, and though she was primarily over the decking, there was still the possibility that she might slip and fall overboard.

He glanced down and caught a glimpse of Hannah climbing up to them. 'Let me try, Michael. I'll coax her down.' When she drew closer, he saw that she'd tied her skirts to each of her ankles.

There was no hesitation in his refusal. 'No.' He wouldn't risk Hannah's safety, no matter that she was already close to them. 'Climb down.'

But she ignored his orders, reaching up higher. The combined weight of the three of them made the line stretch tight. 'You're frightening her,' Hannah insisted. 'I'm a woman. She'll let me help.'

When he was about to argue again, she touched his elbow. 'Stay below us, in case either of us falls.' Mrs Turner had begun singing again, her frail voice turning hoarse.

'Michael, please,' Hannah begged. 'If you try to force her down, she'll fight you. And you'll both be hurt.'

He knew she was right. Though he didn't want to endanger Hannah, he would give her one chance. With great reluctance, he lowered himself below them, to ensure that neither of them fell. He heard Hannah speaking to Mrs Turner softly.

'I've asked him to leave us alone,' she murmured

to the older woman. 'He's gone now and won't harm you.'

'They tried to take him away,' she wept. 'My boy.'

Hannah spoke so quietly to Mrs Turner, Michael couldn't make out what she was saying. He held tightly to the ratlines, watching both of them. Endless minutes passed, and his grip tightened while he watched.

Then Mrs Turner slowly began to descend, with Hannah beside her. Michael kept his hands poised on the lines, prepared to break their fall, if either slipped.

Several of the deck hands had gathered around, and Michael ordered them away. The bo'sun tried to apologise, but Michael cut him off, shielding the women from his gaze. 'I will escort them back to their state rooms,' he said firmly.

Relief filled him up inside that both women were safe on deck. Lady Hannah held Mrs Turner's hand and was speaking quietly to her.

What Hannah had just done was completely un-heard of. Women didn't climb twenty feet in the air to rescue a stranger. It was scandalous, dangerous and right now he wanted to shake her. But he also wanted to hold her tightly, thankful that she hadn't been hurt.

She shouldn't have taken such a bold risk. His

anger and fear built up to the point where he gritted his teeth to keep from lashing out at her.

Though his rational mind pointed out that both of them were all right, it might have been a very different outcome. He couldn't let Hannah take such chances again.

The air was frigid, and Hannah's teeth were threatening to chatter from the cold. Mrs Turner's hands were icy, and Michael led them all back to Hannah's state room, where she found Estelle waiting.

The maid's eyes widened at the sight of Hannah and her windblown, dishevelled appearance.

'Lady Hannah, whatever happened to you?' Estelle looked appalled, but Hannah had no desire to explain herself. Nor did she want a word of this spoken to her mother.

Ignoring the question, she said, 'I ordered you to look after Mrs Turner, but you neglected your duty, it seems.'

Excuses stammered from Estelle's lips, but Hannah had endured her fill of them. 'Enough. Go and help Mrs Turner prepare for bed.'

The maid cast a glance at Michael, and he stared back at Estelle, until she returned her attentions to Mrs Turner.

Hannah was about to help them, when the Lieutenant refused to surrender her wrist, leading her into the dimly lit hallway. He forced her to follow him around the corner to a spot hidden from view.

Keeping his voice in a whisper, he leaned down to her ear. 'Whatever possessed you to do something so dangerous?'

Her teeth started chattering, his words breaking apart the false confidence that was holding her together. She knew it had been perilous, but standing below on the decking hadn't been useful, either.

'I don't know. I just thought…you needed help,' she whispered, thankful when he rubbed her hands to warm them.

'I didn't need you breaking your neck.' He pulled her body close to his, letting his body heat warm her freezing skin. The actions were in opposition to his words. 'You could have been killed.'

'So could you.' She pulled back, trying to calm the chattering of her teeth. 'You asked me to help look after Mrs Turner. And you were frightening her. It seemed like the only way to get her down.'

He said nothing but stroked her hair. His wide hands moved over her scalp, down her back. 'Don't ever do something like that again.' Right now, he was holding her like he didn't want to let go. He fitted his body to hers as though he wanted to shield her from all harm.

Against her better judgement, Hannah embraced him back. In their fleeting solitude, his mouth brushed against her temple. She closed her eyes, wishing to God there weren't so many obstacles between them.

He'd made no promises to her, nor could he. She knew that. All they had was a few stolen moments together. Tomorrow evening, they would arrive in Bremerhaven. And the day after that, she would be left behind at her cousins' house.

He framed her face with his hands. 'Thank you for what you did.'

She braved a smile, startled by his unexpected offering. 'You're welcome. I hope Mrs Turner feels better in the morning.'

'Get some sleep,' he ordered.

'I doubt it.' Her insides were still churning, after everything that had happened, and most especially after the way he'd touched her.

'Michael,' she murmured. 'About what happened between us earlier—'

'It won't happen again,' he swore. He jerked his hands back, as though he couldn't get away from her fast enough. The deep embarrassment returned, for she'd given so much of herself to him. Like a wanton woman, she had laid herself bare before him, seeking the mindless pleasure he'd offered.

'Good,' she echoed. 'That's good, then.' Without another word, she turned back to her room so he would not see the tears.

* * *

Lady Hannah was absent from breakfast that morning. Her maid said she'd taken a tray in her state room, and Michael supposed she needed the extra sleep after the night they'd endured.

Earlier, he'd gone back to the upper deck where they had rescued Mrs Turner. Seeing the narrow ratlines in the morning sunlight made his breath catch. If either of them had fallen overboard, they might have become trapped beneath the large paddle wheel.

He never should have let Hannah climb up. It would have been so easy for her to be harmed or killed. The failure would have fallen upon his shoulders, just as he'd failed his fellow soldiers at Balaclava.

He returned to the promenade deck, but saw no sign of Mrs Turner or Lady Hannah. He wasn't about to knock on her state-room door, for he'd already broken enough rules of propriety. It was better for him to keep his distance and hope that he met her by chance.

After exploring the many rooms of the ship, he found them in the Grand Saloon. Hannah wore a long-sleeved, flounced rose gown adorned with lace. The trim was sewn across her bodice down to a narrow vee at the waist. A matching bonnet with ribbons and more lace cradled her face. Were it not for the dull exhaustion in her eyes, no one would notice anything out of order. Her gaze went to his neck, but he'd hidden the abraded skin with a high cravat.

Beside her sat Mrs Turner, wearing her black mourning gown. The elderly woman beamed, calling out, 'Michael! You will join us, won't you?' In her hands, she held out a deck of cards. 'I am teaching Lady Hannah to play piquet.'

He wasn't certain that was such a good idea. 'I thought ladies weren't supposed to play cards.'

Mrs Turner pulled out a chair. 'Oh, we're not going to be ladies today, are we?'

It was then that he saw the enormous slice of chocolate cake on the plate beside Hannah. She took a bite of the dessert, as if defying the etiquette for proper breakfast food. Watching her devour the cake reminded him of the expression on her face last night when he'd showed her the pleasures of her secret flesh.

He hastily took a seat to hide his reaction to the memory.

Mrs Turner dealt out the cards to each of them. 'I know you've played before.'

He let his gaze rest upon Hannah's face while she ate her cake. 'Yes.'

'Then you'll be able to teach Lady Hannah all that she needs to know.'

He made no response, watching as Hannah's tongue slipped out to lick her fingertip. There were many things he wanted to teach Lady Hannah, and not a single one of them having to do with cards.

Hannah picked up the hand dealt, a sheepish smile upon her face. 'I'm not very good with cards. I was never allowed to play.'

He picked up his own cards, barely glancing at them. 'Why not?'

'My mother believed that any cards were a form of gambling. She didn't want me to risk eternal hellfire.'

'There are far worse ways to sin,' he pointed out.

Hannah's face turned scarlet, as though she were thinking of the time she'd spent in his arms. She forced her attention back to the cards.

'Which of us will be the dealer?' Michael asked Mrs Turner.

'Why don't you take on that role? Let Lady Hannah draw first.'

Michael deferred to the widow's wishes and dealt the cards. He picked up his hand, studying the two jacks and the queen of spades amid the other numbered cards. 'Were you wanting to wager on the game?'

Mrs Turner beamed. 'Well, of course we should have a wager. That's what makes playing cards so entertaining. And wicked.'

'There's nothing wrong with a bit of wickedness…once in a while.' Michael shifted his cards, laying them facedown on the table while he waited for Hannah.

When she glanced up, her gaze settled upon his mouth. He spied the traces of chocolate upon her lips. Right now he wanted to lick it off, devouring her mouth and pulling her close.

'What should we wager with?' Hannah asked, a faint blush of colour upon her cheeks. 'Money we don't have?'

He knew she was referring to the fictional thousand pounds he'd offered in return for her handkerchief last night. 'Not for money.'

'What, then?'

A flash of inspiration struck him, and Michael signalled to one of the ships' waiters. After a brief discussion, the waiter nodded, disappearing behind closed doors.

'Wait and see.'

When the waiter returned, he held a tray of miniature pastries, caramels and confections.

'We'll play for sweets,' Michael said.

'Lieutenant Thorpe, you are a man of genius,' Hannah breathed. Her face beamed with anticipation and a new determination to win.

He rested his wrist upon the table, watching her as she focused on her cards. Mrs Turner explained the rules, urging Hannah to choose five cards to exchange from her hand.

'The seven is the lowest card and ace is the

highest,' the widow explained. 'You should try to exchange the most cards, in order to hold the advantage. Then you will count the number of points in your hand.'

Hannah's mouth was pursed, as though she were contemplating the best combination to discard. After she picked up her new cards, Mrs Turner explained more of the rules while Michael exchanged his own cards.

'The winner of each trick will receive her choice of confections from the tray,' the widow said, reaching for one of the chocolates. 'I had best sample these to ensure that they are of good quality.'

'Shouldn't we each sample a bit?' Hannah offered, eyeing the sweets.

'Not unless you win.' Michael arranged his cards. 'That would be cheating.' After she'd arranged her hand, he asked, 'What is your opening bid?'

Before she answered, Hannah took another glance at her cards. 'What penalty will the loser pay, for losing a trick?'

'There's no penalty for losing. The winner gets the sweets, and that's fair enough.'

'No, Lady Hannah is right,' Mrs. Turner said. 'The loser should pay a forfeit.'

'I will not bleat like a goat. Or sing.' He didn't care what the women wanted; some things were beneath his dignity.

Hannah offered him a stunning smile. 'I think it

should be answering questions. The loser has to tell the winner the truth, no matter what is asked.'

'Even better,' Mrs Turner said. 'We will take turns playing against one another.' From the bright colour in the woman's cheeks, it appeared that she had not suffered unduly the night before. Michael wondered if she had any memory of what she'd done. Probably not.

Hannah won the first trick. Her lips curved upwards with victory as she chose one of the caramels. Her eyes closed as she chewed the confection. 'I could eat a hundred of these,' she breathed.

And didn't he want to be the one to give them to her? The exquisite expression on her face was like a woman in the throes of sexual fulfillment.

Michael focused his attention back on his cards, ignoring the rigid arousal he was forced to hide beneath the table.

'Time for your forfeit,' Hannah demanded. She reached for a glass of lemonade that the waiter had brought earlier, thinking to herself. After a moment, she asked, 'How did you and my brother Stephen become friends?'

Her question surprised him. He'd expected her to inquire about Reischor or about the journey to Lohenberg.

'I met Whitmore at school, years ago.'

Her face turned curious. 'I didn't know you'd gone to Eton.'

Michael dealt the next set of cards, shrugging. 'I did receive an education. My mother insisted on it, though it was an unnecessary hardship.'

Mrs Turner's face turned serious. 'It was important to Mary. She wanted our Michael to have a better life than they could give.' With a smile, she added, 'He was the best student there.'

'Really.' Lady Hannah's mouth softened in thought as she arranged another card.

Michael sensed the unspoken questions. Common men rarely attended schools that educated the upper classes. The truth was, he didn't know why he'd been allowed to attend. The headmaster had never made mention of it, though Michael was certain his fellow students had suspected his humble beginnings.

Knowing that each day he spent at school was another coin taken away from his parents, he felt he had no choice but to excel at his studies. And though he'd learned Latin and French, he'd found little use for it. A gentleman's education didn't amount to much without a title.

In the end, he'd followed the path of several friends, joining the British Army. Whitmore had been his closest friend and had considered a military career as well, before he'd become the heir.

Mrs Turner played against him in the next round, and Michael spied Graf von Reischor approaching. Though he nearly lost his concentration, he managed to win the trick.

When Hannah offered him the tray, he chose a chocolate-dipped cream.

'Take it,' he bade Hannah.

'But it was your win. The sweet belongs to you.'

'My win. My choice.' He held it out, and Hannah smiled before she slipped the confection inside her mouth. The pleasure on her face made the decision worthwhile.

'And what question would you have me answer?' Mrs Turner prompted. She eyed the confection tray with a forlorn look.

He thought a moment. 'Tell me the earliest memory you have of my mother.'

The Graf greeted them, pulling up a chair. 'I hope you don't mind if I join in your conversation.'

'Not at all.' Mrs Turner beamed.

Michael tensed, unsure if he wanted the Graf to hear stories about his mother.

'Mary Thorpe was my closest friend, you know.' Mrs Turner's expression turned distant as she remembered. 'She and Paul worked hard and always remembered those less fortunate than themselves.' She rubbed her chin, smiling wistfully. 'They loved you very much. After so many years of being childless, you were their gift.'

In the fraction of a moment, her voice faded to a whisper. 'You were only three years old.'

He saw the Graf's face narrow. 'Three years?'

The widow frowned at the Graf. 'Until you have won a trick, you are not allowed to ask questions.' She sent the Graf a stern look. 'I believe it's your turn to deal, Lady Hannah.'

Michael chose another sweet off the tray and passed it to the widow, as a silent means of thanks. The elderly woman popped it into her mouth.

'Later tonight, we will arrive at the home of Lady Hannah's cousins,' the Graf informed them. 'They live inland, a few hours beyond Bremerhaven, near the Lohenberg border.'

Michael saw Mrs Turner's hands begin to shake. 'Lohenberg?' she whispered. 'You never said we were going to Lohenberg. You said Germany.'

He hadn't, because he'd suspected she would react in this way. 'We are passing through Germany,' he admitted. 'But the trip to Lohenberg will only be for a few weeks. There's nothing to worry about.'

'No.' She stood up, raising her voice. 'No. You can't go back.'

Go back?

Mrs Turner had turned deathly white, wringing her hands. Turning on the Graf, she demanded, 'You can't force him to go.' Muttering to herself, she pushed the cards away, overturning the tray of confections.

Michael caught her before she could run off.

Hysteria was etched in her face. 'Why?' he asked softly. 'Why can't I go?'

'Because they'll kill you if you do.'

Chapter Thirteen

Later that evening

The coach jostled across the rough roads, while outside, clouds obscured the landscape. The ship had docked at Bremerhaven, and now they were journeying towards her cousins' home near the border.

Hannah had sent Estelle to travel with the Graf and his servants in another coach while she travelled with Michael and Mrs Turner. She didn't want to agitate the older woman after her outburst earlier. It had taken most of the day and a dose of laudanum to calm her down. Now, the slight noise of Mrs Turner snoring was the only sound to disturb the interior of the coach.

In the meantime, Hannah's head was starting to ache, but she pushed away the pain. Only a few more hours, and she could sleep in a real bed. She imagined soft pillows and warm covers.

Michael looked as though he were on the way

to his execution. There was a grim cast to his face while he stared out the window.

'Are you all right?' Hannah asked. 'Is there something I can get for you?' There was a basket of food and drink at her feet, which neither of them had touched. Mrs Turner hadn't yet awakened to take her share of the meal.

'I don't need anything,' he said. But his hands were curled into fists at his sides, his gaze staring out the window.

'You're hoping that this turns out to be nothing,' she predicted. 'That you have no ties to Lohenberg.'

He nodded, his face dark with tension. Though he might deny it, she wasn't so certain his past was that simple. Someone had tried to strangle him after dinner. Not only that, but the widow knew something about Michael's past. Something ominous.

Whenever Hannah had tried to ask Michael about his own journey to Lohenberg, he'd redirected her questions. He, too, was holding secrets.

'What if you are royalty?' she asked. 'Would it be so bad?'

He shook his head. 'There's no evidence of that. Any resemblance to the King is a coincidence.'

'What about Mrs Turner?'

'Mrs Turner has slowly been losing her wits over the past year. Nothing she says can be trusted.'

'She was singing about a lost child last night. What if she was talking about you?'

'She was singing about her son, Henry.' Michael stared outside the window. 'It was her child who was lost. And it was my fault he's dead.' The heaviness in his voice suggested he felt responsible for the widow's madness.

'How did he die?'

Michael rested his hand on his knee, tapping at his hat. 'It was at Balaclava.'

'Tell me what happened.'

He glanced over at Mrs Turner, as though reluctant to speak of it or remember the day.

'Please,' she whispered. 'I want to know.'

At last, he lowered his voice. 'Men were shot down around me, by the hundreds. Myself included.'

'You lived.'

'Only because I fell beneath Henry's body. When the enemy soldiers stabbed their bayonets into the dead, they stabbed Henry. Not me.'

The desolation and bitterness in his voice made her reach out to take his hand. Though both of them wore gloves, she tried to offer him the comfort of touch.

'He was already dead, wasn't he?'

'Yes. But I should be the one dead, not him.' He shook his head in disgust.

'It wasn't your fault that he died. Only God can determine who dies and who lives.' She reached out and took his hand in hers. 'Don't punish yourself for being one of the lucky few.'

He gripped her palm. 'Can't you understand? If I am proven to be the Prince, Reischor wants to place me upon the throne. Why would a man like me deserve a fate like that?'

'Perhaps it's an obligation. A chance for you to make changes that will help this country. What if you could protect others from dying at war?'

He looked away. 'I don't want it, Hannah. I'm not a man who can lead others. It's not in me.'

He exhaled, and the breath was filled with guilt. 'I couldn't even look after my own men, Hannah. How could anyone believe I could look after a country?'

'Because you care about others. And because you're bullheaded enough to do it.' She released his hand, leaning back against the coach.

The throbbing of her headache started to bother her again, and she reached for the vial of laudanum she had given to Mrs Turner.

'Are you having another of your headaches?' Michael asked suddenly.

She shook her head. 'I hope not. Sometimes if I take the laudanum soon enough, it keeps the headache from becoming too bad.'

After she measured out two drops, she closed her eyes, resting her head against the side of the coach.

When the bouncing of the wheels made her clench her teeth, she lowered her head into her hands.

A moment later, she heard Michael removing his gloves. He reached over to her bonnet and untied it, lifting it away. She didn't protest, not wanting to wake Mrs Turner.

With his bare hands, Michael covered her hair, his thumbs massaging her temples. The gentleness of his touch, his desire to take away the pain, made her breath catch.

His thumbs were rough, his fingers slipping into her hair, framing her face. The effects of the laudanum, coupled with his gentle caress, made her relax.

The circling movement of his thumbs and the light pressure on her scalp helped her forget about the headache. She grew less restrained, leaning into his touch.

'I shouldn't let you do this,' she whispered. The more she allowed him liberties, the worse she would feel in a few days when he was gone.

He lifted her hand to his mouth, removing her glove before kissing her hand. 'Nor this.'

The languid heat of his mouth against her skin was tantalising. Seductive. She wanted to sit in his lap, as before, and pull his mouth down to hers.

'If you were a Prince,' she breathed, 'you wouldn't look twice at a woman like me, with all the scandalous things I've done.'

'If I were a Prince…' he nipped at her fingers, sliding the tip of her thumb into his mouth '…I would make you a Princess.'

He caressed her palm, adding, 'I'd lock you up in a tower and come to you at night.' A dark smile crossed his face. 'I'd forbid you to wear anything at all, except your hair.'

She jerked her hand away as if it were on fire. Her skin certainly was. His evocative images made her body ache and her mind imagine things that weren't going to be.

They would never be together, no matter what the future held. The words were part of a game, nothing more.

Michael reached for her hand again, his long fingers twining in hers, almost as if he drew comfort from her presence.

Hannah stared at the door to the coach, knowing she needed to break free of him. Last night, she had allowed him intimacies that only a husband should know. The pleasure could not eradicate her guilt.

'I'll be arriving at my cousins' house tonight,' she said, unable to keep the sadness from her voice. Gently, she pulled her hand away and put on her glove. 'I shouldn't see you again.'

'You're right.' He rested his forearms on his knees, glancing outside at the clouded scenery.

The evening light was fading, night slipping soundlessly over the land. Barren fields overshadowed the greenery, ploughed in preparation for planting. The dismal landscape darkened her mood even more.

What had she hoped? That he would ask her to stay with him? He wouldn't. Not ever, for she doubted if she meant anything more to him than a distraction.

The tiny space inside the coach was starting to close in on her, as though the bars of her exile were shutting out the rest of the world.

Michael didn't look at her again, and Hannah closed her eyes so she wouldn't dwell upon it. The anger and hurt brimmed up inside. Her headache was starting to fade, and she drifted into sleep.

Abruptly, the coach came to a stop. Hannah stared at Michael, wondering what had happened. 'Stay here,' Michael ordered. 'I'll find out what it is.'

'Did something happen to the Graf's coach?'

'I don't know. I'm going to find out.' He stared hard at her. 'But do not leave this coach.'

She forced herself to nod, though she could hear the edge in his tone. Fear penetrated her veins, and she rubbed her arms to warm them.

Hannah looked over at Mrs Turner, who hadn't woken up. That was good, for if there truly was a threat, the widow would only be more frightened.

She strained to hear the men talking. Perhaps the Graf's coach had gotten mired or a horse was having difficulty. It was likely nothing more than that.

But when she heard the sounds of gunfire, she ducked down below the window, grabbing Mrs Turner and pushing her against the seat. The widow opened her eyes briefly, but in her drugged haze, she wasn't aware of what was happening. Moments later, she started snoring again.

The men were shouting, and more gunfire erupted. Outside, Hannah heard the coachman abandoning his seat, joining in with the others.

Oh God, what was happening? It hurt to breathe, and Hannah closed her eyes, praying that no one would be hurt.

It was a foolish thought, for the fighting continued outside. She tried to glimpse the men from the window but could see nothing. When the shouting stopped and the voices grew low, she suspected the worst.

More minutes passed, but she didn't leave the coach. Michael had ordered her not to.

But what if he's dead? her mind offered. *Or wounded?*

What if they needed help, and she was doing nothing but cowering inside the coach? Hannah took a deep breath, then another.

Her hands shook as she turned the door handle, climbing down from the coach. It was getting too dark to see, but from the whale-oil lamps she glimpsed the road. Thank goodness the laudanum had managed to keep her headache from transforming into a vicious illness, like before. But it made her unbearably tired, and she struggled to keep a clear head. Ahead, she heard the Graf issuing orders in Lohenisch.

'Peter, see if the women are safe. Gustav, take my coach and go to the nearest village with the other servants. Arrange for a doctor to meet us at the inn. *Schnelhurt!*'

Though his orders held the undeniable air of command, there was an edge of pain beneath them. As Hannah drew closer, she saw the Graf seated on the ground, with a panicked Estelle and a footman beside the fallen body of Michael. Two other men she didn't recognise lay dead, a few paces away.

'Is the Lieutenant all right?' She rushed to Michael's side, kneeling before him.

'You shouldn't have left the coach, Lady Hannah,' the ambassador argued. 'It's not safe here.' He nodded for the coachman to accompany her back, but Hannah refused to go.

'What happened?'

The Graf released a breath. 'I went with Gustav to investigate and saw that someone had blocked the road. I was shot.' His eyes closed as he fought off the pain. 'Lieutenant Thorpe and the coachman did most of the fighting, but the last one got away.'

Hannah wouldn't leave Michael's side, and once

he was safely clear of the coach, Gustav drove away with the servants. She lifted Michael's head to rest in her lap, and he groaned at the movement. Thank God he was alive.

'Was Lieutenant Thorpe shot, as well?'

'A bullet grazed his arm, but nothing too serious. I'm more concerned about his head injury. His attacker struck him against the coach before Gustav shot him.' The Graf winced at the memory.

'I'm sorry…for endangering you,' he apologized, his voice breaking. 'Until now, I didn't believe it myself. But…there must be a connection to the royal family. Why else would anyone try to kill the Lieutenant?'

'Why indeed,' Hannah remarked, not speaking a word about the earlier attack on board the ship. Changing the subject, she asked, 'What about you? Where are you hurt?'

The Graf slipped back into Lohenisch, almost without realising it. 'I know of at least three bullet wounds.'

Hannah hid her fear, for she didn't know the first thing about tending such injuries. Her stomach tightened with queasiness. 'How bad is it?'

'I'm afraid I cannot walk at the moment.'

Thankful that it was dark, Hannah removed one of her petticoats. If she could stop some of the bleeding, perhaps that would help.

'I already tended to Lieutenant Thorpe's wounds,'

the Graf murmured. Hannah leaned down to examine Michael's head, where she saw bruising and a swollen knot. His upper arm was partially wrapped with a man's cravat, blood staining the cloth.

She tore the petticoat in half, then in half again. 'Who do you believe the Lieutenant really is?'

While she wrapped the Graf's first wound, he answered, 'Most likely the Changeling Prince.'

Hannah tied another bandage around the Graf's knee, while he revealed the tale of the young Prince who disappeared on the night of All Hallows Eve, only to return the next morning.

'He looked slightly different, so the stories say. Not a great deal, but enough to make those around him wonder. He cried often, and he stopped speaking for nearly a year. His nurse thought he'd been bewitched. But the King put an end to the rumours, swearing that the boy was indeed his son.'

'If there was a switch, do you think the King had something to do with it?' Hannah suggested. She tightened the bandage around the Graf's leg, trying to stop the bleeding.

It was then that the Graf seemed to realise that they hadn't been speaking English. 'Exactly how many languages do you speak, Lady Hannah?'

'Five.' Her face flushed, for she didn't want him to think her an aberration. 'Including English.'

'That may prove useful to us,' the Graf mused. 'If you decide to stay with our travelling party.'

What was he suggesting? That she accompany them into Lohenberg? Her first instinct was to protest that, no, she couldn't possibly continue with them. But when she looked down at Michael's unconscious form, her heart shredded into pieces. She worried about him, far more than she should.

At that moment, Michael sat up slowly, clutching his temple. Hannah was saved from further discussion, and she helped to support him with both arms around his shoulders.

'Where are they?' he demanded, rubbing the back of his head.

'Gone, I'm afraid,' the Graf answered. 'Our men weren't fast enough to stop them.'

Michael released a curse and tried to rise. Hannah helped him to steady his balance. 'How badly are you hurt?'

'I'm fine.' He looked down at the Graf. 'What about him?'

'Both of you need to be tended by a doctor,' Hannah asserted. 'He's been shot several times, and I'm not sure if all of the bullets passed through.'

She didn't voice her fear that the Graf might not survive the injuries. She'd never seen a man die before, and she didn't want to think of it.

Turning to the Graf, she asked, 'How far are we from the village?'

'Too far,' he managed. 'Several hours, at least.'

Michael leaned down, and too late Hannah realised that he meant to pick the Graf up.

'Your arm—' she protested.

'It's nothing. Hannah.' Michael emitted a hiss of pain when he lifted the Graf up. The coachman, Peter, moved towards them and helped put the Graf inside the vehicle.

When the Graf was safely inside, Mrs Turner stirred. Her eyes flickered upon Michael and the Graf, and she let out a cry of alarm at the sight of their wounds.

'What's happened?' the widow demanded. 'You're bleeding.'

'Nothing serious.' Michael shrugged it off. 'A minor wound—no need to worry.' Nodding toward the Graf, he added, 'But Reischor suffered worse injuries. I need you to help Lady Hannah tend him while I drive us to the closest village.'

Mrs Turner covered her mouth, her eyes still glazed over from the effects of the laudanum. 'But what happened?'

Hannah cut off further questions, saying, 'I'll explain everything to you, on the way.'

Michael handed her one of the lamps to illuminate the interior of the coach. While the coachman checked the horses and started the carriage back on the journey, Hannah helped Mrs Turner with the Graf's wounds. The petticoats were soaked through with blood, and she blanched at the sight.

Mrs Turner didn't seem at all bothered by the injuries and took charge, offering him a dose of laudanum to dull the pain. The Graf took it gratefully.

As the widow helped tend him, Hannah's thoughts returned to Michael and the story of the Changeling Prince. Whoever believed he posed a threat wouldn't stop until the threat was eliminated.

She stared outside the window, the wretched fear gathering up inside. Though she couldn't grasp what her feelings were, she didn't want anything to happen to the Lieutenant.

Tomorrow, she was supposed to bid him farewell while he continued his journey to Lohenberg.

But she didn't want to leave him. Hannah felt as though she were stumbling blind, without a path to follow. They were at a crossroads, their lives taking different turns. Was it so wrong, wanting to walk with him a little further?

Though she didn't know what would happen, Hannah was certain of one thing. She was not about to be left behind, not when the man she cared about was in such danger.

Chapter Fourteen

Michael knew he was dreaming. And yet, he couldn't push away the strange visions. In the dream, he was a young boy again, holding his mother's hand.

It was a warm afternoon, the air sour with the odours of London. The buzzing of unfamiliar voices and sounds made him stay close to her side.

'It's all right, Michael. You'll be safe now.' She brushed a light kiss on his temple, murmuring words of comfort.

'I'm afraid.' He gripped her leg, burying his face into her side. 'She said they were going to hurt me if I wasn't good. If I didn't do what she said.'

Every stranger, every unfamiliar face, was a threat to him. His stomach gnawed at him with worry and hunger.

'We're going to take care of you now,' Mary whispered. 'No one will ever harm you again.'

'Michael,' he heard Lady Hannah murmuring. 'Wake up.'

He let out a breath, realising that he'd been given a few drops of laudanum. His head felt heavy, his eyes leaden. 'I will. I just need a moment.'

Her hand reached out to his face, her warm palm resting upon his cheek. It was nice. He wanted to stay here a little longer, feeling her hand upon his skin.

'Michael, I need you to open your eyes. Look at me.'

His vision flickered, then cleared as he saw Hannah. From her rumpled appearance, she probably hadn't slept at all. Her hair had been hastily repinned, her long-sleeved rose gown wrinkled. She'd discarded her bonnet on a chair nearby.

Had she stayed with him all night long? By the looks of it, they were inside a room at the inn. 'Where is Mrs Turner?'

'She is for, I mean *with*, Graf von Reischor.' Her face flushed, and she kept staring at him, a worried expression on her face. 'Estelle is helping her.'

'You shouldn't be here alone with me,' he warned. 'Think of what the others will say.'

'I told the innkeeper you were my husband.'

He raised an eyebrow at that, wondering why she would lie. 'And the Graf agreed to this?'

'He was sleeping permanently.'

He frowned, not knowing what she was saying. 'I beg your pardon?'

She flushed again. 'I mean, he was unconscious.' Her mouth pursed tightly, and he couldn't understand why she kept gaping at him.

'What's wrong?' He glanced at his right arm, but the bandage appeared clean. His wound ached a little, but it was bearable. The bullet had only nicked the skin. 'Why are you staring at me that way?'

'Don't you realise what you're doing?'

'I don't, no. Tell me.' He sat up carefully on the bed, swinging his legs over the side.

'Listen to yourself,' she said. 'You've been speaking Lohenisch in your sleep during the past hour, and just now. Another language, Michael. One you claimed you didn't know.'

'I haven't—' he started to say, but then he heard the unfamiliar words. It was as if his voice and his brain were disconnected somehow. He had spoken from instinct, without thinking.

And Hannah had also been speaking Lohenisch, he now realised. It was why she'd made a few mistakes, errors that she'd corrected.

The revelation was like a knife slicing through his throat, cutting away any further denials. There *was* a connection between him and Lohenberg, one he had long forgotten. Somehow, the country was a part of his heritage.

He struggled to speak the language again, but the

words eluded him. The moment he tried to think about what he wanted to say, he couldn't grasp a single sentence.

Hannah placed both hands on his shoulders, regarding him. 'I think we both know that you are not merely a fishmonger's son.'

He didn't want to believe it. The idea of having another life, another family who hadn't wanted him, seemed to shift the ground beneath him.

'Then who am I, Hannah?'

'That's what we're going to find out.'

'We?'

She offered a hopeful smile. 'The Graf cannot possibly travel to Lohenberg in his condition. Not only that, but my cousins do not know exactly when I will arrive. A few days won't matter. I'll come with you.'

He stood up, pressing her hands away. 'No. It's inappropriate for you to travel with us.'

She stared down at her hands, her cheeks brightening. 'I want to help you. You'll need help remembering the Lohenisch language.' Squaring her shoulders, she added, 'After that, I'll leave. You needn't worry that this would be anything more than…than friendship.'

The embarrassment on her face increased his own feelings of awkwardness. He'd misinterpreted her offer, thinking she had changed her mind about being with him.

Damn it all, he didn't know what to do about Hannah. She wasn't a woman he could marry, nor could he become her lover. And yet, he couldn't quite bring himself to push her away, the way he should.

'I can act as your translator,' she offered. 'Without the Graf, we'll attract less attention, and Mrs Turner will be fine with him.'

Alone with her? Was she so naïve to think that no one would notice an unmarried woman and man travelling together? 'Others will speak poorly of you,' he warned.

'Not if they believe I am your wife.' She stood only an arm's length away from him. 'It's a travel arrangement, Michael. Nothing more than that.'

Looking at her innocent face, he saw that she truly thought they could travel together as friends, not lovers.

'Twice, someone has tried to kill me,' he argued. He wasn't going to put her into harm's way, no matter how she tried to convince him. 'It could happen again.'

'Not if we disguise ourselves.' She reached out and touched his coat. 'With the right attire, we could blend in with the others. No one would know we're any different, especially without the Graf to draw notice.' She pulled her hand away once more. 'And we'll find the answers you're looking for.'

He kept silent, pondering her idea. It wasn't sensible at all. To travel alone with Hannah, into a country he barely knew, was risking far too much.

Most of all, she risked her innocence. For if he had to remain at her side every hour of every day, he doubted if he could resist touching her again.

'It's not a good idea, Hannah. It's dangerous.'

She started to protest again, something about all the reasons why he should uncover the past. He silenced her by kissing her.

With his mouth, he ravaged her lips, trying to show her how much he desired her. Her arms wound around his neck, whether for balance or whether in response to his kiss he didn't know. She smelled so good, the jasmine fragrance exotic and tempting. He softened the kiss, sliding his tongue inside her mouth. Coaxing and urging her to give him more, he used his good arm to draw her close.

'Do you feel how much I want you?' he whispered, bringing her hips to his. 'The danger you face is from me, not the assassins of Lohenberg.'

He lowered his mouth to the curve of her neck, whispering upon her skin, 'If you travel with me, pretending to be my wife, I can't promise not to touch you.'

She pulled away, composing herself. 'I'll take the risk.'

* * *

'The Graf von Reischor isn't dead, is he?'

'No,' the servant apologised. 'He survived the assassins we hired. And as for the Prince—'

'Do not call him that. He is only a man with an unfortunate resemblance to the King. A bastard son.'

The servant cleared his throat. 'You are right, of course. But if he is only the King's by-blow, is there a need to kill him?'

'There can be no usurper. No reason to question the rightful heir to the throne. He bears too strong a resemblance to the King.'

'You are right, of course,' the servant confirmed. 'And it will be noticed, once he enters Lohenberg.'

'You cannot allow it. If you have to kill him yourself, ensure that this man poses no threat to the throne.'

The servant bowed. 'It will be as you wish.' Straightening, he inquired, 'Do you wish for me to remain in the Graf's employ? I can continue to watch and inform you of his doings.'

'Yes. And return to me, as soon as it is done.'

'What about the Queen?'

A brief nod. 'See to it that she's kept quiet. Use your connections in the palace and tell no one of the Graf's doings. I don't want any more stories about the Changeling Prince.'

A bag of coins exchanged hands. The servant

gave thanks, but hesitated before departing. 'What of the woman who is travelling with them? She was supposed to be sent to some cousins in Germany, but after the Graf was injured, they were delayed. If she witnesses anything—'

'Dispose of her, if you must.'

Hannah's bottom felt as though it had been beaten with wooden paddles. She clung to her horse, knowing the Graf's servants would pursue them. Reischor would be livid when he learned of her impulsive plan. Not only because they had 'borrowed' horses from his coach, but also because he would suspect they had discovered something about Michael's past.

Yet Michael faced more danger by travelling with the Graf than with her. It might not be the best of circumstances, but he could hide his identity easier if he didn't arrive in a grand coach with servants.

The cool morning air held a mist that clung to the forest tree trunks, an enchanted cloud hiding the green moss. Michael seemed not to notice their surroundings, keeping his gaze fixed ahead. He rode beside her, dressed in grey trousers, a white shirt, black waistcoat and matching jacket. The subdued colors were less conspicuous, and Hannah had chosen a faded blue long-sleeved gown that she'd borrowed from Estelle.

She worried that, by taking horses, they still might

attract notice. Perhaps they should have walked or hired a wagon.

There was no time for it now. Though it was barely past dawn, Hannah feared they hadn't left soon enough.

There was only one road leading into Lohenberg, and as they crossed the border, Hannah saw that Michael kept glancing behind them. Like her, he appeared unsettled about what they had done.

'Is anyone following us?' Hannah asked.

'Not yet.'

Ahead, the road curved toward a small village. Vast fields encircled the farmhouses, ready for planting. Michael led them into the village, surprising her when he stopped the horse at a tavern. 'We'll eat breakfast here.'

His offer surprised her, for she hadn't expected to stop. It was only a few hours more until they reached the capital city of Vermisten. The royal *Schloss* lay on the outskirts, and Hannah was anxious to see it.

He helped her down, but didn't look at all eager to eat. 'Are you certain you wish to stop?' Hannah questioned. 'You don't have to on my behalf. I can wait until we reach Vermisten.'

'We're gathering information,' he said, taking her hand. 'Neither of us has been to the capital city before, and we need to know what we're facing.'

'Know your enemy?' she guessed, thinking of his military background.

'Precisely.'

He led their horses into one of the brick stables, giving a young lad a handful of coins to care for them.

'Those are Lohenberg coins,' Hannah remarked. 'Where did you get them?'

'Graf von Reischor provided me with a purse of coins to spend upon my arrival.' He shot her a side-long glance. 'I doubt if this was the way he intended for me to use them.'

'He puts a great deal of effort toward appearances.' Hannah took his arm as they approached the door. 'But since he cannot accompany us, I think he wouldn't mind.'

Michael took her hand in his. 'Are you ready?'

She nodded. He led her inside the tavern. A dining room was set aside for travelling guests, with several sturdy tables and clean tablecloths. The tables were full and only a few empty chairs remained.

'Good morning,' a thin-faced woman greeted them in Lohenisch. Her grey hair was pulled back from her face, and she wore a white apron over her black gown. When Hannah explained their desire for a meal, the woman answered, 'If you don't mind sharing, I can seat you beside some guests over there.' She nodded toward a table by the window.

'That will be fine,' Hannah answered in the same

language. 'My husband and I have been travelling all morning.'

From the blank look on his face, Michael hadn't recognized the woman's words. He held Hannah's hand firmly as they joined the elderly couple at the far table.

A serving maid approached them after a few minutes. Before she could ask Michael any questions, Hannah interrupted, asking for them to be served breakfast.

Switching to English, she whispered to Michael, 'Do you remember the language any more?'

He shook his head slightly. 'I can't quite grasp it. I feel as though I *should* understand what she's saying.'

'I'll translate for you,' Hannah offered. She noticed that he still hadn't released her hand. Beneath the table, he continued to hold her fingers, his thumb caressing the top of her hand. A breathless ripple of feeling permeated her skin, and she admitted to herself that she wouldn't mind if he held her hand throughout the meal.

'This was a mistake,' he said. 'I shouldn't have let you talk me into this. If I can't even understand the damned language—'

'You will,' Hannah reassured him. 'I promise you, it'll come back to you.'

'It's of no use to me, if I can't recall a thing unless I'm drugged or half-asleep.'

'It's there. I'll help you to remember.' She gave his hand a squeeze, and just then their food arrived.

Hannah noticed the couple beside them had been watching their interaction. The man and woman were trying not to stare, but Michael had definitely caught their attention.

'Hello,' Hannah greeted them in Lohenisch. Though she was well aware that it was highly inappropriate for her to speak before Michael, she didn't see any other choice. They were here to gather information, and she was the only one who spoke the language. At least, right now.

She introduced Michael as Lieutenant Thorpe and herself as his wife. The older man returned the greeting, and Hannah learned that they were Helmut and Gerda Dorfer.

'You are from London?' Herr Dorfer asked in Lohenisch.

'We are.' Hannah took a bite of her sausage and added, 'I have cousins in Germany, and my husband has always wanted to visit Lohenberg.'

'If you don't mind my saying so,' Frau Dorfer spoke up, 'your husband looks very much like our König Sweyn.' Her face softened. 'When he was younger, that is.'

At the admission, the woman suddenly grew fearful, as if she'd said too much. Herr Dorfer sent his wife a warning look, and she fell silent.

Hannah wasn't about to lose the opportunity. Extending her hand to Michael, she sent him a silent signal for coins. Thankfully, he placed a handful into her palm. Hannah slid the money toward Frau Dorfer. 'We are planning to visit the *Schloss* when we arrive in Vermisten. I would be grateful if you know someone who could answer our questions. We would like to seek an audience with the King.'

Frau Dorfer glanced at her husband, who offered a relenting nod. Her hand covered the coins. 'I can answer your questions. I used to work in the *Schloss* as one of the maids before I married Helmut.' Looking uncomfortable, she enquired, 'But why do you seek the King?' Her gaze travelled over Michael once more.

'Ask her if she has heard the story of the Changeling Prince,' Michael said.

Helmut exchanged glances with his wife after Hannah translated. Gerda's face paled, and the pair argued for a moment.

It seemed Frau Dorfer won the disagreement, for she suggested to Hannah, 'Go and speak to the master of the household, BurgGraf Castell. He can advise you and possibly arrange a private audience with the lord chamberlain, Herr Schliessing.' She blushed. 'The lord chamberlain would know what to do.'

After Hannah translated, Michael's face tightened with frustration. Whether from the information or from his inability to speak, she wasn't certain.

She thanked Frau Dorfer for the information, and the woman offered them the name of a respectable inn in Vermisten where they could stay.

'And,' Frau Dorfer added, 'you would be wise to keep your husband's appearance hidden, if possible, until you've been granted the audience. If anyone sees his resemblance to the King, his advisers may refuse to allow you entrance.'

Hannah nodded her thanks to Herr and Frau Dorfer before turning her attention back to her meal. Michael was eating while staring off into the distance, as if trying to recall the forgotten language.

Hannah kept their conversation in English to remain private. 'I don't believe you should seek a private audience with the lord chamberlain,' she admitted. 'It would be too easy for the King to brush you aside, pretending you don't exist. I think we should make use of your appearance.'

'What do you mean?'

'I believe you should confront them directly. Demand to see the King. Find out if you truly are the Prince.'

'Twice, someone has tried to kill me,' Michael pointed out.

'That's exactly why it must be true. Someone considers you a threat. And he wants you dead.'

Chapter Fifteen

They spent the remainder of the afternoon in Michael's own personal version of Hades. Shopping.

He had allowed Hannah to drag him from one shop to the next, while she ordered clothes for him. He'd paid for them with the money the Graf had given him.

Hannah was adamant that he be clothed like a member of the royal household. From sports attire to formal evening wear, it seemed she hadn't missed a single thing. Not even hats, gloves or…undergarments. Michael shuddered at the last shop. Some things weren't meant to be measured or prodded.

'The Graf was right about this,' Hannah had explained. 'It's about appearances.'

'And we couldn't have ordered everything at the first shop?'

'Of course not!' She eyed him as though he'd suggested wearing rags to greet the monarch. 'You need to be seen by as many people as possible today. Then the King cannot ignore your presence. He'll have to help you discover the truth.'

It was also a much greater risk. Michael couldn't abandon his old habits of constantly looking over his shoulder. There had already been two attacks— a third was imminent, and he didn't want Hannah caught up in it. The threat would come—the only question was when, not if. By then, he hoped to have Hannah escorted back to her cousins' home.

Glancing at her, he saw her face bright with enthusiasm. She was enjoying the afternoon they'd spent together, though she hadn't bought a single thing for herself. It struck him as wrong, and he took her to one of the shops, hoping she could have a new dress made.

'There's no need,' Hannah protested. 'Don't waste a penny on me. I'll have plenty of gowns, once my trunks arrive with the Graf.'

But when he saw her eye drawn to the milliner's, he sent her to choose a new bonnet. While she was busy with the shopkeeper, he slipped next door to make another purchase.

The gift cost far more than he'd anticipated, but it was something he wanted Hannah to have. Michael used the last of his own savings, instead of money given by the Graf. He hid the gift inside his pocket, wrapped in brown paper, and made it back inside the milliner's before Hannah realised he'd left her.

* * *

Hours later, after dinner when they were back inside their room at the inn, Hannah sank down into a chair. 'My feet are exhausted,' she said, unfastening her shoes. 'I feel as though we walked twenty miles today.'

He ventured a smile, suddenly feeling anxious to give her the gift he'd purchased. He wanted to see her expression when she opened the parcel.

'Here.' He thrust the box at her without a word of explanation. 'This is for you.'

She set her stocking feet back on the carpet, accepting the box. 'Now when did you get this?' With a soft smile, she added, 'I hope it's something sweet.'

She tore open the brown paper, and lifted open the box. Inside rested a diamond-and-aquamarine ring.

Hannah didn't react, or say a word. She simply stared at the jewellery. He hadn't had but a few minutes this afternoon, but the moment he'd seen it in the shop, he'd known it was meant for her.

'Well, go on. See if it fits.'

He removed the ring from the box and slid it on the third finger of her left hand. 'I can have the jeweller adjust the size, if needed.'

Fate was on his side, for the ring fit beautifully. Hannah clutched the diamonds, staring at him. 'Michael, what have you done?'

'You've told everyone we're married. Don't you think they would wonder why you aren't wearing a ring?'

She shook her head, her face paling. 'You can't afford this. It's too much.'

Though that might be true, his pride bristled. If he wanted to spend his savings on her, that was his choice. And this was something he wanted her to have as a memento of their time together. Something to keep, that would make her think of him.

'Don't worry about the cost.'

She took the ring off, pressing it back into his hands. 'You shouldn't have done this. I can't accept it.'

The small bit of metal seemed to burn into his skin. Why couldn't she?

'Isn't it good enough for you?' The bitter words escaped him before he could stop them.

The stricken look on her face was worse than a slap. God knew he deserved it. He was behaving like a child, sulking because she didn't like the ring. But it was the first time he'd had any money at all to spend on her. And she didn't want the gift.

'You don't understand.' She spoke quietly, averting her gaze. 'I can't accept a ring from you. We aren't really married.'

'No. But it will keep others from talking.' He came and held out the ring in his palm. 'Take it.'

She shook her head slowly. 'This is too much. I can't take a ring made of diamonds.'

'Why not?' He'd expected her to love the jewellery, to be pleased with the setting. Not give him reasons why she couldn't wear it. 'I'm not the only man who's given you jewels, am I?'

'You're not my father or brother. It isn't suitable.'

'Everyone believes I am your husband.'

'Can't you understand?' she whispered, standing up. Her hands covered his. 'This ring means you're making a sacrifice for me. You're giving up too much. I'm not worth that to you.'

'I'll determine what you're worth. And I'll be damned if I give you a ring made of tin.'

She blinked hard, sitting back down again. Her palms rested on her gown, and she refused to look at him. 'I can't take it, Michael,' she whispered. 'Not only because of the cost…but because I would want it to mean something more.'

Hannah heard Michael leave their shared room after he'd shoved the ring back inside his pocket. After he'd gone, she released the harsh tears gathering in her throat.

It was a beautiful ring. A stunning cluster of diamonds and aquamarines that she would be honoured to wear, if it were a true wedding ring.

She drew her feet up beneath her skirts, her corset cutting into her ribs as the unwanted tears streamed down her face. Why had he done this? He knew their arrangement was only temporary. After he had the answers he sought, she would be out of his life. It had to be that way, and both of them knew it.

He'd been so angry when he left. Would he want her to leave now? The thought of travelling to Germany without knowing his fate was like a hand strangling her breath.

She was losing her heart to this man, whether he was a common soldier or a forgotten Prince. Somehow, he'd guessed at the hidden feelings inside her. Her secret, that she wanted to take every stolen moment she could with him, no matter how great the cost. She wanted him to touch her, to make her come alive the way he had upon the ship.

The bedroom seemed unexpectedly empty. Hannah stared at the bed, realising that she'd never truly thought about where they would sleep tonight. Did she dare rest beside him, the way a true wife would?

She sat down upon the coverlet, running her fingers over the worn quilt. Today there had been nothing untoward about his behaviour. He'd endured the shopping trip, letting her order purchases for him, though she could see that he didn't care for it at all.

He must have gone to the jeweller's while she was

trying on bonnets. It had been such a short moment, but he'd seized it. For her.

Well done, Hannah. The man spent a fortune on you, and you cast it back in his face.

But she couldn't let him do it. Not even if he had a fortune to spend. A ring like that, so personal, so precious. It was something she would treasure for the rest of her life.

If she accepted it, the gift would haunt her, reminding her of the feelings she held for him.

She sat up, suddenly afraid of where he'd gone. Michael couldn't go out walking alone, not when it was such a risk. He'd been shot only two days ago. What if someone attacked him?

It was far too dangerous. Hannah pushed her feet back into her shoes, not even bothering to finish buttoning them. She flew down the stairs and pushed her way past the other guests who were enjoying their dinners downstairs.

She found the Lieutenant inside the stables, tending his horse. With a sharp look towards the stable lad, she asked for a moment alone with her 'husband'. The boy tipped his cap and waited outside.

Standing behind Michael, she wondered what she could say. The acrid odour of the stalls surrounded them, not exactly the best place for an apology.

'Michael,' she murmured, 'will you come back inside?'

He didn't turn around at first, but kept brushing the horse's back in slow, even strokes.

'Go back to our room, Hannah. It's been a long day, and I know you're tired. I'll be up later.'

She couldn't bring herself to leave him. By refusing his gift, she'd wounded his pride. She touched the sleeve of his coat, resting her forehead against his shoulder. 'Don't be angry with me.' A thousand excuses tangled up in her mouth, but all of them were a mockery of what she was feeling right now.

'I'm not angry.' His clipped voice belied the words. 'It was an inappropriate gift. You were right.'

'It was a beautiful ring,' she said, stepping between him and the horse. Trapped in his arms, she gave him no choice but to look at her. 'And if circumstances were different, I would be proud to wear it.'

'But they aren't.' He set down the brush and let his hands rest on her waist. In his eyes, she saw disappointment, masked by duty. Didn't he understand why she had refused the ring? Didn't he know that she was trying to keep both of them from being hurt?

'Go back, Hannah. I want a moment to myself.'

She couldn't do it. If she left him right now, the breach would only widen. He'd sleep on the floor and within another day or two, she would be inside a coach, bound for Germany.

He's going to break my heart, she thought. *But there wasn't another choice, was there?*

She stood up on tiptoe and kissed him. Her arms wrapped around his neck, while she tried to show him what she felt. The desires she couldn't voice, the forbidden yearning to steal whatever moments she could.

At first, he didn't kiss her back. But as she pressed her mouth to his, slowly tempting him to yield, she felt his arms tighten.

His kiss was tentative at first, as though he weren't sure she truly wanted him. Hannah gripped his neck, hoping he would respond to her invitation.

'Don't hold back from me,' she whispered, when his mouth broke free from hers. 'Not tonight.'

Michael brought her against the door to one of the stalls, lifting her up while he kissed her hard. 'I'm no good for you, Hannah.'

'I don't care any more. I need you.' She held on tight, shuddering when his thigh slid between her legs. Hard and firm, he nudged her, making her ride him.

Though anyone who happened upon them would only see a husband and a wife caught in an embrace, beneath her skirts, he made her feel completely vulnerable.

'Take me back upstairs,' she whispered.

'In a moment.' He took her mouth roughly, his hands dragging through her hair. Pins fell everywhere while he kissed her, his tongue teasing in the intimate act she feared. Her mouth was numb, swollen from his kiss, while she ached between her legs. When he pressed his thigh between her legs again, she couldn't stop the shattered gasp that escaped. It was like the night upon the ship, only this time, the impact was far greater.

That night, she'd suspected they would not become lovers. But now, she wasn't certain how far she would let him go.

Michael slid her down, touching his head to hers. 'What are you doing, Hannah?'

She shivered, fighting to catch her breath. 'I think you know.'

He grabbed her hand and pulled her outside the stable. Hannah knew the stable lad could have guessed what happened to her, for her hair was falling about her shoulders, her face flushed with unfulfilled need.

When they reached the doors to the inn, Michael stopped short. 'Go up to our room and wait for me there. I'll only be a moment.'

She fled up the stairs, not looking at any of the guests and praying they weren't staring at her dishevelled appearance. When she reached her room, she took off her shoes again, blindly pulling at the remainder of pins that held up her hair.

Oh, heaven. What was she about to do?

She stared at the solitary bed and the flickering

candle illuminating the small space. Everything about this room was primed for a seduction. One she wasn't ready for.

It was too easy, falling into his arms within the stable. Now that he'd given her a moment alone to think, her mind was screaming out every lecture her mother had ever given.

Never let a man touch you, unless he is your husband. Not even a kiss. And especially never let him see so much as a bared ankle.

The door opened, and Michael stood with something hidden behind his back. Hannah craned her neck to see what it was, and then spied a covered plate.

Michael removed the cover and revealed a thick slice of cake with buttercream icing.

Hannah didn't smile, though it appeared mouthwatering. Glancing at the dessert, she mentioned, 'You…forgot to bring a fork or a spoon.'

'No, I didn't.'

She didn't know what he meant by that, but sensual images of him feeding her from his fingertips suddenly erupted in her mind.

Michael set the plate down upon the dresser and closed the distance. He moved behind her, his hands upon the buttons of her gown. Though Hannah tried to relax, her skin had gone cold. It was easier to imagine surrendering to him when he was kissing her, not allowing her to think.

Instead, his hands flicked over the buttons of her gown, one by one. Her mind was raging that she should stop him and hold fast to her innocence. Her body tensed as more and more skin was revealed.

'I know you're afraid,' he whispered, dropping a kiss on her nape, 'but you have no maid, and you cannot sleep in your corset.'

He was offering her the choice, she realised. He would not ask for more than she was willing to give.

'If you'd prefer, I could ask one of the maids downstairs to come up and assist you.'

She let out a shaky breath. That would be the easiest course of action, but it would also raise unnecessary questions about why she wasn't allowing her husband to unfasten her gown.

'It's all right,' she managed. 'You can help me.' Her heartbeat clamoured in her chest, punctuating the indecision building up inside her.

'Will you turn down the lamp?' she whispered. 'I don't want you to see me.'

He didn't answer. Instead, he came around to face her. He made no further move to undress her, but the gown sagged about her shoulders. 'Do you want me to sleep somewhere else?'

'No. You can't.' Not only was it too expensive to hire out a second room, it wasn't safe to be apart.

He stepped back, waiting for her command. Hannah clutched the edges of her gown, as if trying to hold together the last remnants of her up-bringing.

Michael seemed to be weighing his own decision. In the end, he walked towards the hearth and sat down in one of the chairs, his gaze averted from her.

It was like she'd already lost him. And it hurt, worse than anything she could imagine. This man had taken care of her when she'd needed him most. He didn't live by the rules, but by his judgement. And she knew there would never be another man like him in her life.

If she did marry, it would be to a titled lord who would expect her to bear his children. She'd met dozens of them over the last year, and not a single one would come close to the intense feeling she held for Michael Thorpe.

She wanted to know him intimately. To feel his skin upon hers and to know that he cherished her. There was not a doubt in her mind that if she let him make love to her, it would be the worst sort of rule to break. It would also be wonderful.

Her moments of freedom were slipping away, with every hour. This might be their only night together. And she wanted it, no matter that it was wrong. No matter that he could never be hers.

Hannah let her gown slide down, baring her corset and chemise. She untied the petticoats, step-ping free of them.

The long walk across the room was the most frightening she'd ever taken. But in her heart, she knew she would hold regrets if she did not reach out to him now.

In the candlelight, he would see every part of her body. Right now, shivers prickled over her skin as she walked in front of him. Wearing only her under-garments, she laid herself bare, offering herself.

And still Michael didn't move. His eyes stared into hers, as though he didn't know what to think of her actions. Kneeling down before him, Hannah reached out to remove his coat. Her fingers shook as she untied his cravat and unbuttoned his waist-coat. Abruptly, Michael's hands suddenly closed over hers.

'You don't want this, Hannah. I can see your fear.'

She'd never been so bold in all her life, but more than anything else was the fear that he would turn her away.

'I am afraid, yes. And I know that I should ask you for help with my corset and sleep far away from you.'

He waited, and she touched her hand to his heart. Despite the calm mien he presented, his pulse was racing. 'I know what I should do,' she repeated again. 'But I want this night. Give me a memory I'll always have.'

Chapter Sixteen

Her body tensed when Michael reached the laces that tightened her corset. He loosened the stays, and his fingertips caressed the thin fabric of her chemise. Almost instantly, her nipples puckered. As he helped her remove the corset, the stiff panel brushed against her breasts. A pang of arousal echoed within her core, and the awakening of desire began to silence the voices of her mother's warnings and her conscience.

Layers of clothing fell away until she wore only the thin chemise and drawers. Michael had removed his shirt, and in the firelight, his bare skin was golden. She reached out to his wounded upper arm and saw that the angry skin was healing. The abrasions on his neck were also fading.

'Does it hurt?'

'Sweet, there's only one thing I'm feeling right now. And it's not the kind of pain you're thinking of.' He glanced up at the mantel. 'The candlestick is there, if you need it to bash my head.'

She almost smiled, but the overwhelming nerves were gathering strength. 'How do you want to… do this?' Perhaps if she had an idea of what was expected, she could calm the anxiety boiling inside her. 'I don't know what I am supposed to do.'

'I'll start by kissing you.' His voice rumbled against her ear as he slid her chemise and drawers away. Before she could comprehend that she was no longer wearing anything at all, his mouth came down on hers.

Hot, feverish feelings permeated her, sending flames of desire over every part of her body. Michael picked her up in his arms, laying her down upon the bed. Her hair fell across the pillow, and he caressed the length. A moment later, he turned around and removed his trousers and undergarments. She caught a glimpse of his taut backside, the rigid curve of his hip. When he turned around, he was holding the plate of cake and there was a wicked gleam in his eye.

He wanted to eat, now? Confusion caught her sensibilities, making her wonder what he intended.

Michael walked towards her naked, his erect manhood jutting forward. A flash of panic flew through her mind, for she couldn't imagine him joining with her. He sat down beside her on the bed, setting the plate down.

'Open your mouth,' he ordered, breaking off a morsel of cake.

A distraction. That's what this was, she realised. Something to calm her down.

She tasted the sweet creamy icing, but it did nothing to alleviate her apprehensions. Michael kissed her again, devouring the traces of buttercream from her lips. She clung to him, startled by the feeling of his bare skin upon hers. Her breathing quickened as he ran his palms down her spine and over the curve of her bottom.

'I know I shouldn't do this,' he murmured, lowering his mouth to her shoulder, drifting downwards to her breast. 'But I've given up trying to resist you.' He dipped his finger into the cake icing and touched it to her nipple. 'It's too late now, sweet. I intend to spend the rest of the night taking you apart.'

With that, he covered her nipple with his mouth, swirling against her skin with his tongue. He licked the icing off, sucking hard while she shuddered at the sensation. She was bending to him, growing moist between her legs.

Michael turned his attention to the other breast, kissing it with the same attention while he flicked the erect bud of the first nipple with his fingers. Tormented by his touch, she fought to catch her breath.

'You're more delicious to me than any cake,' he murmured. 'I could taste you all day.' His mouth drifted lower, down her stomach toward the soft hair covering her mound.

His cheeks were smooth against her thighs, and she clamped her legs tight, afraid of what he might do next.

He lifted his head up, staring at her. In the dim light, his hazel eyes held the warmth of chocolate, with green flecks. 'I'm going to give you a night to remember, Hannah. Trust me.'

He pressed a kiss upon her stomach, his hands reaching beneath her spine to her hips. He drew his palms over her bottom, pressing her close to his face.

Oh, sweet God. He wouldn't taste her there, would he?

He dipped his finger into the icing, brushing a small amount upon her cleft. A moment later, her hands dug into the sheets, a keening cry erupting from her throat as he covered her intimate flesh with his mouth.

He nibbled at her delicate skin, arousing her until she arched deeply, shaking with the ferocity of his wicked tongue.

The rising crescendo of need burst forth in a release that made her cry out. She tried to sit up, but he held her down, her legs splayed as he worked her again with his mouth.

'I can't. Michael, I can't do this. It's too much.'

In answer, he slid two fingers inside her wetness,

stretching her. It sent her over the edge once more as he entered and withdrew.

'Touch me,' he urged, pulling her hand to his shaft. She had never felt a man's flesh before and had never realised how soft and smooth it was. Her thumb caressed the tip, and she felt moisture there.

As she dragged her hand along the length, she watched him hiss with pleasure. He let her explore him, feeling the change in skin texture, and the way he grew even harder in reaction to her touch. When she began to glide her hand up and down, he caught her wrist and pushed it aside. 'Not tonight. This night is for you.'

Michael turned her on to her side, while he came up behind her. Raising her leg over his, he placed his manhood between her thighs. 'When you're ready for me, I'm going to be inside you.'

He cupped both of her breasts, nipping at her shoulder with his mouth. His thick erection nudged an inch within her, and Hannah trembled at the feeling. As he continued to caress her nipples, rolling the tips while he teased her wetness, she pleaded with him, 'Michael, I need…something. But I don't know what it is.'

He moved his length between her legs. 'Sweet, don't rush. I want this to be good for you.' Slowly, gently, he eased himself into her body. He didn't force her, or hurt her. Just a gentle sliding, back and forth. The thickness of him was like a caress inside her body, each time going a little deeper. His thumb moved to the ridge at the top of her womanhood, stroking her while he sheathed himself partway inside her. 'I want to see you come apart again,' he murmured, coaxing the wet heat.

Her body ached, squeezing him while he rubbed the small hooded opening. She felt herself rising up again, reaching for the intense pleasure. He held back from her, slowing his pace. Tears escaped her eyes, and she shivered violently against his hand.

'Come for me,' he commanded. And with another stroke of his hand, she soared. He pushed the rest of the way inside her, filling her up until they were fully joined. Though the fit was tight, she held him close, shocked at the wonder of it.

Her hips arched as he pulled back and slid home once again. The tenderness of his penetration made her heart weep for this act of love.

But she sensed he was holding back, trying not to hurt her. The position of being on her side felt too cautious, and she wanted him to know the same fulfillment.

She eased away from him, lying on her back and bringing him atop her. With her hand, she guided him inside once more, raising her knees. 'Take what you need from me, Michael.'

His face turned to stone, his body growing harder

within her. He plunged inside, quickening his pace. She gripped him, holding tight as he rode her hard.

A moment later, he pulled her hips to the edge of the bed. He stood up, lifting her legs high while he filled her. His face transformed with his own pleasure, tight with suppressed need. She met each stroke with her hips, offering a counterpressure. It wasn't enough. Michael gripped her hard, thrusting his body inside her until at last, his face tightened, and he let out a low groan.

He collapsed on top of her, their bodies still joined. Hannah felt a wetness from his warm seed, and she reached down to run her hands over his backside. She wrapped her legs around him, squeezing him in a different sort of embrace.

No wonder men and women never talked about this. She'd never dreamed that the intimacy would be this wild, this pleasurable.

'How are you feeling?' he asked, his voice husky.

'I feel beautiful.' And she did. Languid and re-laxed, as though it were the most natural thing in the world to be naked with a man.

'Hungry?' he prompted, withdrawing from her.

'A little.' She let him feed her cake from his fin-gertips, and she licked the icing, watching his eyes grow dark with desire once again.

'You're going to kill me if you keep looking at me

like that.' He ran his hands over her flesh. 'I won't be able to get enough of you.'

Hannah locked her arms around his neck. 'I don't mind.'

Later that night, after he'd made love to her twice more, he straightened the bed sheets. 'Time to sleep.' She was about to curl up next to him when he dropped a pillow on top of her.

'What is that for?' She tried to move the pillow away, but he laid it in the centre of the bed. When she reached out, she felt the presence of the two pillows set lengthwise down the middle of the bed.

'I'm setting up a barricade on the bed. You'll sleep on your side, and I on mine.'

A pillow barricade? What on earth?

'You don't want to sleep beside me?' she asked, confused at the gesture. 'Is something the matter?'

'Sweet, if you come anywhere near me again, I won't be responsible for what happens.' His body weight settled on his side of the bed. 'I'd suggest you stay over there, if you want any sleep at all.'

She smiled in the darkness and huddled beneath the coverlet. Was he truly serious about being unable to resist her?

A moment later, a hand nudged at her cheek. 'You're on my side,' he said.

'I'm on the edge of the bed! If I move any further, I'll fall off,' she protested.

His leg tangled up in hers, beneath the pillow barricade. 'You're still on my side.'

When she realised that his long leg was sprawled all the way across the bed, hanging off the end, she started to laugh. 'If you had your way, this entire bed would be your side.'

'It is. I'm just letting you borrow it.' He withdrew his leg, his hand reaching for hers.

Lying on her back with their palms entwined, Hannah released the laughter building up. 'You don't like to share, do you?'

'Not at all. And I'll never share you.' His hand moved up to caress her face with his knuckles. And when at last, she heard the quiet sounds of his breathing, her heartbeat wouldn't calm at all.

For this was the sort of marriage she'd dreamed of. A handsome husband, teasing her. Making her feel beloved. Lying beside him at night, whispering secrets in the dark.

Please don't let him be the Prince, she prayed. For if he was, he was as good as lost.

Michael rose before the sun came up, letting Hannah sleep. She was curled up on her side, her palm slightly open. He dressed in silence, slipping outside the door. He reached into his pocket and found the ring, still there. At first, he'd planned to return it to the jeweller's. But after last night, he wasn't certain.

He didn't know what had come over Hannah, why she had given herself to him. She'd refused to accept a ring from him, telling him that she would want it to mean something else.

Was she saying she wanted to marry a man like him?

It was foolish to consider the possibility. He was better off living on his own. He couldn't take care of her in the manner she deserved.

Grimly, he thought of their impending visit to the *Schloss*. The cynical side to him didn't believe it would accomplish anything. A man like him... becoming a Prince? He simply couldn't believe it could ever be true. They would take one look at him and toss him out.

But if he were a Prince, he'd have the means to take care of Hannah. He could make her a Princess.

You're not capable of protecting a wife. Don't even consider such a thing.

Being with Hannah last night had changed everything. He'd become her lover, and it had been better than anything he'd ever imagined.

Sweet, fiery and passionate, she'd swept him away. He'd been conscious of her every move, her every sigh.

He fingered the ring in his pocket, and continued towards the innkeeper. He thought of hiring a maid to help Hannah dress, but in truth, he wanted another excuse to touch her again. Instead, he ordered a tray of food to be sent up for their breakfast.

While the innkeeper's wife went to prepare the food, the innkeeper paused. In halting English, he offered, 'Lieutenant Thorpe, some men arrived last night. They were searching the inn for a man of your description. I thought you should know.'

He suspected it was the Graf's men. But it could also be the men who had attacked their coaches. There was no way to be sure. Nonetheless, it was not safe for them to remain here any longer. Michael thanked the innkeeper and went upstairs with the tray of food.

Hannah was already awake and struggling to dress herself. 'Good morning,' she said, offering a hesitant smile. 'Could you help me with this?'

'Of course.' He set down the tray and came up behind her, his hands grazing her shoulders. With both hands gripping the corset strings, he tightened her stays.

'Why in the name of God do women torture themselves this way?' he grumbled. He'd worried about hurting her, but Hannah had only laughed and told him to pull it tighter.

He'd much rather have unlaced her, baring her soft, pale skin. As it was, he stole another kiss, trying to quench the need for her body. Her mouth moulded to his, her arms wrapping around his neck.

The dark desire to have her again took control

without warning. He wanted to strip her down, making love to her until she trembled with pleasure.

But Hannah broke away from him, her face crimson with embarrassment. 'Michael, I've been thinking. Last night when we…were together, well…I don't think we should…do that any more.'

Her sudden refusal bruised his pride. He reached into his pocket, touching the ring. *This was her choice,* he reminded himself. And perhaps it was better that way.

'You're right.' He shrugged as if he didn't care one way or the other. But he knew he'd become too tangled up with thoughts of her. Their time together would be short enough, and the more they became involved with one another, the worse it would be to say goodbye. 'Last night was a bad decision for both of us.'

She paled, but nodded her head in agreement. 'I had no regrets at the time. But what if…there's a baby?'

He lost his breath at the very thought. He'd been caught defenceless by her, unable to think beyond the staggering desire. A baby. An innocent child, who would look to him as a father, a provider.

Harsh visions struck him down, of a child crying out for food. Of Hannah wearing a threadbare dress, her hands worn from scrubbing floors. Would that be their lives, if he remained a soldier? He couldn't let that happen.

'If there is a child, I'll take care of you.' He voiced the words she expected to hear, though the idea of giving her anything less than the life she had was horrifying. He prayed that there would be no child, no lasting consequences of their forbidden night together.

'All right.' But she didn't look overjoyed by the prospect either.

Michael turned his back, gathering up the edges of his thoughts. 'I received word that men are looking for me. We shouldn't stay here tonight.'

'Where do you want to go?' Hannah moved in front of him for assistance with the buttons running down the back of her dress. Though he fastened them for her, the feel of her skin beneath his hands only re-ignited his hunger.

'The *Schloss*. For now, at least. We'll decide where to stay afterwards.' Michael offered her the tray of food, choosing a scone for himself.

Hannah picked at the food, as though she didn't like that idea. 'We have to speak to the King. There's no other choice. But I can't shake the feeling that something terrible will happen if we do.'

She pushed her plate aside and donned her pelisse. After putting on her bonnet, she tied the ribbon beneath her chin.

'It's a risk, yes.' But a necessary one. Michael

wanted the answers, if for no other reason than to close this part of his life away. More than ever, he felt on the verge of unlocking the secrets of his past. Perhaps just by visiting the *Schloss*, he would sense something.

Hannah finished putting on her gloves and regarded him. 'Should we wait for the Graf to arrive after all? He knows more than we do about the royal family.'

'True. But at the moment, we have the element of surprise,' he murmured. Finishing his breakfast, he rose and picked up his hat. 'We'll do as Gerda suggested. I'll ask to speak to the master of the household, or possibly the lord chamberlain.'

'Should I request an audience with the Queen, while you do that?' she suggested. 'I might be able to find out more.'

'No. We should remain together. Especially if others believe we're married.' His gaze fell upon her hand.

Hannah saw the direction of his gaze. She let out a shuddering breath and removed her glove. 'All right. I'll wear the ring, but only for a few days. After that, I'm returning it to you.'

Michael withdrew the ring from his pocket and slid it on her finger. He held her hand a moment longer than he should have, but she refused to look at him.

In her eyes he saw the self-flagellation, the anger

at herself for breaking so many rules. He wanted to say something to make her feel better. But what could he say? He'd been selfish, indulging in the night he'd spent in her arms. Even afterwards, with the shield of pillows between them, he'd needed to know she was close.

Hannah had fallen asleep holding his hand. It had felt nice, watching over her while she dreamed. She was far too good for the likes of him, but it was too late to undo what had transpired between them.

She adjusted the ring on her finger. 'I hope you find what you're looking for today, Michael.'

So do I.

With her hand in his, he led her down the hallway and towards the stairs. Below, he heard the din of voices gathering. It sounded as if someone important was here. Instinct made him keep Hannah behind him.

When he reached the bottom of the stairs, people seemed to swarm from every angle. A group of soldiers came forward, armed with muskets. They cleared through the crowd, forming a line at the bottom of the stairs.

'His Royal Highness has asked to see you,' the Captain of the Guard announced.

Not the King. The Prince.

Michael glanced back at Hannah. He reached back to take her hand, bringing her beside him. 'I suppose we're going to get our audience after all.'

Chapter Seventeen

'Not her,' the Captain corrected, in halting English. 'Only you.'

Of course, Michael thought. It didn't surprise him that the Prince wanted to address him alone. It was the easiest way to eliminate the threat.

When the Captain started to argue, Michael cut him off. 'My *wife* comes with me.'

All around, he heard the buzz of voices. Though he couldn't understand all of the Lohenisch words, he overheard them discussing the Changeling Prince. He tried to shield Hannah from the throng, but several of the men and women crowded too close.

That was it. Michael stopped walking with the soldiers, levelling the crowd with his anger. 'You do not touch her. Ever.'

He guided Hannah to walk in front of him. The soldiers eyed him with distrust, as if they thought he would try to escape. Not at all. He had every intention of accompanying them to get his answers.

It didn't bother him that he was about to face the Prince of this country, the man who stood to lose the most.

His immediate concern was Hannah's safety. And though a part of him feared that it could be a trap, these men didn't have the look of executioners. He'd seen soldiers who had been commanded to kill a man. The emptiness in their eyes and the grim reluctance were evident. No, this was duty. And so he kept Hannah close to him and kept another eye upon their weapons.

The soldiers escorted both of them towards a cart drawn by horses. The primitive transportation would have insulted anyone of true noble birth. Hannah eyed it with the greatest reluctance. Even so, she said nothing as Michael lifted her up. In English, she whispered, 'Why did they come for you? Do you think your enemies have found us?'

'More likely word has spread of our arrival, after yesterday.'

'I don't like this.' Hannah shook her head, her gaze focused upon their muskets. 'One of them said it was for our protection, but it doesn't feel right.'

'I agree.' At the moment, he didn't want her to leave his side. 'If they try to separate us, send word to the Graf immediately.'

'I'm not worried about myself,' Hannah whispered. 'I'm worried about you.' She gripped his hand, and he traced the ring upon her finger.

Though she'd sworn she would only wear it for a few days, he didn't want it to leave her hand. The delicate jewel was a means of keeping other men away from her.

'I can take care of myself, Hannah.'

She still didn't look convinced.

When they arrived at the *Schloss*, she craned her neck to study it. The stone walls gleamed in the light, the pointed towers reminding Michael of a fairy-tale castle. A sudden memory took hold, of walking through a flower garden, and a dark-haired woman smiling at him.

He'd been here before. There was no doubt of it in his mind.

'Do you suppose they'll lock you inside one of those?' Hannah pointed to one of the towers, only half-teasing.

He didn't smile. Truthfully, he had no idea what to expect from this audience. The soldiers helped them disembark from the wagon, and they were led to a private entrance.

The stone exterior of the *Schloss* had an older foundation that was built centuries ago, while newer grey stones formed the upper levels. Glass windows reflected the morning sunlight while wild roses formed a pink-and-green hedge against the side. Six large chimneys rose from the topmost towers, reminding him that this was a modern

Schloss and not an ancient crumbling castle from hundreds of years ago.

'Lieutenant Thorpe and Mrs Thorpe, please follow me.' The Captain escorted them through the back entrance and down a long hallway.

A winding stone staircase led to the upper levels, and when they reached the first floor, the Captain stopped and opened the door leading to a small parlour. Motioning a female servant forward, he said, 'Mrs Thorpe, you may await your husband here.'

Hannah eyed the small sitting room, her gaze searching Michael's.

'She stays with me.' He wasn't going to be separated from her until he knew what to expect.

'I am sorry, Lieutenant Thorpe. Fürst Karl wished to speak with you alone. We must obey his orders.'

Michael stared at the Captain. 'I am not subject to his rule. And Lady Hannah remains at my side.'

He was well aware of the insult from the way the Captain stiffened.

'Michael, I think you should go with them,' Hannah interrupted. Leaning close to his ear, she added, 'I may learn more about your circumstances if we are apart.'

'Not this time. Not until we've met them.'

For long moments, the Captain seemed hesitant to disobey, but at long last he signalled for them both to follow. He led them up another flight of stairs to a large room with a set of four Gothic windows.

Light spilled into the chamber, illuminating a grand piano flanked by delicate French chairs. Long blue curtains hung around the windows, giving the room a touch of warmth.

But there was no warmth coming from the man seated in a leather armchair at the far end of the room. His expression was grim, a man who radiated anger and hostility.

Michael kept Hannah's hand in his as he stared at the man. Though the dark hair was slightly lighter, the Prince's face was nearly a mirror image of his own.

'I suppose you've come here, hoping the King will acknowledge you.' Fürst Karl stared at the man and woman who sat down before him. The gossip in Vermisten had risen to a fever pitch, the people wondering who the Lieutenant really was. The old stories of the Changeling Prince were resurfacing, and Karl sensed his grasp upon the throne slipping.

The legends and stories were just that—fictional tales born of superstitions. He refused to believe that anyone else could ever usurp his place as the Crown Prince of Lohenberg. All his life he'd devoted himself to Lohenberg, his beloved country. But his kingdom was drifting toward chaos if he didn't settle this problem.

The man seated across from him was, without a

doubt, a half-brother. Michael Thorpe, a lieutenant in the British Army, and most likely his father's bastard son.

Whether or not his ailing father had heard of the man's arrival, he couldn't be sure. But Karl would go to any lengths necessary to protect his mother. The Queen didn't need to know about her husband's indiscretions. She'd endured enough punishment over the years, from her own weak mind.

Mad Queen Astri, locked away from the world for her own good. Few people dared to talk to her any more, for it only provoked another bad spell. Even his father avoided his wife, behaving as though he'd been widowed years ago. And as far as Karl was aware, only the Graf von Reischor had met with the Queen.

Now this.

'What is it you want?' Karl demanded, continuing to speak English to the couple. 'Money?' The idea of paying a single *pfennig* to this man, to keep him away from Lohenberg, was repulsive.

'I came here for answers.'

The Lieutenant stared back, as though making a comparison between them. Karl tensed, for this man looked more like his father than he did. It unnerved him.

'How old are you?' Karl asked.

'Twenty-six.'

The same age, then. Karl bit back a curse, furious

with his father. How could Sweyn have done such a thing? He might have understood it, if the Lieutenant were a younger man. Astri's madness had cast an unforgivable shadow over the *Schloss*. It would have been understandable, if his father had sought comfort in another woman's arms.

But the presence of this man suggested something else. Perhaps Astri had known of her husband's infidelity. Perhaps that had pushed her past the brink of reason.

It made him sick to think of it. Karl leaned forward slightly, staring harder at the Lieutenant. There was no doubting the resemblance between them. It only fuelled his anger toward the King.

'We share the same father, obviously,' the Lieutenant said, 'but I wonder about our mothers. Which of us was truly born of the Queen? Should we ask her?'

Never. The idea of forcing Astri to endure this man's presence was unthinkable.

'The Queen will not see you.' Prince Karl stood and went to stand by the window. 'She sees no one.' Not even him. His mother had barely acknowledged him during his entire childhood. That wasn't about to change.

'What if I spoke to her?' the woman spoke up suddenly. 'Surely Her Majesty would not feel uneasy about my presence. I am no threat.'

Karl hadn't given the Lieutenant's wife much

thought. She'd remained quiet throughout their discussion, but from the confident way she held herself, he suspected there was more to her than he'd first suspected. She was beautiful, certainly. But there was something uncommon about her, too. An air of quality, as though she belonged here.

Even so, he could not let anyone see the Queen.

'No one,' he repeated. Right now, he wanted to be rid of both of them. Though Karl loathed the idea of bribery, he didn't see that he had much of a choice. 'Return to London, and do not set foot in Lohenberg again. I'll see to it that you receive compensation.'

'We're not leaving,' the Lieutenant argued. 'Not until I've spoken with the King and Queen.'

Karl raised his hand in a silent signal to one of his guards. 'Show the Lieutenant and his wife out. Be sure they reach the borders safely.'

He wanted them gone from the *Schloss*. Out of Vermisten, out of his life. The sooner they were back in England, the better. If he had to use force, he wouldn't hesitate. This was about protecting his family.

The couple didn't argue, but the Lieutenant stood, facing him. His gaze held the promise of a threat. In Lohenisch, he said calmly, 'I didn't ask for this. But I swear to you, I'll have my answers. And so will you, whether you want to hear them or not.'

* * *

Michael couldn't seem to catch hold of the thousand-and-one thoughts racing through his mind. Confronting the Crown Prince had been like having his face smashed against a mirror. He'd seen traces of himself in the man's features. His half-brother. But which of them was illegitimate?

His thoughts returned to his parents. They had lied to him, letting him believe that he was their flesh-and-blood son. Had it been out of love, to protect him from harm? Or had they stolen him away?

His earliest memories of Mary Thorpe were of a woman who had soothed him, rocking him to sleep. Ever patient and loving, he'd never had any reason to doubt her. He still didn't want to.

He held fast to Hannah's hand, for she was his only constant presence in this ever-changing chaos. She grounded him, keeping him from losing his mind.

God in heaven, he didn't know what to do. It was clear that his life was a missing piece in this strange puzzle. But did he possess a birthright? Could he make the transition from pauper to Prince, if it were true?

The soldiers escorted them to the front of the *Schloss* just as Graf von Reischor arrived with his servants. The ambassador's face was nearly grey with exertion, and his footmen carried him towards them.

'Coming here alone was a mistake,' the Graf said without prelude. 'You have no idea the threats you could face.'

'Twice, men have tried to kill me,' Michael retaliated. 'I know precisely what we face.' With a hint of satisfaction, he added, 'And yet there hasn't been an attempt on my life since we left your side. Why do you suppose that is?'

'You should have waited for me,' the Graf insisted. His footmen eased the ambassador to a standing position. A moment later, Reischor motioned the servants away and lowered his voice. 'What happened?'

Was I right? he seemed to be asking.

'The Prince ordered us to leave,' Michael answered. 'His guards are escorting us to the borders.'

His reply fuelled the Graf's indignation. 'I didn't tell you to speak with the Fürst. Of course *he* wouldn't want you in the *Schloss*.'

'We weren't given a choice,' Hannah interrupted, her hand squeezing Michael's in an attempt to calm him. 'This morning the Prince sent men to the inn, and we were brought before him.' Keeping her voice just above a whisper, she added, 'He feels threatened by Michael.'

'Well, of course he would.' The Graf straightened, sending a thoughtful glance toward the *Schloss*. 'It seems we will need to alter our strategy.'

He spoke quietly to his own men, ordering them to

escort Michael and Hannah to his hunting lodge. 'I will join you there this evening, after I have spoken with Her Majesty.'

'The Prince says the Queen will see no one.'

'He means they won't allow it.' The Graf's face hardened with frustration. 'They accused her of madness and locked her up. No one wants to admit that she was right, all along.'

'Right about what?'

'About you being stolen away.' The Graf cleared his throat. 'But this is not the place to discuss it.'

He signalled to the Prince's guards. 'My servants will drive Lieutenant Thorpe and his...companion to the border. You may return to your duties.'

The Captain looked suspicious, but he obeyed. Within seconds, the Graf's servants surrounded them, and they continued walking towards his coach.

'My driver will bring you to my hunting lodge after he's certain you aren't followed out of Vermisten,' the Graf told them.

Hannah wasn't convinced. 'The Prince will order us out of the country, if he discovers we're still here.'

The Graf appeared irritated at her concern. 'Your presence is not required, Lady Hannah. If it bothers you, my men can escort you to your cousins' house in Germany, even now.'

She looked uncomfortable and turned to Michael,

her eyes searching his. He didn't want her to leave, not yet.

'I need someone I can trust, to be my translator.' Michael took her hand in his. He didn't mention that he was starting to remember the language. Best to let others believe he couldn't speak a word.

When they reached the coach, the Graf's gaze flickered toward their joined hands. Michael saw the instant the Graf noticed the ring upon Hannah's hand.

'Have you gone and done something foolish?'

Hannah blushed, covering the ring with her hand. 'Not really. It was a gift. If others believed we were married—'

The Graf's face tightened with disgust. 'I hope, for the sake of the Lieutenant's future, that not too many people believe it.'

Her face paled, and Michael tightened his hand on hers. This wasn't her fault, and he'd not let the Graf lay the blame upon her. He held up the ring. 'I've protected her reputation with this.'

'You shouldn't have brought her here,' the Graf protested. 'Her cousins are probably already wondering where we are.'

'We've been gone only two days,' Michael pointed out.

'And do you intend to keep her with you, as your—?'

'Don't say it.' Michael was about to move towards him when Hannah stepped between them.

'It's all right,' she said slowly. Looking the Graf squarely in the eye, she said, 'I have no intention of interfering with the Lieutenant's future. I will return to my cousins' house soon enough.' She released his hand, taking a step away. Her face was perfectly composed, showing no trace that she felt anything.

She was right, of course. That was the proper thing to do, and Michael should never have allowed her to come with him. But the idea of her leaving him, returning to a house of strangers who would help her marry a foreigner, made him want to take her hand back again.

After he helped Hannah into the coach, Michael asked, 'Where is Mrs Turner now?' He'd believed she would be safe, remaining with the Graf.

'She is staying at an inn with Lady Hannah's maid and the other servants.' The Graf visibly winced. 'She was not pleased about the journey here.'

Michael didn't doubt that. 'Bring her to the lodge, if you would. I want to speak with her as soon as possible.' Abigail Turner had known his mother since he was a small boy. She might be able to shed light on whether or not Mary Thorpe had ever been to Lohenberg.

The Graf nodded, though he didn't appear enthused about the idea. 'As you wish.'

Inside the coach, Hannah appeared shaken by the interaction. From the way she wouldn't meet his gaze, Michael suspected she was considering leaving.

Did he want to be a part of this royal family, though he was undoubtedly the black sheep? Instinct made him consider leaving it behind. They didn't want him—of that he had no doubt. But if he turned his back upon them, he would not see Hannah again. He was torn between a life he didn't want and a woman he did.

The journey towards the border was a jarring, rough ride. The miles passed, and still he didn't speak to Hannah. She was twisting the ring around her finger, deep in thought. When the afternoon sun began to drift lower in the sky, she turned to him and asked, 'What did you think of the Prince?'

'I think he's afraid.' As any man would be, when faced with an unexpected piece of the past.

'What about you? Are you afraid of what will happen?'

He shook his head. 'I'm not the one with a king-dom to lose, sweet.'

'He's your brother, isn't he?' She looked troubled by the prediction, as though she didn't want it to be true.

He nodded. 'I'm probably a bastard son. They'll want to be rid of me, for appearance's sake.'

She shook her head, meeting his eyes with her own. 'I don't believe that, Michael. I saw the portrait of the King in the library. You are the very image of your father.' Deep green eyes stared into his. 'If anyone is a bastard son, it's the Prince.'

Chapter Eighteen

Hannah stared out the window of the coach, feeling more and more uneasy about their circumstances. Now that Fürst Karl and Michael had met, she didn't doubt that the threats would worsen.

Michael rested his wrists upon his knees, glancing outside at the forest. 'I don't think there can be a good outcome for me, Hannah. There's too much at stake.'

'But if the Kingdom rightfully belongs to you…'

'I don't want it,' he admitted, shaking his head. 'I know nothing about Lohenberg. I was brought up in England as a fishmonger's son. I couldn't be a Prince, even if I wanted to.'

He'd already discarded the idea; she could see it on his face. He didn't believe he was capable of governing the people. But he was the sort of man who had seen the darker side of poverty. He would know, better than anyone, how to help those who were less fortunate.

She rested her hands upon her skirts, leaning towards him. He needed to put aside his doubts and reach for the future he deserved. 'You could. And I think you were meant for this.' Thinking a moment, she asked him, 'If it weren't for you, how many more men would have died at Balaclava?'

'I didn't save enough.'

'But many more lived.' She reached out to touch his cheek. 'You're a man who takes care of others. Your men. Mrs Turner.' She forced him to look at her. 'Me.'

'I'm no good at it, Hannah.' He glanced at the lavish gilt interior of the coach. 'I don't belong in a *Schloss* like that.'

'And what if they are your real family? You'll simply turn your back on them?'

A harsh laugh escaped him. 'They turned their back on me.'

'You don't know that. There are a thousand things that might have happened. Give it a chance. Find out the truth.'

'And what about you?' he asked quietly. 'What will you do if we find out I'm the Prince of this country?'

She stared at the ring on her hand, turning it over to hide the diamond-and-aquamarine cluster. 'I suppose I'll go to Germany.'

He took her hand and turned the ring back to

reveal the stones. Shrugging, he said, 'I need you to translate for me. After that, it's your choice.'

There was no mention of wanting her there. She had hoped he would ask her to stay, to tell her that she meant something to him. But he didn't appear to care whether or not she stayed. It battered her foolish dreams, and she berated herself for even thinking of it.

Crestfallen, she chose her words carefully. 'You're remembering more of the language every day. You were born knowing it; it's only a matter of time before you remember everything. You don't need me.'

Tell me you do, she pleaded silently. *Let me believe that last night was important to you.*

But he said nothing.

Hannah glanced outside so he couldn't see her eyes brimming with tears. 'The Graf was right. We shouldn't have pretended to be married.' Her face felt brittle, and her throat tightened in a struggle for control.

'You want to leave,' Michael murmured softly.

'I want you to ask me to stay.' The words slipped out, and she longed to take them back. 'I know I shouldn't have come with you here. It was wrong.' One of the tears slipped free against her will. 'But...I didn't want to leave you.'

Blood rushed to her face, as she laid her confession bare before him. 'I wanted to be with you, for however long that would be. And I don't regret letting you share my bed.'

He moved across the coach to sit beside her. With his thumbs, he brushed the tears away. 'If I were a better man, one who could take care of you, I wouldn't let you go. I'd damn the consequences and force you to stay with me.' He held her gloved hand to his face. 'But there are people who want me dead. It might be best if you stayed with your cousins, where you can be safe.'

She shivered, rubbing her arms, though the air was still warm. 'Is that what you want?'

He leaned in, touching his forehead to hers. She could feel the warmth of his mouth against her cheek, the hushed breath between them. The feverish burn of desire crept over her, the need to feel his body pressed close.

'You know what I want. And there's nothing honourable about it.'

Spirals of need threaded through her, and Hannah softened beneath the onslaught of Michael's kiss. The sensual pressure of his mouth and tongue loosened her doubts. Without words, he was coaxing her, silencing the warnings in her head.

When he broke away, it took a moment to steady her breathing. Every memory of last night came crashing through her mind. The touch of his hands, the feeling of his body joining with hers.

She needed to be with him, even if it meant being

his mistress and not his wife. And though she knew he would break her heart in the end, she would take whatever moments she could.

Michael couldn't sleep. Though he'd been given the best room in the Graf's hunting lodge, the soft featherbed offered nothing in the way of true comfort.

When he heard the door creaking open in the middle of the night, he reached under his pillow for the knife he'd hidden. Slowly, the footsteps drew closer. He held his breath, waiting. It was a risk, for he didn't know who was approaching or why. It might be someone trying to kill him, or it might be a servant who'd forgotten something. But then, a servant would have knocked first.

It was risky to wait, if the assailant had a gun. He held his position for as long as he dared, while the footsteps came even nearer. There was a faint scent of faded herbs, like a lavender sachet that had been trapped in a drawer for too long. A familiar perfume, but one he couldn't quite place.

When he sensed the person standing by his bed, he charged forward, with the knife drawn. 'Who's there?' he demanded.

A woman gasped, and he reached out to turn up the lamp. The dim glow illuminated the room, revealing the presence of Abigail Turner.

'Mrs Turner, what are you doing here?' he demanded.

She trembled, her face white with fear. He realised he was still holding the knife, and he set it down.

'I wanted to talk with you.' She sat down in a nearby chair, her voice quaking. 'Since you didn't heed my warning, I wanted you to understand. They're going to find me, and then I can't say what will happen.'

She spoke as though she'd done something wrong. He half-wondered if she was having one of her spells again. 'Find you?'

Raising her chin, she nodded. 'I was supposed to give you to them.' Her lower lip trembled, and she shook her head, her face tight with unshed tears. 'But how could I let them kill you? You were a boy…just a boy.'

He was having trouble understanding what she meant. 'Are you saying, you are from Lohenberg?' he ventured. 'This is your country?'

She glanced away. 'I haven't been back in over twenty-three years. I never wanted to return… after…what I did.' She gripped her arms, her voice fading softer. 'They took my husband, you see. They said if I didn't give you over to them, they were going to kill Sebastian.'

He stared hard at her curling grey hair and her soft brown eyes, but could not tell if it was the truth she spoke. She reached out and cupped his cheeks with her hands. The tears did spill over now, and she wept openly for her loss. Michael held her hands, trying to offer her comfort, though his mind was reeling from her revelation.

Though he didn't want to cause her more emotional pain, he needed to understand. 'You abducted me from my family,' he said slowly. 'Because these men took your husband.'

She nodded. 'I was in the Queen's service and was one of a few women who could get close to you.'

'Who were these men? Who hired them?'

'I don't know,' she wept. 'They came to me on All Hallows Eve. There was a masked ball that night, and everyone, even the guards, had masks.'

She wiped her tears, adding, 'I imagine that's how they were able to get inside the palace without anyone noticing. I was supposed to take you away from your nurse and bring you to a coach that was waiting outside. With all the other carriages for the ballroom guests, no one would notice it.'

'How did you get past the guards?'

'I told them I was taking you outside, to the gardens where the Queen was waiting. They believed my story and let me pass.' She lowered her head in self-loathing. 'They trusted me. I didn't know until later that the hired men had put another child in your place.'

Michael didn't allow a single emotion to be

revealed. He struggled to keep back the surge of resentment. Mrs Turner had known about his past, all these years, and had never once said a word about it. She'd known that his parents were not his own.

But if he revealed any of his frustration now, she might slip into a fit of madness, and he'd never hear the entire truth.

Carefully, he asked, 'What happened after you took me from my nurse?'

She continued weeping, clutching her hands together. 'I almost gave you over to them, God forgive me. You were asleep in my arms when I got inside the coach.' Her hand went to her middle. 'But I had recently learned that I was expecting a child of my own. Henry.' A mournful smile crept through her tears. 'And I thought about how I would feel if anyone harmed my own child. I couldn't bring myself to do it. Even if it meant losing Sebastian.'

She dried her eyes, seeming to pull her thoughts together. 'I stopped the coachman and bribed him to drive me home instead.' Her gaze turned solemn with regret. 'I suppose we were both having regrets.'

'I gathered up all the money and jewels that I could, and I used it to buy our passage to London,' she continued. 'I kept you for a few months until I was about to give birth. It was then that I met Paul and Mary Thorpe. They were childless and they promised to take care of you and help me with my own baby.'

Mrs Turner let out a heavy sigh. 'I was afraid of anyone finding us. I also knew I would have to live in poverty for the rest of my days. It was the only way to avoid notice.'

He'd often wondered how Mrs Turner had managed to survive, without a husband to support her. He'd always believed it was his parents' charity.

'Did my parents know about my past?'

She shook her head. 'It would have made them uncomfortable to know you were a Prince. They'd have treated you like a bit of glass, and then what sort of man would you have grown into?'

She took a deep breath, blowing her nose in the handkerchief he gave her. 'I told them you were orphaned in Lohenberg, and that I'd promised to find a home for you. I let them raise you as they chose. But the one thing I insisted on was your education. Dear heaven, how I pestered Mary about that. I told her that you might be a fishmonger's son, but you deserved a chance for a better future.'

'How could they possibly have afforded my schooling?' Michael voiced aloud. 'I never understood it.'

'I sold some jewels I'd kept from Lohenberg.' She dabbed at her eyes. 'Mary let Paul believe that she'd inherited a small sum from an aunt who died.' She patted his cheek. 'You needed it more than I did.'

'What happened to your husband?'

Silent tears rolled down her face. 'I've never known. I haven't seen Sebastian since that night.' She shivered at the memory. 'I hoped that somehow he managed to survive. But I couldn't write to him or ever learn what happened; otherwise they might have found you.'

The burden of her secret seemed to grow lighter, now that she had laid it before him. But Michael felt its weight suffocating him. He didn't want a royal life, or the difficulties it would bring.

'I sent the last of my funds to bring you back from Malta, after I learned you were wounded,' she admitted. 'I had hoped that both you and Henry would return.'

Michael embraced her while she wept for her son. With Abigail Turner's confession, he could no longer deny the truth staring him in the face. He would have to confront the impostor Prince Karl, as well as the King and Queen. God help him.

Mrs Turner leaned her head on his shoulder, patting his back. 'I am sorry for keeping this from you, Michael. I thought the only way to save your life was to keep it a secret.'

She was asking for his forgiveness, but right now he was having trouble thinking clearly. He forced himself to give her a light squeeze, but inside, his thoughts were churning.

Mrs Turner pulled back from him. Her face still held the melancholy, but it was soon replaced by stubbornness. 'I will go to Queen Astri in the morning and tell her everything.'

He wasn't so certain that was a good idea. 'We've already been forbidden to see the Queen. I don't think—'

'I was one of her ladies-in-waiting for over five years. The Queen will see me.'

'Not if she believes you stole her only son.'

Mrs Turner's face crumpled up with tears, as though he'd struck her across the face. But she needed to understand that any contact with the *Schloss* would mean her own imprisonment, possibly death.

'If you try to speak with her, you'll face punishment for what you did. The men who took your husband might find you again; they know I'm still alive. It's too grave a risk.'

'I have to atone for what I did. I have to bring you back to her, so she knows that I never meant to betray her.'

'In time. I will face her first, before you.' He crossed his arms in front of him. 'But even if she does agree to see me, she might not believe it. There's no proof that I am her son, except for my resemblance to the King.'

The corners of Mrs Turner's mouth turned up. 'You're wrong, lad. There is proof that you are the Prince.'

He waited for her to continue, and she came up behind him. 'You have a scar here.' She pointed to his left leg. 'On the back of your calf.'

Michael had seen the scar before, but he'd never remembered how he'd received it.

'When you were two years old,' Mrs Turner said, 'you loved climbing up on tables, no matter how your nurse tried to stop you. One day, you fell backwards and cut yourself on one of your toys. You cried and your mother held you while they stitched up the wound.' Mrs Turner stretched her thumb and forefinger to show the size. 'It's naught more than this large. But only a few members in the palace knew about it.'

She grew solemn. 'You're going to get your throne back, Michael Thorpe. I promise you that.'

Michael spent the last few hours of the night pacing. Mrs Turner's confession made it impossible to deny his past any longer. Now he had to decide whether or not to seek the Kingdom he'd lost.

He threw on a pair of trousers and a shirt, not bothering with a waistcoat. Tiptoeing outside his room, he moved down the corridor and towards the back stairway. The Graf's lodge was not large, though it was luxurious.

He didn't know what drew him towards Hannah's bedchamber. It wasn't the desire to intrude, but a deeper need. If he could sleep beside her, he sensed he could calm the tangled state of his mind.

The Graf had given her a room on the opposite side of the house. Although they had kept up their ruse of marriage to the outside world, Heinrich von Reischor intended to uphold Hannah's virtue as best he could.

Quietly, Michael opened the door to her room and moved inside. Though he doubted if she'd hidden a knife under her pillow the way he had, he whispered, 'It's Michael. Are you asleep?'

'I was,' Hannah replied, rolling over and blinking at him. 'What is it?'

He closed the door behind him, thankful to find that she was alone. Without another word, he crossed the room and lay down beside her in the bed.

She wore a thin cotton nightgown, and her body was warm from sleep. A light fragrance of jasmine clung to her hair. Michael curled around her, holding her close.

She didn't ask for explanations, but softly ran her fingers over his arm. A reassuring touch, one that helped to calm his troubled spirits.

'Stay with me tonight,' she whispered.

He kissed her temple in answer. Though his body was already responding to her nearness, he forced the desire away. Right now, he just wanted to sleep beside her.

'You can tell me, you know,' she whispered. 'Whatever is bothering you.'

'In the morning,' he promised. 'Right now, I've the need to hold you.'

She rolled over on to her side, propping up her head on her hand. 'Tell me.'

He explained Mrs Turner's confession, all the while finding an excuse to touch Hannah. He ran his fingers over her shoulder, down to the curve of her hip. 'I hardly know what to do any more. The throne isn't something I want.'

Her hand came up to his face, and she pressed her lips to his in a soft kiss. 'If Queen Astri is your true mother, she'll want to know what happened to you.' She pressed closer to him, stroking his spine. The gesture made him grow hard, and he fought to gain control over his body's instincts.

'They're strangers to me,' he admitted. 'I know nothing of the way they live or how I should act.'

'I'll help you.' Hannah ran her fingers through his hair. 'I'll come with you to the *Schloss* for a few days.'

He pulled her on top of him, holding her close. The edges of her nightgown slid up around her legs, and when he reached down to correct the hem, he realised she was naked beneath it.

His palms moved over her bare bottom, and his

manhood swelled against the soft spot between her thighs. She tensed, and he felt the prickle of goose-flesh on her skin.

'Michael,' she breathed. It was neither a protest, nor an invitation. He sensed that she desired him, too, but was trying to resist him.

He cupped her face, drawing her in for a kiss. His frustrations, his uncertain future, were making it impossible to think clearly. And right now, if she was willing, he wanted to forget.

She kissed him back, her mouth warm and wet. He rocked her hips against his, and she shuddered at the contact. His palms squeezed her soft bottom, while his shaft strained to break free.

'I want to be inside you,' he murmured against her mouth, sliding his hands beneath her nightgown to cup her bare breasts. The fierce need burned inside him, and if she allowed it, he wanted nothing more than to turn her over and fill her body with his own.

She stilled, and her hands captured his wrists, pulling them away. 'Michael, no. I can't.' Hannah extricated herself from his embrace, and he noticed that her fingers were bare, unlike a few hours ago. She must have removed the wedding ring he'd given her.

His desire was instantly replaced with wariness. 'I didn't come here to seduce you. I'm not going to force you into anything you don't want.'

She sat up and drew her nightgown over her knees. In the fragile garment, she looked like an innocent maiden about to be sacrificed to a dragon.

'I was wrong. I thought I could be your mistress.' She gathered up the bed sheets like a shield.

He took several deep breaths, feeling as though he were walking upon a precipice. 'I told you. If there's a child, I will provide for both of you.'

She shook her head slowly. 'We made the mistake once. Not again. If I bore a child, you would resent me.'

He couldn't understand what she meant. 'I would never resent you.'

'I thought that if we were together, even if I were nothing but your mistress, you might eventually want to marry me.' She lowered her head. 'It was a foolish thought. As the Crown Prince, there is no chance of it.'

'I don't live by the decisions of others.'

She ignored him. 'You could marry a Princess. Or a duchess. Anyone you please.'

His anger ignited. 'Do you think I give a damn about social status?' He stood, his shadow falling over her. 'Are you demanding that I marry you? Because I don't think that's what you really want.'

His fury erupted. 'You want a man with a title and several estates. You want a respectable name and separate bedrooms with an adjoining door. When you sit at your dinner table, you want a man at your side whom others admire. Not a man like me. A soldier, responsible for the deaths of hundreds of men.'

She spoke not a word, and he realised he'd been hoping for her argument. He'd hoped she would deny it. But he suspected he'd been her temptation, a sinful indulgence that she didn't want forever.

'If I thought you wanted me, I'd find a minister right now,' he murmured, sitting down. 'I would make you a Princess. But you wouldn't say yes, would you?'

Because she knew where he came from. She knew who he truly was—a man from the streets.

For the longest moment, Michael stared into her bleak face. Waiting for her to tell him he was wrong. Waiting for her to embrace him or offer words of reassurance.

'No, I wouldn't,' she said at last. Her face was pale, but determined. 'I'll help you acclimate to the *Schloss*. And after that, I'm leaving for Germany.'

The door closed behind Michael, and Hannah buried her face in the pillow, weeping hot tears. The wretched pain of forcing him to leave her was more than she could bear.

His idle remark, that he'd make her a Princess, made her shudder. He didn't know what it was like to live in a gilded cage, the way she did.

Hannah understood exactly what it was to have

her appearance inspected every few hours, her food selected based on what would keep her figure slender, and her life ordered to a stringent set of rules.

For a Princess, it would be far worse.

The hot tears caught up in her throat, for it had taken every bit of her willpower to hold firm on the decision. She had fallen in love with Michael Thorpe, but not once had he spoken of his feelings toward her. And the thought of living in a *Schloss*, hoping for a scrap of affection or a night in his arms, was too much to bear.

She'd rather be the wife of a nobleman or a commoner. Someone who would let her have a taste of the freedom she'd never possessed.

Michael's life would be controlled by the strings of politics, his future no longer under his control. If he were the Crown Prince, he couldn't avoid his fate.

But she could.

And though it broke her heart into a thousand pieces, she couldn't endure life as a Princess unless he loved her back.

Chapter Nineteen

Though he was healing from his bullet wounds, the Graf von Reischor was still unable to walk. While Michael waited in the coach with Lady Hannah, the older man's servants used a wheeled chair to push him into the *Schloss*.

'Do you think he'll manage an audience with the Queen?' Hannah asked, watching as they disappeared inside.

'I have no doubt of it.'

'What about the royal guards? The Prince ordered us to leave the country. Surely, they won't allow it.'

'They haven't seen us yet. For now, they believe the ambassador is paying his respects to the Queen.'

They waited for nearly two hours before the Graf returned to the coach. The man looked exhausted, but satisfied. To Michael, he said, 'I've arranged an audience. The King has agreed to meet with us, overruling Fürst Karl's orders.'

'What about the Queen?' Hannah asked. 'Will she see us?'

The Graf nodded. 'We will see her first, before our audience with the King. But we must be careful, because Her Majesty is confined to one of the towers. Visitors are rare, and I would caution you not to upset her.'

Would the Queen be like Abigail Turner, with fleeting moments of clarity? Michael wondered. Or had she crossed past the point of rational behaviour?

The Graf took assistance from the footmen, who helped him back into the chair. Michael adjusted his gloves, while his doubts and apprehensions rose higher.

Hannah closed the door to the coach for a moment, keeping her voice low. 'When you encounter anyone at the *Schloss*, do not allow them to touch you,' she said. 'Royalty may never be touched without permission to do so.'

He gave a nod, trying to memorise her instructions.

'Wait for a footman to ask permission to take your coat,' she continued. 'You must stand and allow him to take it off you.'

He stared at her. 'Do you mean to say I am not allowed to remove my own coat?'

'Others will be responsible for dressing you and undressing you,' she answered. 'A valet will be assigned to you, and you must permit him to carry out his duties.'

'As if I were nothing more than a child?'

'No. Because it is your right to be waited on by others.'

'What if I refuse?'

'You mustn't.' She glanced back at the *Schloss*. 'Already there will be those who doubt your right to be Prince.' She took his hand and pleaded, 'Trust what I say. It will be easier if you obey the rules that are expected.'

He glanced down at their joined hands. Hannah tried to jerk her fingers back, but he held them in his grip. Beneath the glove, she still wasn't wearing the ring he'd given her.

'Should I tell them that you are my translator, my mistress or my wife?' he demanded.

For an infinite moment, she looked into his eyes as though he were crushing her heart. He'd expected a firm refusal, as well as a reminder that she would only stay for a few days. Clear green eyes watched him with an unnamed emotion.

'Tell them whatever you want,' she said.

Why in God's name couldn't women simply state what they desired instead of hiding their true thoughts behind a set of good manners?

A servant opened the door to the coach, and a chill swept over Michael at the thought of meeting the Queen. He disembarked and reached up to help Hannah down.

'Don't do that again,' she murmured. 'You're royalty. Let a footman help me down.'

He couldn't believe what he was hearing. Did she expect him to behave as though he owned the earth and everyone else was privileged to be in his presence? From the way she followed, a discreet distance behind him, it seemed that was exactly the case.

Servants carried the Graf up two flights of stairs, to a private drawing room within one of the towers while they followed behind. When Michael waited for Hannah, she shook her head. 'This is your audience, not mine. I will await you here.' She pointed to a wooden high-backed chair.

'Do as you please.' He turned his back on her, unable to conceal his anger. What was the matter with her? He couldn't understand why she was behaving like his subject instead of his equal.

Before he could think upon it further, he was led into a private room. The Graf's men seated him in a chair, and the ambassador was pale from overexertion.

'Lieutenant Thorpe.' The Graf struggled to rise to his feet. 'May I present to you Her Majesty, Queen Astri of Lohenberg?'

At the Graf's bidding, the servant opened another door, leading to a room Michael hadn't noticed before. After a moment, he moved forward without making a sound.

A woman was seated, staring out the window. Iron bars had been fastened in front of them, and a lady-in-waiting sat nearby, embroidering the hem of a gown.

Michael didn't know what to say. He'd never been in the presence of a queen before, much less one who was possibly his true mother. In the end, he knocked softly upon the door frame.

'Your Majesty...' he began.

Her head turned at the sound of his voice. When she saw him, her hands began to shake. Her eyes welled up, and she pointed to him.

'Come closer,' she murmured. And he saw that she was not at all mad. Her hazel eyes were the same as his own, and he saw similarities between their facial features.

'Graf von Reischor told me that he'd found you. I didn't believe him.' She beckoned for him to draw nearer, and Michael forced himself to come and sit beside her.

The Queen's dark hair held no traces of grey. It was braided and wound into an elaborate coiffeur, adorned with jewelled hairpins. She wore a black moiré gown trimmed with black velvet.

'They told me I was mad, when I said that the boy they gave me was not my son. No one would believe me.' She stared at him. 'You look a great deal like the child I lost. Are you he?'

'I don't know.' But something about the Queen's voice, the soft tones of it, was familiar. 'I thought I was Michael Thorpe. I don't remember anything about this country or anyone else.'

She reached out to him. 'May I?' He gave a nod and she touched his cheek, studying his face closer. 'How did you end up in London?'

'Abigail Turner claimed she took me away, when men were trying to kill her husband. She hid me in London these past twenty-three years.'

'Abigail Turner.' The Queen's face darkened with rage. 'She deserves to be put to death for what she did.'

'She saved my life,' Michael countered. He explained what Mrs Turner had told him, and all the while, the Queen listened with an unreadable expression.

When he'd finished, he said, 'I wouldn't blame you if you didn't believe a word I said. Why should you? I'm a stranger claiming that I could be your son.'

'You don't want this throne, do you?' the Queen said slowly.

'No.' He strode away from her, even knowing that it was rude. 'I wanted to believe that Mary Thorpe was my mother. I wanted to go back to my life as a lieutenant in the British Army.' He folded his arms across his chest, switching to Lohenisch. 'But I can't deny the memories I have. Nor this language.'

When he turned back to face the Queen, her gaze met his.

'You're not a lieutenant, are you?' With her posture ramrod straight, she rose and walked towards him. 'Show me your left calf.' He raised the leg of his trousers, lowering his sock until he bared the scar.

Her hazel eyes glistened, and Queen Astri covered her mouth with her hands. 'You're the son I lost. Fürst Karl.'

'My name is not Karl,' he protested. 'I am Michael.'

'Yes. Karl Peter Michael Henry, Fürst of Lohenberg.' She drew closer, staring at the scar. 'It was in the wrong place, you see. The scar on the boy they gave me. *His* scar was just above his ankle. Yours was below the knee. But the King wouldn't believe me. He told me that the boy was our son. The scar was enough to convince him. He had me locked away, believing I'd gone mad when I said the child wasn't ours.

'May I?' she asked, and once again he realised that she was treating him like royalty, requesting permission before she touched him.

Her arms went around him in an embrace, and awkwardly, he stood still, not sure of what to do.

When she moved away, her eyes were wet. 'You don't know me. I'm aware of that, but it's been so very long.'

Another tear rolled down her cheek, combined with a laugh. 'I was right, you see. They didn't believe me, but I was right. The boy they gave me wasn't you.' She removed a handkerchief and wiped her eyes. 'I thank God you're alive.'

The door to the Queen's antechamber opened, and Fürst Karl entered. He strode forward, bowing to the Queen, but his eyes blazed with fury.

'Your Majesty,' he greeted her. To Michael, he said nothing.

'Get out,' she ordered Karl, pointing at the door. 'I've no wish to see you.'

'My lady Mother, I—'

'Out!' she shrieked. 'Leave my presence! I am not your mother, and you are not my son!' Her face filled with loathing, and Michael glimpsed the Prince's shuttered expression.

'If you have need of me—'

'I would never call you, if I had the need. You are nothing to me but an impostor! Lying traitor!'

The Prince sent Michael another dark look, bowing as he made his way out of the chamber.

The Queen apologised as soon as the door closed. 'Tonight, I will order a welcoming feast for you, my son. And the world will know the truth of who is the real Prince.' Her face curved in a smile. 'They have only to look upon your face to see it for themselves.'

But despite her happiness, Michael hadn't missed the hatred upon Karl's face. He'd just deposed a man who had been born and bred for the throne. And he had no doubt that Karl would fight for his kingdom.

Hannah ducked behind the tall wooden chair when Fürst Karl exited the chamber. Anyone could have heard the Queen's rejection, and from the iciness on the Prince's face, it was clear he was furious.

He stopped in front of the chair. 'You may as well come out, Mrs Thorpe. Your gown gives you away.'

Hannah straightened, realising he was right. 'I didn't mean to pry. I was simply waiting upon my… that is, the…Lieutenant.' She didn't say Prince, for it would only fuel the Prince's rage.

Fürst Karl stepped forward, his eyes burning. 'I ordered both of you to leave my country.'

Hannah drew upon every facet of her training to respond. 'I understand how angry you must be with us. But—'

'You understand nothing.' The coldness in his voice was lined with pain.

Hannah prayed she could somehow ease the Prince's anger and reassure him. But this was a man who was about to lose everything. His home, his title…even his family. No words would take away the loss.

'You didn't live here your entire life, did you?' she began. 'Do you remember what it was like before the palace?'

The Prince seemed taken aback by her questions. Rightfully so, she supposed. Royalty was never meant to be interrogated.

'I never lived anywhere else.'

'You might not remember it,' she offered, changing tactics. 'But surely, if you think back to your earliest memory, you know of a time when you were frightened.' She stepped closer to him, her own fears quaking inside. 'When you were but a small child, pushed into a world you didn't understand.'

Careful, Hannah. Don't make him angrier.

But his face remained blank, as though she hadn't spoken at all.

'I can understand why you might resent Lieutenant Thorpe,' she said gently. 'To find out that your life was not what you thought it was…anyone would be angry at the changes.'

'Nothing has changed,' the Fürst insisted. 'And I won't let him do anything to upset the Queen.'

The Prince's protective nature over his mother made Hannah's heart ache. She doubted if Queen Astri had ever accepted Fürst Karl as her son. In her mind, Hannah imagined a lonely boy, trying to win his mother's love. And never succeeding.

'Lieutenant Thorpe came to find out the truth. Not to hurt anyone, especially not the Queen.' She could see the pain in his eyes, of a man whose life was crumbling at his feet. 'Talk to him, I beg of you. If the two of you would come to an understanding, there might be a way to compromise.'

Her words made the Fürst stiffen. He crossed the hallway, coming to stand directly in front of her. 'There cannot be a compromise, Mrs Thorpe. Lohenberg is my homeland, and I will die before handing my throne over to a stranger who knows nothing of our country.'

'He is your brother, by blood,' Hannah said quietly. 'And regardless of the conspiracies that happened years ago, the two of you should put your differences aside. Try to work together.'

The Prince shook his head. 'It's not possible.'

Hannah looked into his eyes, noting the trapped frustration. 'Lieutenant Thorpe is a good man. And I believe you are, as well.'

'I care little about what anyone thinks of me. Least of all, the wife of a lieutenant.'

Her expression grew strained. 'I am the daughter of a Marquess. Not the wife of a lieutenant.' Steeling herself, she admitted, 'I lied about being married. It was merely a way to stay with him.'

'You're in love with him, aren't you?'

She didn't answer, trying to keep the bottled-up emotions from spilling over. 'I want him to be happy. Whether he is a soldier or a Prince.'

The Prince's expression grew taut. 'You want to become a Princess.'

'No.' She took a deep breath. 'Actually, I'd rather be a soldier's wife.' Glancing toward the Queen's chambers, she added, 'I know what it is to be imprisoned in a life like this. To be measured and inspected. And still never be good enough.'

The Prince's gaze met hers, and she thought she detected a softening. For a moment, she saw herself mirrored in him, and wondered if he, too, craved his freedom.

'You will always be a Prince here,' she ventured, touching her own heart. 'A man who loves Lohenberg as you do would make a strong adviser.'

'I'd make a better king,' the Prince responded. His chin raised up, and he added, 'Your days in Lohenberg are coming to an end. Rest assured, Lady Hannah, I'll let no one take what belongs to me.'

Hannah waited the remainder of the morning for Michael, but when he finally emerged from the King's chambers, she caught only a glimpse of him before the servants led him away. After they disappeared down the corridor, the Graf hobbled out, sinking gratefully into the chair offered by his servants.

'They accepted him, then?' Hannah asked. 'Did the audience go well?'

'It did. And I should imagine they will formally acknowledge him as the Fürst within a day or so.' The Graf gave a relaxed smile. 'There's no need for you to stay any longer.'

Hannah didn't return his smile. 'I promised I would remain for a few days.'

'There are others who will help him to assimilate. He does not require your assistance.'

'Trusted servants?' She shook her head. 'Not yet. There were two attempts on his life already. He needs someone to watch out for him, to make sure he's safe.'

'He'll have guards for that.' The Graf motioned a servant forward. 'Escort Lady Hannah back to my coach.'

'Forgive me, Graf von Reischor…' the maidservant curtsied '…but the Queen has already ordered a bedchamber prepared for Lady Hannah.'

Hannah held back her sigh of relief. Her thoughts were so tangled, right now all she wanted was to rest in Michael's arms, to feel the warmth of his body beside her. But he hadn't spoken to her, nor even glanced in her direction when he'd left with the Queen. She tried to ignore the disappointment settling in her stomach.

As she followed the maidservant to one of the

guest rooms, she was startled to cross paths with guests she'd met aboard the *Orpheus*.

'Why, Lord Brentford,' she greeted, surprised to see the Viscount. 'And Miss Nelson. This is a surprise.'

The Viscount beamed, returning the greeting. 'I was delighted that the König accepted my request for an audience,' he explained. 'And, of course, we simply *had* to bring Ophelia to meet the royal family. My wife insisted on it.'

Miss Nelson glanced at her father, clearly uncomfortable. She twisted her hands, not offering a greeting or any remark to Hannah.

'Where is Lady Brentford?' Hannah asked, curious as to why the Viscountess was not with them.

'Shopping.' The Viscount winced. 'She claims that Ophelia needs a more dramatic gown for tonight, and she's having a gown altered.'

'Perhaps I'll see all of you at dinner this evening,' Hannah offered.

'Perhaps,' Lord Brentford replied. 'We are hoping Ophelia will be presented to the Crown Prince. After all, he has not yet chosen a bride.'

Hannah wasn't certain how Lord Brentford had wormed his way into the *Schloss*, but it was clear he wanted an advantageous marriage for his daughter.

'Good afternoon to you both,' she bid them in

parting. Lord Brentford's broad smile never faded as he continued down the corridor.

The maidservant, Johanna, showed her to a room decorated in shades of green and cream. Though it was small, each piece of furniture was exquisite, with warm shades of wood and shining brass handles.

Hannah gave instructions for her trunks to be delivered to the *Schloss*, along with her maid Estelle. Johanna promised to make the necessary arrangements.

An hour later, when Johanna returned with Estelle and the trunks, Hannah asked her maid, 'Where is Mrs Turner?'

'She remained at the Graf's estate,' Estelle answered. 'On his orders.'

Likely to keep her safe, Hannah mused. Still, she wished for the woman's friendly presence.

Behind the two maidservants, a tall, elegant lady entered the room. Her grey hair was pulled into a neat coiffeur, and she wore a flounced maroon dress with draping sleeves.

'I am Lady Schmertach, head of the Queen's ladies-in-waiting,' the woman introduced herself. 'There are certain rules that all guests must abide by, and I am here to see to it that you understand them.'

Were all guests greeted this way? Hannah wondered. She felt rather like a child in the schoolroom, preparing to receive instructions.

After Lady Schmertach seated herself upon the velvet sofa, she cleared her throat. 'First and foremost, you are not to address the King or Queen under any circumstances. Should they choose to speak with you, they will send an attendant to fetch you.'

Rather like a pet dog, Hannah thought. While she listened, Estelle and Johanna began helping her to dress. She noticed that they had selected a rose damask gown flecked with silver threads. It had not been one of her favorites, and she interjected, 'I would prefer the violet tarlatan with the flowers embroidered on the overskirt.'

Lady Schmertach's expression hardened. 'I was not finished explaining matters to you, Lady Hannah. Please do not interrupt. Courtesy is another rule by which we abide here.'

Years of Hannah's own training in courtesy prevented her from snapping out her own retort at the Queen's lady. She bit her lip. 'You were saying?'

Estelle continued working with Johanna, fitting the rose dress over Hannah's corset. Hannah hid her displeasure, waiting for the older woman to finish her lecture.

'You will be seated at the end of the table, along with the other unmarried ladies.'

A little pang squeezed at her heart. So, Michael

had not told anyone that they were married. She should have expected it, for it gave her a means of leaving the *Schloss* without anyone noticing.

Lady Schmertach continued her long diatribe, explaining that she should not expect to dance with Fürst Karl, nor to be introduced. 'Royal marriages are not fairy tales,' she insisted. 'They are political alliances that benefit both countries. So you must not allow yourself to fall into the common belief that he will notice you.'

Johanna picked up a hairbrush and began to comb Hannah's hair into a severe knot that pulled at her face. Hannah was beginning to feel like a doll, dressed up in ribbons and lace, unable to move without someone pushing her limbs into place.

'Do you understand all that I have instructed you?' Lady Schmertach asked. 'Have you any questions about how to conduct yourself this evening?'

'No.' She understood perfectly well that she was to remain exactly in her chair and to keep a full distance from the royal family.

'Good. Graf von Reischor has informed me that your cousins will arrive shortly to escort you back to Germany.' With a prim smile, she rose from her chair. 'I hope you enjoy the hospitality this evening.'

Hannah's temples ached from the tight hairpins, and she ordered Johanna and Estelle to leave her alone. When they had gone, she stripped away every pin until her hair hung down below her shoulders.

What is the matter with me? she wondered. *Why can't I tell them what it is I really want?* The words of protest seemed weighted down by years of obedience.

There was a soft knock on the door. Hannah called out, 'Enter', expecting one of the maids to return.

Instead, Michael stepped inside. He closed the door behind him, seemingly surprised to find her alone.

Hannah stood, wondering if she was supposed to curtsy before him. He hadn't changed his clothing from this morning, and his cravat hung crooked at his throat as if he'd tugged at it. She resisted the urge to correct it. 'Was there something you needed?'

His dark gaze fixed upon her. 'Yes. There's something I needed.'

All the blood seemed to rush to her face, and prickles rose up on her skin. Whether it was nerves or simply the intense awareness of Michael, she didn't know. She forced herself to sit down.

'The Graf gave you the chance to leave, earlier today,' he began. 'But you didn't take it. Why?'

She drew on one of her gloves. 'Because I promised I would stay here for a few days longer. To help you grow accustomed to your new life here.'

'Is that the only reason?'

No. I didn't want to leave you. 'What other reason would there be?'

His gaze swept over her gown, but he made no comment. 'I saw that Viscount Brentford and his family are here.'

'Yes, I spoke with him and Miss Nelson.' She grimaced. 'Though they don't know you're the real Prince. I suppose it doesn't matter whether it's you or Fürst Karl. And it won't be the last time you'll be pursued by eager fathers and daughters.'

'Does it bother you?' He folded his arms across his chest.

Of course it bothered her. But she couldn't do anything about it. 'What do you expect me to say? That I'm jealous?' Her shield of calm collapsed into pieces. It wasn't women like Miss Nelson who bothered her. No, it was the soldier's mask that never revealed a hint of Michael's feelings.

'No. You wouldn't be, would you?' he responded. 'I can see that you've made your decision already.'

She crossed the room and stood in front of him. 'What decision? What decision have I ever been allowed to make? You've already made up your mind about me and what you think I want. Just as Estelle and Johanna have decided what I'll wear and how my hair should be arranged. And Graf von Reischor has decided that I'll be returning home to my cousins.'

She rose from her chair and crossed towards him.

With a not-so-gentle push, she said, 'My decisions don't seem to matter in the least, so why bother asking?'

He caught her in his arms. 'Because I don't believe what you told me this morning.' He tilted her face to his, their mouths the barest breath apart. 'I don't know which is worse…forcing you to live a life you don't want…or letting you go.'

His hazel eyes were full of desire, his mouth achingly close to kissing hers. God help her, she needed him so much. Being without him was going to rip her heart apart.

'Make your decision, Hannah.' He pressed the ring into her palm. 'Either become my Princess in truth. Or leave.'

He withdrew from her embrace, walking away. When the door closed behind him, she stared down at her rose gown. She didn't care for the colour, nor did she want to wear the pearls Estelle had chosen.

She hated herself and what she had become. And then her gaze fell upon a list Estelle had made, detailing everything Lady Schmertach had instructed.

Whether it was a list of reminders or a list of orders, Hannah didn't care. She tore the paper into tiny pieces, ripping apart all the expectations.

This was her life, was it not? If she wished to wear

violet, she could. If she wanted to wear her hair down, who were the servants to tell her otherwise?

The years of fettered isolation were drowning her. She didn't know if she could stand living in this isolated, rigid palace of rules. But there was one thing she wanted more than anything in the world, one man worth fighting for.

She slid the aquamarine-and-diamond ring upon her finger and threw open the door to her room. Picking up her skirts, she raced down the hall. When she rounded the corner, she nearly crashed into Michael.

He caught her before she fell, his hazel eyes questioning. Hannah didn't speak a word, but took his hand in hers, leading him back to her bedchamber. Once they were inside, she turned the key in the lock.

'What do you want?' he asked. His eyes stared hard at the ring upon her hand.

'I don't want to wear this gown tonight,' she answered. 'Nor these pearls.' She reached behind her neck, fumbling with the clasp. Her hands were shaking, her heart pounding in her chest.

Michael came up behind her, his warm hands resting on her nape. With the flick of his thumb, he unfastened the necklace.

'Now the dress,' she ordered. 'Help me. Please.' She wanted his hands upon her, removing all the layers between them.

I don't care that this is wrong. I don't care, I don't care, I don't care.

But Michael took his time unfastening the dozens of buttons, his fingers touching her with unbearable slowness. With each release, her skin erupted with goose bumps. She was waiting for him to kiss her, but he held himself back.

Hannah removed her petticoats, standing before him in her corset and undergarments.

'Am I to play your lady's maid?' he murmured.

'No. You're going to play my husband.' She reached up to kiss him, and their mouths came together in a heated frenzy. He stripped off his coat, and she helped him with his waistcoat and shirt until his chest was bared to her. Hannah kissed his skin, moving her mouth over his pectoral muscles, the marbled skin that was everything she wanted.

He unfastened her corset, turning her to the wall as he unlaced her stays. His hands cupped her breasts, pushing away more clothing until both of them were naked. Her palms pressed against the wallpaper and behind her, he moved close so that his erect shaft slid between her open thighs.

With his fingertips, he teased her breasts. His mouth moved over her shoulders and down her spine until he eased the tip of himself inside her, from behind.

She bloomed with moisture, aching for him. As he slid deeper, he murmured, 'This isn't the proper way to make love to a lady.' With himself still inside her, he guided her to move towards the sofa, leaning over the side. She cried out with exquisite pleasure as he filled her from behind.

'I don't care about what's proper any more,' she breathed. 'Just be with me now.'

He withdrew, then penetrated her again. 'I am at your command.'

Chapter Twenty

Michael kissed Hannah's shoulder, her hair falling against his face as he plunged inside her. He couldn't stay away from her, no matter how hard he tried. When he was with Hannah, the emptiness of his life and his past failures all seemed to dissolve. She made him feel whole again.

No kingdom was worth being without her.

She was close to her release, and he pushed himself against the wetness, driving her nearer to the fulfillment she craved. Half-sobs were coming from her, but the long smooth strokes weren't giving her what she needed.

'Hold on,' he urged. Bracing her hands against the couch, he took her roughly. The increased tempo and pounding of his body inside hers made her breathing quicken.

His erection grew harder, and as her body tightened around him, squeezing him in her liquid depths, his control was splintering apart.

Michael pinched her nipples, coaxing her, 'Reach for it, Hannah.' He didn't care how long it took; he would be her slave if it meant bringing her the pleasure she needed.

He reached down to caress the fold of flesh that would help. The touch of his hand made her buck against him, and the counter-pressure of her hips sent his own release blasting through him. At last, she emitted a shuddering gasp, her body trembling wildly. Her inner walls climaxed around him, and he groaned, pulling her hips tight against his own.

For a moment, he rested his cheek against her back, no longer certain he'd be able to walk. No woman had ever made him feel this way. He couldn't possibly let her go. She was his to protect, his to care for.

He withdrew from her, sweeping her into his arms and taking her to bed. They lay facing one another, skin to skin. He kissed her lips, apologising, 'I didn't hurt you, did I?'

Her cheeks were glowing, her green eyes luminous. 'I felt like a conquest of war.'

He lowered his forehead to hers. 'I'm sorry. I rather lost my head.'

She shivered, and he held her tighter, her bare breasts teasing his chest. 'I wasn't thinking clearly, either.'

His leg moved atop her hip. 'We could stay here.

Scandalise all of them by remaining in bed.' He kissed her mouth. 'Then you'd have to marry me.'

She looked away, her face disconsolate. 'Michael, be serious. This is your future. It's where you belong, and you need to choose a wife who can endure a life such as this.'

He didn't like the tone in her voice. 'And that wife isn't you?'

She didn't answer, and he let her pull away from him. With only a sheet covering her, she looked fragile and uncertain. His frustration deepened, for he couldn't understand why she was so reluctant to become a Princess.

He ran his hand over the curve of her body, down to her bottom. 'I'm not a man who begs, Hannah. Either become my wife or don't. It's your choice.'

Without another word, he dressed and left her bedchamber.

'You have not done as I asked,' the voice said. 'The Lieutenant must not be allowed to take the throne. I want him removed.'

'I am so sorry, my—'

'Apologies are unacceptable. Either dispose of him or you will not like the consequences. You have a wife of your own, I believe.'

'She is innocent,' the servant insisted. 'Please, I beg of you. Don't bring her into this.'

'You will not presume to tell me what to do. Take

care of the Lieutenant and use any means necessary. Even Lady Hannah, if need be. Is that understood?'

'It is.'

'Good. The King must not recognise Michael
Thorpe as his son.'

The servant bowed. 'I will see to it.'

It took all his restraint to allow another man to
dress him. Michael stood while the valet helped
him out of his afternoon attire and into the formal
black cloth coat and white cravat. The Graf had arranged for his belongings to be sent to the *Schloss*,
along with the clothing Hannah had ordered from
the tailor.

When he saw the reddened skin on Michael's arm
where the bullet had grazed it, the valet asked, 'Do
you require a new bandage, my lord?'

'It's all right.' The minor wound had healed
enough that he could put it from his mind. The neck
abrasions could be hidden with his cravat. He preferred it this way. It was easier to blend in with the
nobles, not drawing attention to himself.

He was going to face a battle of a different sort this
evening, though he'd prefer not to do so in public.
Tonight would be a test, and he suspected that his
half-brother, Fürst Karl, would be in attendance.

But not the King.

Michael tensed at the thought of the audience,

earlier in the afternoon. It had been brief, for the frail ruler was hardly able to receive guests. When the Graf had whispered to him about Michael, the ageing monarch had tried to sit up. With long grey hair and a short beard and mustache, his father appeared far older than he was. But the King's eyes had held intelligence and curiosity.

An unexpected memory had flashed through Michael. Of apples, strangely enough. Without asking permission to leave the King's side, Michael had gone over to a bowl of fruit in the corner, retrieving a single apple.

Holding it before the King, he said, 'You used to peel these for me. With a jewelled dagger.'

He kept speaking, not knowing if what he was saying made any sense at all. 'I used to sit on your lap and you would try to peel the entire fruit in one long piece. You promised that one day you would give me the dagger.'

The King's expression had paled at the story. And Michael had shown him the scar.

'She was right,' the King whispered, before his eyes closed. 'Tell the Queen…she was right.' The monarch gripped the sheets, and the palace physicians surrounded him, making further conversation impossible.

It bothered him, to have caused the older man further distress. Yet, there was nothing to be done about it. He now understood why the Graf had been so insistent on bringing him to Lohenberg with all haste. It was doubtful that the King would live much longer.

Graf von Reischor arrived at his door a few minutes later. Escorted by two servants, they pushed him in the wheeled chair.

'You should remain in your bed until you've healed,' Michael chided.

'Nonsense. This is a dinner, and I'll be seated most of the time. A man has to eat.'

And a man had to manipulate, Michael thought. As he walked alongside the Graf, he couldn't suppress the sense of foreboding. This dinner was going to go very badly; he had no doubt.

They arrived just before the seating of the guests. Michael remained behind the others, despite the Graf's insistence that he stand near the front.

Michael watched the guests, nodding politely to Viscount Brentford and his daughter. He sensed their gazes upon him, and the light murmur of gossip.

Though he waited to catch a glimpse of Hannah, there was no sign of her. He was about to enter the banquet hall, when all of a sudden murmurs of surprise came from behind him.

The throng parted, with a sea of curtsies and bows as Queen Astri made her entrance. She wore a champagne-coloured silk gown trimmed with silver and gold embroidery, and two ladies-in-waiting helped manage her train. A moment later, the Queen approached him.

Michael remained standing while the women around him fell into curtsies. He gave an awkward bow to his mother.

'Will you join us, Fürst Michael?' she asked.

A hundred sets of eyes stared at him, agog at the Queen's announcement. Michael moved forward, unsure of where to stand, and not knowing whether to offer his arm or not. The Graf discreetly motioned for him to walk behind her.

Michael continued in the royal procession, still hoping to see Hannah. But once he had joined the Queen at the head of the table, he had to turn his attention to her. His mother's face was alight with happiness, as though her joy could not be contained. Throughout the meal, she peppered him with questions while he did his best to answer.

'Was the King all right after I left?' he asked her at last.

'I wouldn't know.' Astri's expression turned shadowed. 'He locked me in that tower for over twenty years. Tonight was the first time I was allowed to come and go as I pleased. I have the both of you to thank for it.' She cast a gaze at the Graf, and her face softened. Michael detected a faint blush behind the ambassador's countenance.

'The King has accepted you as his son,' the Queen said. 'And I am grateful that you have been returned to me at last.'

Throughout the remainder of the dinner, Michael waited for Hannah's arrival. When the hours dragged on, his concern sharpened. It was considered unforgivable to leave a monarch's side without prior permission, but he was beginning to see no alternative.

After the dishes had been cleared away, he stood and made his apologies, excusing himself. The Queen's expression faltered, but she gave him a wave of dismissal.

The people in the banquet hall stared at him, but he didn't care about being rude. Right now, he needed to find Hannah and learn what was going on.

When at last he reached her room, he threw open the door without knocking. Her room was empty, with no trunks, no belongings. The bed was made, and there was no sign that she'd even stayed in the room.

Something was wrong.

Michael strode down the hallway and when he caught sight of a maid, he cornered her. In Lohenisch, he demanded, 'Did you see Lady Hannah leave?'

'Y-yes, sir,' the maid stammered. 'Her cousins

arrived, and she went to Germany with them an hour ago.'

He stepped backwards, cursing. He never thought Hannah would actually leave him, but it appeared she'd already done so. He had believed she would give him a chance, that a Marquess's daughter might let herself love a soldier.

It seemed he'd been wrong.

'Lieutenant Thorpe,' a matron's voice interrupted. 'Might I have a word with you?'

Michael turned and saw Lady Brentford waving at him. He had no desire to speak with the Viscountess, but perhaps he could excuse himself.

'Lady Brentford, I'm sorry, but this isn't a good time.'

Her gaze turned knowing, and she smiled. 'No, I suppose it isn't. You were rather close to Lady Hannah, weren't you? I know more about why she left. If you'd care to hear her reasons, why don't you join me for a few moments?' She began walking towards one of the sitting rooms.

He didn't at all believe Hannah would have confided in the Viscountess. However, he had so little information, perhaps she might have something to offer.

Once they were inside, she closed the door. Michael's gut warned him that Lady Brentford's intentions were not altruistic. Particularly since she had a stepdaughter of marriageable age.

'What is it you want, Lady Brentford?'

She gave him a serene smile. 'I want to see everything put back the way it should be. And we both know that after tonight's dinner, there will be rumours about you.'

'I hardly care about the gossiping tongues of women who don't have anything better to do.'

She flinched slightly. 'Well. Be that as it may, I think you will have an interest in this matter.'

He waited for her to go on. She walked around the edge of the salon, behaving with a familiarity that seemed out of place. 'This isn't the first time I've been in the palace, you know.'

He didn't respond. She traced her hand over a porcelain figure of a shepherdess. 'I was a longtime companion of König Sweyn. His mistress, you might say.'

Horror washed over him when he stared at her.

'No, I am not your mother,' she said, voicing his fears. 'But I think you know the man who *is* my son.'

'Karl,' he said slowly.

'Yes, Karl.' Lady Brentford walked towards the door, stopping before it. 'The King and I were lovers, even after he married Astri. When the Queen became pregnant, she denied him her bed. It was easy enough to coax him back into mine. But it was short-lived. Soon enough, he went back to her and sent me away.'

'Did he know about Karl?'

'I tried to tell him, but the Queen refused to let me into the *Schloss*. So, I decided that if I could not take my rightful place on the throne, my *son* would.'

Michael sensed a ruthlessness, a woman who would stop at nothing to get her desires. He edged his way towards the door, to prevent her from leaving.

'It took a great deal of planning to switch two children,' he said. 'I presume it was you who hired the men?'

A grim smile crossed her mouth. 'Yes. I had to marry the Viscount for his money and influence, a year after Karl was born. Brentford never knew anything about my son. I paid a woman to keep him in the village, far away from us. And my husband was so occupied with his beloved little girl, born from his first wife, he didn't care whether or not I gave him a child.'

'You waited years,' Michael said. 'I was three when you made the switch.'

She nodded. 'I had to wait until Brentford was traveling abroad, before I could come back to Lohenberg with Karl. It took time to choose the right men who could hide amongst the palace guards. And of course, every detail had to be right. Even the scar upon Karl's leg. I carved the wound myself, when he was two,' she said, with a note of pride.

Knowing that she'd hurt her own child made Michael even more tense. 'You want him to become the King.'

'If he is king, then my blood will be part of the royal line, just as it always should have been.'

Michael chose his next words carefully, for he knew it was too late for Karl to claim the throne. Not after the Queen had formally acknowledged him tonight. 'What do you want from me?'

Her icy smile grew thin. 'I want your life, in exchange for Lady Hannah's.' She opened the door, her eyes narrowed. 'Karl will not lose what I've worked so hard to gain.'

Hannah's throat was raw, and her eyes were burning. She didn't know what had happened, but one minute, she was preparing for the banquet, and the next, she was opening her eyes inside a darkened coach.

A man sat across from her, a revolver in his hand. 'So, you're awake, are you? Good.'

'Where are you taking me?'

He smirked. 'Away from the *Schloss*. Once Thorpe learns you've been taken, he'll come after you. I imagine he won't want anything to happen to a pretty one like you.' He tipped the revolver towards her.

Hannah's heart clamoured, realising that they meant to lure Michael to her and then kill him. She closed her mouth, not wanting to provoke her attacker by asking more questions. She wondered if he'd been sent by Fürst Karl.

Closing her eyes, she leaned her head against the side of the coach. Once again, she'd been taken captive by a man against her wishes. Only, with Belgrave, she'd relied upon Michael to save her. This time, she had to save herself.

Remain calm, she urged herself. *Think of your options.*

Her hands weren't bound, but jumping from a moving coach was dangerous. If she fell badly, she could break her neck. But then again, once she reached their destination, her escape options would be worse. They'd probably tie her up. And if Michael did come to rescue her, after they'd killed him no doubt they would take her life as well.

She stared down at her violet gown. The skirts were going to be a problem, hindering her escape. But perhaps if she removed the petticoats, the gown wouldn't billow out so much.

'How much further are we travelling?' she asked her guard.

The man shrugged. 'An hour, perhaps.'

There was a chance he would fire his gun at her, but more likely he needed her alive, in order to lure Michael. Her best chance of escape was now.

Hannah pretended to settle back against the seat, but she inched the back hem of her gown to rest above her hips, so that she was no longer seated upon it. The front of the gown covered the numerous petticoats, but now she could reach the ties that bound the skirts. With her fingers working quickly, she untied them. The man didn't seem to notice her efforts, since it was so dark.

When the last petticoat was unfastened, Hannah stared at the coach door. She would have to open it in one swift motion, stepping free from the petticoats and leaping from the moving coach.

Her common sense told her that this was not a good idea. She would probably tangle up in her skirts and fall on her face.

In her mind, she could almost imagine what her mother would say. 'A proper young lady would never dream of trying to escape. She would simply fold her hands in her lap and wait calmly to be killed.'

Hannah grimaced, and began easing the petticoats past her hips, keeping her lap covered with the dress.

Her pulse was pounding so hard, it was a wonder the man hadn't heard it. Her courage was waning with every second, while her brain screamed out all the things that could go wrong.

Before she could stop herself, she reached for the door handle and threw herself outside the moving carriage. Her body struck the ground hard, and a vicious pain rolled over her as she tumbled off the road. Every inch of her would have bruises, she was certain.

But she was alive.

The sound of male voices shouting made her aware that she couldn't stay for long. They would search for her, and she mustn't be found.

Without the petticoats, her gown hung down low, and she gathered up the hem with both hands. Thank heavens her dress was violet; it would keep them from seeing her clearly. Ignoring the pain, she held fast to her skirts and ran towards the forest. She didn't know where she was or how far she was from the palace.

Her chest ached from running so hard, but she forced herself to keep going. For this time, her life depended on it.

Chapter Twenty-One

Michael reached out and seized Lady Brentford's arm. He twisted it behind her back and forced her into the corridor. 'Where is she? By God, you're going to tell me or—'

The woman laughed at him, and when he looked into her eyes, he saw the true face of madness. 'If you kill me, you'll never find her.' Half-choking on her laughter, she didn't seem to care that she was caught. 'Never, never,' she sang.

At the end of the corridor, he saw Queen Astri approaching with her guards. The men came forward to surround them, and the Queen's face hardened at the sight of Lady Brentford. 'I forbade you to show your face here again.'

Lady Brentford's laughter ceased. With a sly smile, she attempted a curtsy, though Michael kept his grip firm. 'Queen Astri.' Disrespect coated her tone.

'She is the woman responsible for kidnapping

me years ago,' Michael told the Queen. Though he didn't want to offend his mother, she needed to understand the Viscountess's actions. 'Karl is Lady Brentford's son. She had hoped he would take the throne.'

The Queen's expression didn't change. 'I've always known that Karl was the result of one of my husband's liaisons. It's the only reason others believed he was the King's son. They thought me mad when I claimed Karl was not my child.' She shivered as though from a sudden chill. 'But I always knew. The scar was wrong.'

Queen Astri turned to her men and commanded them, 'Chain the King's whore in the south-west tower. Let her know what it is to be a prisoner.'

Immediately, the royal guardsmen came and took Lady Brentford into custody. The Viscountess didn't look at all concerned by her fate; instead, she continued to laugh.

'Find her if you can, Lieutenant. Remember— your life, for hers.'

'Her men have taken Lady Hannah captive,' Michael explained to the Queen, after the guards took Lady Brentford away. 'With your permission, Your Majesty, I need men to help me find her.'

The Queen laid her hand on his. 'I will grant you my assistance.' Her hazel eyes hardened. 'But you must promise that afterwards you will assume your place as the Crown Prince.'

Though he understood the the Queen's desire, he didn't want to endanger Hannah. 'Not until Hannah is safe.'

The Queen's face tensed. 'This woman means a great deal to you, doesn't she?'

He met her gaze, leaving no room for disagreement. 'She is going to become my Princess.'

A soft smile touched her lips. 'Then you'd better find her.'

Karl fully intended to get drunk. He'd nearly finished off one bottle of brandy and was intent on starting another when he'd overheard laughter in the hallway.

He'd stumbled to the door, intending to slam it shut. But then he'd seen Lieutenant Thorpe standing in the corridor, forcing a woman forward while guards approached them. The woman's face had haunted his nightmares.

Frozen, he'd stared at them, only half-hearing the revelation that the laughing woman was his mother, the King's mistress. He'd not seen her face in years, but the memory of her cruelty struck him to the bone.

For so long, he'd believed the visions were bad dreams. But they had been real.

The Viscountess had come to visit him, inspecting him and ordering him to stand up straight. When it wasn't enough to meet her standards, she'd locked him in a cupboard, screaming at him.

And the knife. Karl shut the door to the study, the vivid memory terrifying, even after so many years. She'd wielded a blade, cutting into the back of his leg while he'd screamed.

He reached for the bottle of brandy, draining it with one last swallow. He closed his eyes, recalling the night he'd been brought to the *Schloss*. He'd been taken from his nurse, crying. The Viscountess had warned him not to speak. And fear had silenced his tongue for nearly a year.

He set down the bottle, no longer knowing what to do.

I know what it is to be imprisoned in a life like this, Lady Hannah had said to him. *And still never be good enough.*

Damn her, she'd seen right through him. She'd tried, in her own way, to reassure him. But Karl knew it wasn't going to be all right. He wasn't the Crown Prince, only a bastard. The years of hard work and patriotism had meant nothing.

His fingers closed around the neck of the empty brandy bottle, the blunt pain clouding out everything. And suddenly, he crashed it into the hearth. Glass shattered everywhere, like the pieces of his life.

Without thinking, he strode out of his study and

into the corridor. He found a servant and gave the order to prepare a horse and fetch his cloak.

He knew that Lieutenant Thorpe had taken a group of soldiers with him to find Lady Hannah and bring her back. They didn't need his help, and Karl wasn't nearly drunk enough to join his half-brother in the search.

But perhaps, though he'd lost his birthright, he could prove his worth in another way. Perhaps being a Prince didn't have to be by blood.

But by actions.

Hannah continued walking through the forest for the next hour, to hide from the men searching. Her entire body ached, and she had bruises up and down her arms and legs. The urge to cry kept rising up, but she reminded herself that tears weren't going to help her get back to Vermisten.

She kept away from the main road, knowing that the men would expect her to follow it. Several times, she stopped, waiting for the moonlight to illuminate her way.

But after another hour, the forest ended, and she had no choice but to venture out into the open. She waited, praying, *Dear God, don't let them find me.* As she walked parallel to the road, she tried to keep hidden.

But still, her thoughts were caught up in Michael. This afternoon, when he'd returned to her, she'd disobeyed so many rules. Lying in his arms, letting herself be with him, had been one of the most glorious moments of her life. And though her courage had faltered, she now knew that she loved him, whether he was a common soldier or a Crown Prince.

It would break her heart if she never saw him again. She wanted him, more than anything else in the world. And though her feet were blistered and her body was bruised, her heart ached even more.

I don't want to live without him.

All her life, she'd been told what was right and proper. She'd been given rigid rules, expected to be a perfect lady at all times. For so long, she'd lived under that shadow, allowing others to make decisions for her.

She'd blamed everyone else for her lack of freedom, when one simple word would have changed everything: no. A Princess lived under a rigid set of expectations, true. But she did not bow to the whims of anyone. A true Princess gave commands and decided which rules were meant to protect her and which were meant to control her.

Hannah sat down in the tall grass, resting her feet for a moment. She needed to stop being a lady. And start being a Princess.

Her eyes were blurred with tears when she stood up. In the distance, she heard the sound of a horse approaching. Hannah ducked into the underbrush, her heart thundering in her chest.

When the rider drew closer, she caught sight of his face in the moonlight, and her heart nearly stopped. He moved his horse off the roadside, directly towards her.

Hannah couldn't breathe, couldn't move. Then he stared at the very spot where she was hiding. At his side, she saw the gleam of a revolver.

His voice was cool and resolute. 'Did you lose your way, Lady Hannah?'

Despite hours of searching, all they found along the main road was an abandoned coach and a pile of discarded petticoats, nearly twenty miles from the *Schloss*. The road was covered in ruts, made by the wheels of hundreds of coaches. There was no way to tell what had happened to Hannah.

Michael cursed, and wheeled his horse around, doubling back the way they had come. He must have missed something. But what?

The Captain of the Guard approached. 'Forgive me, Your Royal Highness. I believe we should spread out our search in a different direction.'

'She can't be much further from here. The clothes were hers; I'm certain of it. And I'm not leaving her alone.' He touched the revolver at his side, hoping he found Hannah before anyone else did.

The night had begun to fade with the rising of

the sun. Amber rays slid over the horizon, the sky dipped in shades of violet.

Michael spurred his horse faster, searching along the edge of the road. He studied the carriage tracks for anything out of the ordinary, wishing to God that he could find something.

And then, it was as if the Almighty answered his prayer. He pulled his horse to a stop and saw it. There, in the dust, he saw the fragment of a violet gown. Just a small tear, but he knew without a doubt that it was hers. It lay near an open meadow, and he noticed tracks leading away from the road.

'This way,' he commanded the men.

As he tracked her through the field and east of the city, he kept the scrap of fabric clenched in his palm. *I'm going to find you,* he promised her. *And God help the man who took you.*

Michael increased the punishing pace, relying upon the bent grasses to guide him. Then, only a few miles east of Vermisten, he sighted a single horse carrying two people. The woman wore a violet gown, leaving no doubt it was Lady Hannah.

Michael rode as fast as he dared, the palace guards joining behind him. With the company of these men, he was certain they could intercept the rider.

But something made him pause. His soldier instincts told him that this was too easy. A trap, perhaps.

He decreased the pace, only slightly, and the palace guards joined him on either side.

The first bullet struck a guard on the outer perimeter, dropping him from his horse. Michael spied the glint of a rifle from behind them. A small group of six men flanked them on both sides, and his own soldiers were within range of the gunfire. Michael charged his mount faster, and the guards followed.

It reminded him of Balaclava, in that fatal moment when he'd tried unsuccessfully to lead his men out of harm's way. And right now, their opponents were gaining on them.

He wasn't going to reach Hannah in time.

If he didn't get these men away safely, all of them would die. And he'd sworn he'd never let anything happen to her.

The leadership of these men was on his shoulders, all of their lives dependent upon the decision he would make. And though doubts rose up, strangling his confidence, a sudden clarity emerged from his fear. He couldn't control the outcome, but he could give an order that might save them.

One of the men turned and tried to fire back, but his shot flew wide. Time to act before anyone else was shot.

Michael signalled them closer. 'Four of you go to the left and take cover near those rocks. The rest of you go to the right and leave me here. I am their target, and it will give you a better chance of picking them off.'

'We can't leave you unguarded,' the Captain argued. 'Our orders are to protect your life.'

'I won't remain on horseback,' Michael countered. 'If we fire from three directions, we'll get them. If we try to outrun them, Hannah will be caught in the crossfire.'

'Your Royal Highness, I'm not certain—'

'Do it,' Michael commanded. 'If you don't, we die.'

With a quick nod of his head, the Captain gestured for half of the men to follow. The other four went right, and Michael wheeled his horse around, reining the animal to a stop. He dismounted, taking cover on the ground.

In this position, he was reminded of the battleground again, surrounded by the enemy. It was familiar, and yet different, for *he* had given the orders this time. Not for the glory of war or the honour of a country—but to save the men.

No longer was he afraid of failing them, of being responsible for their deaths. Instead, he'd given them the chance to save themselves. Their fate lay in God's hands and in their skill.

His guards fired from both directions, and Michael took careful aim at the centre rider. His first shot was out of range, but the second struck its target. They kept up a steady stream of gunfire, but in the meantime, he was losing Hannah while the rider was taking her further and further away. With a glance behind him, Michael saw her disappearing on the horizon.

He expelled a curse, forcing himself to concentrate. The attackers attempted to scatter, but three more shots ended the battle.

Afterwards, the men rejoined him. The Captain looked shaken, but thankful for his life. 'Your Royal Highness, are you all right?'

Michael nodded. 'Send two men to retrieve our fallen man. The rest of you, follow me. We still have to rescue Lady Hannah.'

He mounted his horse, and reloaded his weapon with ammunition given over by the Captain. Urging his steed faster, he rode as fast as the animal would take him. With each mile, his dread intensified.

He couldn't lose her. Hannah belonged to him as surely as she held his heart. And though she had voiced arguments, trying to convince him that she wasn't worthy of being a Princess, he wasn't going to accept them. He would keep her at his side, both to protect her and to love her.

At the crest of a hill, he saw the pair of them near the city borders of Vermisten. The rider had stopped, and he held Hannah captive.

Michael drew his weapon. Right now he couldn't

risk firing it, for fear of striking Hannah. He kept up the unyielding pace until at last he reached them.

And when he saw that it was Fürst Karl who held her, a suffocating rage came over him.

His guards joined him, surrounding the pair with weapons drawn. The impostor Prince had his own weapon, but did not reach for it. Instead, he lifted Lady Hannah down from the horse. Hannah raced to his side, and Michael turned to his guards, signalling. 'Take him away. He is guilty of kidnapping Lady Hannah.'

He dismounted and crushed Hannah into his embrace. Gripping her hard, he couldn't calm the racing of his heart. Her dress was ragged, the hemline dragging on the ground. Tangled brown hair hung across her shoulders, and her arms were reddened and bruised.

'Michael, no. The Prince didn't—'

He shushed her, covering her mouth with his. 'He's going to answer for every bruise I see.'

She drew back, not allowing him to kiss her fully. 'Let him go. He was keeping me away from the gunfire, not running from you.'

In her eyes, he saw unyielding stubbornness. And though he had trouble believing that Karl would lift a finger to help them, Hannah stepped back from him and turned to the former Prince. 'Thank you, Your Highness.'

The Prince's mouth tightened, but he nodded. Just as he was about to leave, Michael called out to him. Karl turned, his expression taut and unreadable.

'You have my gratitude.'

The former Prince met his gaze, then turned away. Though Michael still didn't trust him, Hannah was right. Karl had found her, keeping her away from the gunfire. He owed the man for that.

'You came for me,' Hannah whispered. She kissed him, winding her arms around his neck. The simple touch of her lips made him forget about everything but her. He didn't care about anyone around them, nor what they might think. He was simply glad she was safe.

When Michael pulled back, he cupped her face, examining Hannah to be sure she was all right. 'I'm sorry that you had to endure such a terrible night. I should have made sure you had better protection.'

'I don't blame you for it.' She stifled a yawn, leaning her head against his chest. 'I'm just glad you found me.'

'Hannah, I was angry, and I said things I didn't mean.' His fingers traced the line of her jaw. 'I love you, and I'm offering you a choice. I want you to marry me, whether you want to be a Princess or merely a lieutenant's wife.'

She stood up on tiptoes, lifting her mouth to

his. 'I love you, Michael. And wherever you go, I will go.'

'Even if it means having to endure this life, with all the trappings of royalty?'

She sent him a mysterious smile. 'Oh, I don't intend for it to be a trap. Not any more.'

Chapter Twenty-Two

Three days later

'Lady Hannah, you simply must wear white,' her maid Estelle argued, holding up one of her mother's lists. 'Lady Rothburne specifically listed this gown in her instructions, should you attend a formal occasion.'

'No, I disagree. White would make her brown hair stand out too much,' Lady Schmertach argued. 'She needs something softer, more feminine.'

The two ladies were battling between an embroidered ivory silk gown and a pale sea-green gown trimmed with antique lace. Tonight, the King was planning to formally acknowledge Michael as the Crown Prince to the people of Vermisten. In turn, Michael intended to announce their betrothal. The entire palace was buzzing with the news.

Hannah ignored the two bickering ladies and opened the door to her wardrobe. Staring at her choices, she selected a crimson silk gown trimmed with ribbons and pearls. It would bare her shoulders, with only slight wisps of fabric as sleeves on her upper arms. With long white gloves, the gown would be vibrant, commanding everyone's attention.

'I will wear this.'

Both women gaped at her. 'But, Lady Hannah, that colour is too scandalous,' Estelle burst in.

'It's the sort of dress a courtesan would wear,' Lady Schmertach interjected. 'Not a Princess.'

No, it wasn't at all the dress a Princess would wear. At least, not a Princess who would be subservient to the wishes of those around her. Not a Princess who would hide behind lists and rules, wondering if she was behaving like a proper lady.

No, it was the gown that a confident woman would wear. A woman who was making her own rules.

Hannah's smile was serene. 'I have made my decision.'

'But, my lady, you can't possibly—'

'You will abide by my wishes, or you will both find yourselves in another post.' Hannah sent them a cool, commanding look, and her message was clear. After exchanging looks, both women dropped into curtsies.

My goodness, that felt good. Liberating, actually. She'd never given orders before, always letting others dictate her decisions.

'Do you...wish to wear the diamonds or the rubies, my lady?' Estelle ventured.

'The rubies,' Hannah pronounced.

She held out her arms, waiting for them to finish dressing her. Estelle clamped her mouth shut and obeyed. Though Lady Schmertach appeared horrified, she, too, assisted the maid. When they had finished, a soft knock resounded at the door.

Lady Schmertach answered it at Hannah's bidding, and a footman came forth with a message. 'The King has requested your presence, Lady Hannah. He wishes to speak with you about your betrothal.' The servant bowed and stepped back into the hall, waiting to escort her. She couldn't exactly keep the King waiting, so she followed the footman, with Lady Schmertach trailing as a silent chaperone.

Hannah felt more than conspicuous in her red gown, particularly for a royal summons. It was one thing to wear a shocking dress for a court ball; it was another to wear such a garment in front of a dying king.

The footman led her into the King's chambers, where she saw the monarch seated in a high-backed, upholstered chair.

Hannah fell into a deep curtsy. 'Your Majesty, I received your summons.' It was the first time she had ever been in the presence of a king. Her nerves grew rattled, and she was afraid of somehow saying the wrong thing.

The King was not old, but illness had drawn away his strength. His grey hair hung at his shoulders, deep wrinkles set within his eyes. Yet she sensed a ruthless air of authority. His gaze passed over her gown with disapproval. 'I understand that my son wishes to marry you. And that you are the daughter of an English Marquess.'

'Yes, Your Majesty.'

'Why would you believe that you could possibly understand the role of a Princess? Do you think yourself capable of ruling at his side?'

No, she didn't know anything about ruling a country, any more than Michael did. But beneath his pointed questions, she saw a man who was trying to intimidate her.

Be polite, she warned herself. 'I can learn what I need to know.'

The King regarded her with dismissal. 'You haven't any idea what the life of a Princess is like. I suppose you believe that Princesses sit around all day wearing diamonds and choosing new gowns.'

His callous remark sent all of her years of good manners and training up in flames. Hannah counted silently to five, then ten.

'No, that's not what I believe at all.'

'You want to marry my son because you want to become royalty, isn't that right?'

'I am going to marry Michael Thorpe,' she said firmly. 'Not a Prince or Fürst, or whatever else you want to call him. I am going to marry the *man* I love, not his title.'

Before the King could add another sardonic remark, she plunged forward. 'And, yes, I know exactly what the life of a Princess is like. She has rules to obey, expectations to live up to and countless advisers telling her what she should and shouldn't do.'

Hannah picked up her skirts and stood directly in front of the King. 'And I would likely be the worst sort of Princess you'd ever have. Do you want to know why?'

The King shook his head, but she spied a gleam in his eyes.

'Because I refuse to live like that. I don't care at all whether I should be wearing a white gown or pearls or a crown. Or whether I should host a garden party or an evening soirée.' Her hands clenched into fists at her side.

'I care about whether the man I love is safe at night. I care about a widowed woman, Mrs Turner, who risked her own life to save his. And I care about a man who is about to lose not only his kingdom tonight, but his own father. Just because he was born on the wrong side of the sheets.'

When she was finished, her lungs were burning. But Hannah met the King's enigmatic gaze with no regrets.

'You're wrong, Lady Hannah,' the King said.

'You wouldn't be at all the worst sort of Princess. You'd be the kind of Princess I would want my son to marry.'

The King reached out for her hand, and smiled. 'After the ceremony, I have no doubt you will tell me all the changes I need to make to my kingdom.' He coughed, signalling to a servant for his medicine. Then he leaned back against the chair to rest.

Hannah's face turned the same shade as her dress. 'My mother would be appalled at what I've just said to you.'

'I prefer a woman who speaks her mind. And—' the King's smile turned wicked '—that is a fetching gown, I must say.'

For the ceremony, Michael had ordered thirty guards to surround them, with more men disguised as townspeople to infiltrate the crowds for the greatest protection.

'We don't need an army,' Hannah protested, taking his hand in hers. 'It's only a ceremony and a blessing. The King will acknowledge you as his son, and there will be a ball tonight. You're behaving as though we're about to go to war.'

'I'm going to keep you safe.' Michael studied every angle of the men, ensuring that each one was in his place. Stealing a glance toward Hannah, he added, 'As beautiful as you look tonight, I wouldn't be surprised if someone else tried to take you away from me. And I'd rather not murder a man in the midst of the ceremony, all things considered.'

'I'm so glad you decided to take your place as Prince.' Hannah leaned in and pressed a kiss upon his cheek. The diamond-and-aquamarine ring sparkled upon her hand. Though the Queen had tried to get her to wear an heirloom betrothal ring that belonged to one of his great-grandmothers, Hannah had refused.

'I don't have a choice,' Michael admitted, 'but it's the right thing to do.'

Though he had not been raised to a life of privilege, he could use his past experience to help the people. He could be a better Prince, precisely because he understood their hardships and could relate to them. The guardsmen, in particular, had already begun treating him as their ruler. Word had spread about how he had led them against Lady Brentford's men and saved their lives.

'You should consider Karl as one of your advisers,' Hannah suggested, with a smile. 'I've never met a man so devoted to his country.'

'I don't entirely trust him.' Michael still felt a lingering resentment that Karl had found Hannah first. And despite her claims that the Fürst had been honourable, Michael couldn't believe the man's motives were selfless.

'I hope you don't mind, but I asked a guardsman to check on Lady Brentford,' Hannah said. 'Even though the King sent away the Viscount and his daughter, I have a bad feeling about her imprisonment.'

'There were three men guarding her,' Michael insisted. What he didn't tell her was that he, too, had gone to ensure Lady Brentford remained imprisoned. The Viscountess had laughed at him again, swearing that he would never become king.

'Nothing will happen,' Michael promised.

'I hope not.'

They could not engage in further conversation, because it was time to join the King and Queen on the dais. Hours of political speeches preceded the King's formal announcement. Though König Sweyn had to lean upon his servants to stand before the people, his proclamation was clear and undeniable. Michael was his true son and would inherit the throne.

Michael hardly heard a word of the King's speech. His gaze studied each and every member of the crowd, for fear of someone threatening Hannah. But when the archbishop approached to give the blessing, Michael had no choice but to leave her side.

A flicker of motion caught his attention. He saw Karl, standing amid the crowd, only a few feet away. There was a look of determination in the former Prince's eyes, just as he raised his revolver.

Michael threw himself towards Hannah and the gun exploded.

Chapter Twenty-Three

A servant who'd been close to Michael dropped forward upon the dais, a knife clenched in his hands. Blood pooled from his chest, and Hannah recognised him as one of Reischor's footmen. He'd been sent to assassinate Michael.

She covered her mouth with her hands, while Michael pulled her tightly to him. Her hands were shaking, and she couldn't let go.

Chaos erupted below them in the crowd, guards surrounding Karl. But Hannah couldn't dwell upon it, for her mind was centred on the danger. Michael could have been killed just now, and she couldn't bear the thought of losing him.

'Are you all right?' she asked, gripping him tightly.

Michael shook his head. 'Stay here with the guards. I need to speak with Karl.'

'He saved your life, Michael,' she reminded him. Though the shot had been risky, if Karl hadn't taken it just now, Michael would be dead. Hannah shuddered to think of it.

He touched her cheek. 'I won't let him be harmed.'

Michael walked back on the dais, shielded by the King's men. Karl held his ground, meeting Michael's gaze with a steadfast look of his own. It was the look of a man satisfied with the outcome.

The crowd studied the two men, both sons of the King. Murmurs of the Changeling legend were whispered. Every last citizen of Vermisten stared at the pair, shocked and fascinated by the mirrored faces.

Karl attempted a bow, but Michael stopped him. Instead, he crossed forward and offered his hand to his half-brother. In doing so, he acknowledged Karl as an equal, granting him the highest honour.

'It seems I owe you my thanks a second time,' Michael said, his voice loud enough for all to hear. 'Brother.'

One month later

'You aren't supposed to be here,' Hannah chided, when Michael slipped inside her chamber. 'If my mother finds you, she'll beat you across the head with her parasol.'

'I doubt it. She's too eager to have you marry into royalty.' He lifted her hand, where the diamond-and-aquamarine engagement ring sparkled.

'She's going to send me into an asylum,' Hannah groaned, just thinking of her mother's excitement over the past few weeks.

'Don't worry. Mrs Turner will keep your mother occupied.'

Hannah ventured a smile. Abigail Turner had been granted a full pardon by the King and Queen, and had rejoined the Queen's ladies. The castle staff was aware of her condition, and Mrs Turner had a servant of her own to tend her, when necessary.

The remainder of the time, she was under the care of her husband, Sebastian, who had escaped his captors and had hidden in Denmark the past twenty-three years. Hannah still smiled to think of their reunion, the elderly couple embracing as though it was their wedding day.

Michael kissed her deeply, and a secret thrill heated her blood. She couldn't believe this man was going to be her husband tomorrow.

When he pulled back, he offered, 'I spoke to Karl this morning. He seemed surprised at the estates and land I granted to him. But I thought it was only fitting, since he is to be an adviser.'

'It wasn't his fault that he was caught in the middle of this,' Hannah said.

'I agree. Queen Astri isn't pleased, but the King is acknowledging him as his illegitimate son and granting him an honorary title.'

Michael's hands moved down the silk of her gown, and he nipped at her chin. 'Do you want to be late for dinner tonight?'

Before she could answer, the door burst open. Lady Rothburne clapped a hand over her mouth. 'Hannah! What on earth are you thinking, being alone with a man in your room?'

'Michael is going to be my husband tomorrow,' she pointed out.

'Well, he isn't right now.' Lady Rothburne made a shooing motion with her hands. 'And I'm certain that His Royal Highness *can wait.*'

Michael sent her a secret wink, nodding to the women as he made his exit. His palace guards followed him, once he was in the hallway.

Lady Rothburne began discussing the wedding flowers and decorations, arguing in favour of roses instead of lilies. Hannah ignored the conversation, for she didn't really care what kind of flowers there were at the ceremony.

'And, Hannah, you really should change the gown you're wearing. That amethyst colour...why, it's scandalous. No decent woman would wear such a thing to dinner.'

Hannah simply ignored her mother's chiding. She had livened up the colours of her wardrobe, after Michael had sent her shopping for her wedding trousseau. Afterwards, many of the ladies of the court had followed her example. 'This par-

ticular gown was a gift from the Queen, Mother,'
Hannah added, enjoying the look of astonishment
on her mother's face.

'Well. I suppose it must be perfectly appropriate,
then.' Lady Rothburne touched her heart and gave
a happy sigh. 'I can hardly believe that my little
girl is going to be a Princess. It's what I've always
dreamed of.'

Hannah would have wed Michael if he were a
beggar, but didn't say so.

'And your cousins, Dietrich and Ingeborg, were
surprised beyond belief to hear about your engagement. I cannot believe you never once visited
their estate in Germany.' Her mother fanned herself, her cheeks flaming. 'Oh, the scandals you've
caused.'

'It was never my intention to worry anyone,
Mother.' She hadn't revealed any of the attempts
on their lives, not wanting to make her mother any
more agitated than she already was. 'And everything is going to be fine. No one cares about the
past.' Particularly herself.

'I must admit, this is all so unfamiliar to me,'
Christine blustered. 'I hardly speak the language
well enough, and the customs are so different.
Why, I'm not even certain how I should behave at
the simplest of society functions!'

Hannah drew her mother into an embrace, hiding

her laugh. 'Don't worry, Mother,' she said, drawing back with a broad smile. 'I'll make you a list.'

'You were meant to be a Princess,' Michael said, as he knelt before Hannah, gently massaging her sore feet. 'Queen Astri was quite proud of you.'

Hannah's ladies-in-waiting had helped her to remove the wedding finery, and his new wife wore a simple nightgown trimmed with lace. He didn't intend for Hannah to wear it much longer.

Their wedding day had been nothing short of a fairy tale, with a horse-drawn carriage, the ceremony itself held inside St Mark's Cathedral in Vermisten. He'd been spellbound at the sight of Hannah in her cream silk wedding gown and the diamond crown the Queen had insisted that she wear.

Around her neck, Hannah had worn the diamond necklace from that night at the ball, so many months ago. Just seeing it nestled against her throat brought back so many memories of the time when he had rescued her from Belgrave. And he understood that she'd worn it as a reminder of that night when they'd spent hours together.

'Are you disappointed not to be a soldier any more?' she asked, helping him to remove his shirt.

'I can help the troops more as a Prince,' he admitted. 'I've arranged to send fifty men from Lohenberg, to deliver supplies to the front. The general was most grateful, even if he did grant me an honourable discharge from the British Army.'

Hannah's palms slid over his bare skin, and he leaned in to kiss her throat. The heady fragrance of jasmine swept over him. 'What about you?' he murmured, lifting the hem of her nightgown, sliding the silk up her thighs. 'I've imprisoned you in this life, as my Princess. Any regrets?'

'None at all.' She inhaled with a gasp when he lifted the nightgown away. 'I was wrong to think this would be a prison. It's only a prison if you let others command you.'

'Princess, I am at your command.' Michael knelt at her feet, touching her long legs, kissing her soft skin. He caressed a path up to her breasts, teasing and tasting her until her hands dug into his hair. 'What are your orders?'

'Take off your clothes.'

Though her tone was teasing, he obeyed. When he was naked, Hannah's arms encircled his neck, and he kissed her deeply. Skin to skin, he possessed her, letting her feel how very much he loved her.

Michael lifted her into his arms and strode over to the bed. Dropping her on to the coverlet, he reached for her discarded crown. With a teasing smile, he laid it upon her head. Like a pagan princess, she captivated him.

'What are your orders now?' Michael covered her

body with his, enjoying the way she trembled with desire.

'Love me,' she whispered, reaching up to kiss him. The warmth of her mouth evoked a searing desire and the need to join their bodies together.

Michael lowered his mouth to her skin, marvelling that she belonged to him now. His Princess and his beloved wife.

'Always,' he promised.

Epilogue

Hannah sat upon the floor of the drawing room, serving tea to a stuffed bear. Emily Chesterfield, the Countess of Whitmore, had her own skirts tucked over her feet while their daughters offered chocolates to the other doll guests. Diamonds and priceless jewels hung from the little girls' necks, while heirloom tiaras rested on their heads.

'I don't know about you, but I'm not going in,' the Earl of Whitmore announced, nodding at Michael, who stood in the doorway with him. 'They might make us wear a crown.'

Hannah smiled and rose to her feet. 'Michael already has to wear one on formal occasions,' she told her brother, as she drew closer to the men. 'It's the price of being a Prince.'

Michael kissed her hand in greeting. 'May we join you for tea?'

The Countess got up from the carpet, holding the hand of his daughter, Charlotte.

At the age of four, Charlotte wore her hair in two

braids, one with a pink ribbon and one with purple. She'd inherited her mother's beauty, but her stubbornness was a trait of her grandfather.

'Papa, you have to sit by me.'

Michael allowed Charlotte to take him by the hand, leading him to a chair. His daughter chose a chocolate biscuit from the tea tray and stuffed it into his mouth. 'I made these, with Aunt Emily's help,' she explained.

He brought her up to sit on his knee. 'They are delicious.'

Charlotte sent him a sunny smile and wound her arms around him. Her sapphire-and-diamond crown dipped below her forehead, and he adjusted it on her head. Pride and contentment filled him up inside, along with the gratitude that he could now give his wife and daughter everything they would ever need.

Hannah came up beside them, and Michael took her hand in his. As their daughter chattered with her cousin Victoria and the Countess, he met his wife's gaze. Love shone from Hannah's smile, along with silent amusement.

Charlotte jumped down from his lap to serve tea to the dolls, and Michael turned to Hannah with a wicked gaze. He glanced down at his lap and whispered, 'There's room.'

'No, you wretch.' Hannah rested her hands on

his shoulders, laughing in his ear. 'That would be improper.'

'I like being improper,' he whispered back. 'We could be quite improper later.'

'Yes, later,' she promised.

He stood up from the chair and reached out to adjust her crown. Hannah's smile transformed at the touch of his hands. In his eyes, he let her see all the desire he held, and how much she meant to him. How much he loved her.

Taking his hand in hers, Hannah sent him a soft smile of her own. 'Or sooner.'

* * * * *

HISTORICAL

Large Print

REAWAKENING MISS CALVERLEY
Sylvia Andrew

Lord Aldhurst rescues a cold, dazed lady one stormy night – and now the nameless beauty is residing in his home! Horrified at her growing feelings for her handsome protector, she flees to London, where she regains her status as the *ton*'s most sought-after debutante. Until she sees James's shocked and stormy face across a ballroom….

THE UNMASKING OF A LADY
Emily May

While she dances prettily by day, the *ton* doesn't know that by night Lady Arabella Knightley helps the poor – stealing jewels from those who court her for her money. Upon discovering it's Arabella, Adam St Just should be appalled. Instead, captivated by her beauty, he proposes to unbutton Lady Arabella…or unmask her!

CAPTURED BY THE WARRIOR
Meriel Fuller

With the country on the brink of anarchy, Bastien de la Roche will do what it takes to restore calm. So when he captures the spirited Alice Matravers, a servant to the royal court, he charms her into gaining an audience with the King. Could Alice's courage and kindness begin to mend Bastien's shattered heart…?

 MILLS & BOON

HISTORICAL

Large Print

INNOCENT COURTESAN TO ADVENTURER'S BRIDE
Louise Allen

Wrongly accused of theft, innocent Celina Shelley is cast out of the brothel she calls home and flees to Quinn Ashley, Lord Dreycott. Lina dresses like a nun, looks like an angel, but flirts like a professional – the last thing Quinn expects is to discover she's a virgin! With this revelation, will he wed her before he beds her?

DISGRACE AND DESIRE
Sarah Mallory

With all of London falling at her feet, wagers abound over who will capture the flirtatious Lady Eloise and her fortune. Dashing Major Jack Clifton has vowed to watch over his late comrade's wife, but her beauty and behaviour intrigue him. The lady is not what she seems, and Jack must discover her secret if he is to protect her…

THE VIKING'S CAPTIVE PRINCESS
Michelle Styles

Dangerous warrior Ivar Gunnarson is a man of deeds, not words. With little time for the ideals of love, Ivar seizes what he wants – and Princess Thyre is no exception! But to become king of Thyre's heart, mysterious and enchanting as she is, will entail a battle Ivar has never engaged in before…

 MILLS & BOON

HISTORICAL

Large Print

COURTING MISS VALLOIS
Gail Whitiker

Miss Sophie Vallois has enthralled London Society, yet the French beauty is a mere farmer's daughter! Only Robert Silverton knows her secret, and he has other reasons to stay away. However, Sophie is so enticing that Robert soon finds that, instead of keeping her at arm's length, he wants the delectable Miss Vallois well and truly *in* his arms!

REPROBATE LORD, RUNAWAY LADY
Isabelle Goddard

Amelie Silverdale is fleeing her betrothal to a vicious, degenerate man, while Gareth Denville knows that the scandal that drove him from London is about to erupt again. In Amelie, Gareth recognises a kindred spirit also in need of escape. On the run together the attraction builds, but what will happen when their old lives catch up with them?

THE BRIDE WORE SCANDAL
Helen Dickson

From the moment Christina Atherton saw notorious Lord Rockley she couldn't control her blushes. In return, dark and seductive Lord Rockley found Christina oh, so beguiling… When Christina discovered that she was expecting, Lord Rockley knew he must make Christina his bride…before scandal ruined them both!

MILLS & BOON

HISTORICAL

Large Print

LADY ARABELLA'S SCANDALOUS MARRIAGE
Carole Mortimer

Sinister whispers may surround Darius Wynter, but one thing's for sure—marriage to the infamous Duke means that Arabella will soon discover the exquisite pleasures of the marriage bed…

DANGEROUS LORD, SEDUCTIVE MISS
Mary Brendan

Heiress Deborah Cleveland jilted an earl for her true love—then he disappeared! Now Lord Buckland has returned, as sinfully attractive as ever. Can Deborah resist the dark magnetism of the lawless lord?

BOUND TO THE BARBARIAN
Carol Townend

To settle a debt, Katerina must convince commanding warrior Ashfirth Saxon that *she* is her royal mistress. But the days—*and nights*—of deceit take their toll. How long before she is willingly bedded by this proud barbarian?

BOUGHT: THE PENNILESS LADY
Deborah Hale

Her new husband may be handsome—but his heart is black. Desperate to safeguard the future of her precious nephew, penniless Lady Artemis Dearing will do anything—even marry the man whose brother ruined her darling sister!

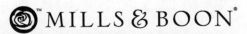 **MILLS & BOON**

V